Michael Strogoff or, The Courier of the Czar

Modern English Translation Book I - Illustrated

Juan José Piedra

QuantumDigitalPublishing.io

Copyright, Michael Strogoff - Book I & II

Contact us: Reviews@AuthorJuanJose.io

Book Design, Cover & Chapter Illustration Art and NFTs by: Juan Jose Piedra

Michael Strogoff Printable Art &

NFT Collections: QuantumDrive.io/MichaelStrogoff
Author WebSite: AuthorJuanJose.io

Author X.com: AuthorJuanJose

Manuscript Editor: Dr. Jessie Keener - https://drjessie.life/

Book I - Old English - Author Jules Verne - First edition March 2025

ISBN 978-1-967405-00-8 (eBook) – ISBN 978-1-967405-01-5 (Paperback) – ISBN 978-1-967405-02-2 (Hardcover)

Book II - Old English - Author Jules Verne - First edition March 2025

ISBN 978-1-967405-03-9 (eBook) – ISBN 978-1-967405-04-6 (Paperback) – ISBN 978-1-967405-05-3 (Hardcover)

Book I - Modern English - Author Juan José Piedra - First edition April 2025

ISBN 978-1-967405-06-0 (eBook) – ISBN 978-1-967405-07-7 (Paperback) – ISBN 978-1-967405-08-4 (Hardcover)

Book II - Modern English - Author Juan José Piedra - First edition April 2025

ISBN 978-1-967405-09-1 (eBook) – ISBN 978-1-967405-10-7 (Paperback) – ISBN 978-1-967405-11-4 (Hardcover)

Box Set - Book I & II - Modern English - Author Juan José Piedra - First edition August 2025

ISBN 978-1-967405-22-0 (eBook) – ISBN 978-1-967405-23-7 (Paperback) – ISBN 978-1-967405-24-4 (Hardcover)

Contents

About The Author

Juan José Piedra

John Joseph Stone, Juan José Piedra

John Joseph Stone, writing under the pen name **Juan José Piedra**, is a **Science Fiction, Steampunk Science Fiction, and Historical Fiction** author and artist whose work seamlessly blends rich storytelling with visually captivating artwork.

His notable works include **illustrating the cover and chapter art** for *Michael Strogoff, or the Courier of the Czar* by **Jules Verne**. With **17 chapters in the first book and 15 in the second**, John's illustrations bring the adventurous world of 19th-century Russia to life. Additionally, he has created **full-color, high-resolution printable images**, available as **NFTs and free downloadable artwork**, along with meticulously designed **Asiatic Russian maps and illustrated scenes** from the novel.

Currently, **Juan José** is developing an **eight-part Steampunk Science Fiction novella series**, chronicling the **evolution of steampunk technology;** from the age of **steam, coal, and wood to high-tech advancements and space travel**. This ambitious project aims to **span the entire fictional history of steampunk innovation**, offering readers a deep, immersive journey through time and technology.

Inspiration & Background

John Joseph's writing is fueled by **extraordinary real-world experiences**. Having spent **over 40 years in the Secret Space Program** while serving in the **USMC Special Section Division**, he brings to life ideas and themes that stretch the boundaries of what most would believe possible; making science fiction the perfect medium to share his vision.

His experiences go beyond classified operations; John has **traveled and lived all over the world**, immersing himself in diverse cultures and perspectives. These global experiences have **broadened his understanding of life and humanity**, giving him a unique lens through which he crafts his stories; offering readers more than just fiction, but reflections on **our world, its possibilities, and its hidden truths**.

Attention to Detail & Creative Vision

A meticulous creator, John Joseph is deeply committed to **historical and technical accuracy** in his works, ensuring that every **story, illustration, and world-building element** is both immersive and authentic. His dedication to precision, combined with an artistic vision, results in stories that are **both intellectually rich and visually stunning**.

Personal Life & Creative Passions

John Joseph is **happily married** and currently resides in **Mérida, Mexico**, where he finds peace in cultivating a lush garden of **Taro, Avocado, and native Mexican trees**. His love for **creating visually compelling imagery** extends beyond writing; he designs **art pieces that inspire, tell stories, and stand as works of art in their own right**.

Connect & Explore More

X: https://x.com/AuthorJuanJose

Books: QuantumDigitalPublishing.io

NFTs, Illustrations and Printable Art: QuantumDrive.io

Contact: authorjuanjose@proton.me

Forward - Michael Strogoff

How Are These Books Unique?

1. Clear & Comfortable Reading: Designed for an enjoyable reading experience, this edition is formatted in 12pt EB Garamond font for excellent readability.

2. Expanded Glossary for Old English Editions: A comprehensive glossary is included at the back of the book to help readers easily understand historical terms and phrases.

3. Beautifully Illustrated: Both volumes feature high-resolution 300dpi illustrations, ensuring stunning print quality. Book I includes 17 chapter illustrations, while Book II has 15, totaling 32 unique images. Plus, enjoy a FREE downloadable version, perfect for printing or setting as wallpaper!

4. Modern English Edition – Coming Soon! We're currently working on a modernized version that updates the language to a smooth, reader-friendly 20th-century style, making this classic adventure even more accessible.

5. Exclusive NFT Collection – Coming Soon! We've also created a series of exclusive NFTs for Michael Strogoff, offering a unique way to collect and engage with this timeless story. Stay tuned!

Jules Verne's Michael Strogoff, or The Courier of the Czar is a thrilling adventure novel set against the vast and treacherous landscapes of

19th-century Russia. The story follows Michael Strogoff, a loyal courier entrusted by Czar Alexander II with a perilous mission: to deliver an urgent message to the governor of Irkutsk and warn him of an impending Tartar rebellion. With telegraph lines cut and enemy spies lurking at every turn, Michael must travel over 5,000 miles from Moscow to Siberia, crossing forests, rivers, and the formidable Ural Mountains while evading capture by treacherous forces. His duty demands unwavering courage and resilience, as failure could mean the fall of Irkutsk and disaster for the Russian Empire.

In Book 1, Jules Verne's Michael Strogoff, or The Courier of the Czar follows the fearless courier of Alexander II on a perilous mission across the vast, treacherous Russian Empire. Tasked with delivering a crucial message to the governor of Irkutsk, Strogoff braves Tatar invasions, the Siberian wilderness, and relentless foes while maintaining his disguise. Along the way, he encounters journalists, spies, and the cunning Ivan Ogareff, a traitor bent on bringing the empire to its knees. His journey is a test of endurance, loyalty, and sheer willpower.

In Book 2, the saga deepens as Strogoff faces greater trials after being captured and subjected to a brutal mock execution, leaving him presumed blinded. Against all odds, he pushes forward, relying on his instincts and unwavering patriotism to reach Irkutsk before Ogareff can unleash his treachery. As the Tatars tighten their grip, Strogoff's final confrontation with his nemesis becomes a defining moment for Russia's survival. Verne masterfully blends historical drama, adventure, and espionage in a gripping tale of duty and heroism at the heart of the empire.

Prologue - Michael Strogoff I & II

Michael Strogoff I & II

From the frozen wastes of Siberia to the fortified cities along the Irtysh, whispers of rebellion rode upon the air, carried by merchants, Cossacks, and exiled men who knew too well the signs of coming strife. Across the vast and treacherous expanse of Asiatic Russia, where the Czar's grip stretched thin over steppe and mountain, the great empire trembled beneath the weight of an unseen enemy.

To the west, Saint Petersburg schemed in its gilded halls, while in Moscow, generals pored over maps marked with the ever-shifting borders of loyalty and betrayal. To the east, beyond the great rivers and dense forests, lay the frontier, a world where the authority of the Russian crown was measured not in decrees but in the speed of a courier's horse.

It was upon the Postmaster Roads that the empire lived and breathed. These arteries of communication, stretching thousands of versts through perilous terrain, were the veins of the Czar's will, binding the farthest reaches of his dominion. Across these routes, the couriers rode, men of iron endurance, bound by duty, carrying dispatches that could mean the difference between war and peace, between loyalty and rebellion.

And now, as the Tartar hordes gathered under the banners of an unseen leader, the fate of the empire depended more than ever on those men who rode alone into the storm.

In the city of Omsk, where the Siberian winds carried the scent of damp earth and the whisper of fate, one such man prepared for the road ahead. Michael Strogoff, a courier of the Tsar, stood at the threshold of history, unaware that he would soon become its author.

For the empire could not afford failure. The enemy moved in silence, striking in the darkness where no warning could be given. The couriers of Russia were all that stood between order and chaos, and of all those who rode, none would bear a burden greater than the one that now approached.

The dispatch was coming. The message that would change everything.

And when it did, Michael Strogoff would ride.

ASIATI

USSIA
Juan Jose Piedra
© 01/01/2025
QuantumDigitalPublishing.io
Michael Strogoff
or, The Courier of the Czar
Book I

Chapter One

A FÊTE, A CELEBRATION AT THE NEW PALACE

With urgent news that demanded immediate attention, General Kissoff, his boots striking the marble floor and medals clanging, burst through the large, ornate wooden doors to bring this news to the Czar. As the aging general hurried through the palace corridors, his face reddened from the rushed pace of his journey.

"Your Majesty, we've received a new message."

"Where from?"

"From Tomsk?"

“Has anyone lost communication beyond there?”

"Yes, sire. Since yesterday."

"Send hourly updates to Tomsk, General. Keep me informed of any developments."

"As you command, sire," General Kissoff replied with a bow.

This exchange took place around 2 AM, while the grand celebration at the New Palace was reaching its pinnacle of magnificence.

Throughout the evening, the military bands of the Preobrajensky and Paulowsky regiments had filled the air with an endless stream of dance music, polkas, mazurkas, schottisches, and waltzes from their finest selections. The brass instruments gleamed under the crystal chandeliers as uniformed musicians performed with practiced precision. Countless pairs of dancers swept across the palace's grand ballrooms, their elaborate gowns and dress uniforms creating a swirling kaleidoscope of color against the marble floors. Only a short distance separated the elegant ballrooms from what locals called the "stone house," a weathered granite structure whose dark past contrasted with the radiant glow next door.

The court's grand-chamberlain received excellent support in carrying out his complex and sensitive responsibilities, his every command executed with swift precision by an army of attendants and servants. High-ranking officials, including grand-dukes with their military assistants and palace chamberlains, supervised the dance arrangements, scrutinizing every detail from the spacing between couples to the exact timing of each musical piece. The grand duchesses sparkled in their diamond jewelry, their tiaras and necklaces catching and scattering light like captured stars, while ladies-in-waiting displayed their finest attire, establishing the standard for wives of military and civilian officials in Moscow, the historic "city of white stone." When music signaled the start of the national dance at such gatherings, each step measured and dignified. The scene became magnificent as elaborate costumes, flowing lace-trimmed gowns, and medal-decorated uniforms moved through the ballroom in perfect synchronization, illuminated by countless chandeliers whose light multiplied in the many mirrors adorning the walls, creating an endless reflection of splendor that seemed to stretch into infinity.

In the New Palace, the grand saloon stood as the most magnificent of all chambers, providing an elegant backdrop for the parade of distinguished guests and ladies in resplendent attire. Above, the ornate ceiling's gilded details had mellowed with age, creating a subtle sparkle like distant stars.

Heavy damask curtains and door hangings cascaded in luxuriant folds, their embroidered patterns catching the light in a kaleidoscope of deep, shifting colors. Crystal sconces lined the walls between towering mirrors, their flames dancing and multiplying on the reflective surfaces. Floors, polished to a mirror sheen, displayed intricate geometric patterns crafted from rare woods, while marble columns rose from floor to ceiling, their fluted surfaces etched with delicate acanthus leaves and crowned with gilt Corinthian capitals. Even the air itself seemed charged with refinement, perfumed by the subtle fragrances of beeswax candles and exotic flowers arranged in towering porcelain vases.

Curved windows illuminated the grand halls like a blazing fire, cutting through the darkness that had enveloped the palace earlier. A striking contrast caught the eye of guests who weren't dancing, their faces bathed in golden warmth and deep shadow as they moved about the space. Those resting by the windows could make out the shadowy silhouettes of the old city's many towers, domes, and spires against the night sky, each architectural marvel etched in stark relief against the star-studded heavens. Below the ornate balconies, guards marched back and forth in silent vigil, their rifles resting on their shoulders while their spiked helmets gleamed like flames in the palace's radiance, brass buttons and medal ribbons catching every stray beam of light. The rhythmic footsteps of patrolling sentries echoed off the stones below, matching the steady tempo of the dancers above, creating an unconscious harmony between duty and revelry. Guards called out passwords between posts, their voices carrying through the cool night air, and trumpet notes pierced through the orchestra's music, signaling changes in the watch. Further below the front of the palace, dark shapes blocked the light streaming from the New Palace's windows, these were boats gliding down the river, whose waters, dimly lit by scattered lamps, lapped against the lowest terraces with a gentle, hypnotic rhythm that seemed to underscore the evening's grandeur.

General Kissoff addressed the host, celebrating the courtesy reserved for monarchs; the host wore a modest chasseur guard officer's uniform, its dark green fabric showing signs of regular wear. His understated attire didn't stem from pretense; rather, it reflected the natural preference of someone who prioritized function over fashion. His simple dress stood in sharp contrast to the lavish outfits surrounding him, as he moved among his entourage of Georgian, Cossack, and Circassian guards, a dazzling company adorned in the resplendent military dress of the Caucasus region.

The towering figure moved among the gathered crowds, his friendly manner and serene face masking an undercurrent of worry that ran deeper than the Neva's waters. He passed between groups with minimal conversation, offering only brief nods and polite smiles, indifferent to both the young guests' peals of laughter and the serious discussions of high-ranking officials and European diplomats stationed at the Russian court. A few of these shrewd political observers, skilled at reading faces through years of diplomatic service in the most demanding posts from Vienna to Constantinople, noticed signs of unease in their host's expression but couldn't pinpoint its cause. The slight tension around his eyes, the occasional distant look that crossed his features, these were subtle tells that spoke volumes to those trained to notice such things. None dared to ask him about it.

The commanding officer of the chasseurs was determined not to let his concerns dampen the celebrations, maintaining his composure with the same discipline that had served him throughout his military career. Given that he wielded authority over what amounted to an entire world's population, from the Baltic shores to the Pacific coast, the ball's cheerful atmosphere continued uninterrupted, a testament to both his self-control and the respect he commanded.

General Kissoff remained in place, awaiting permission to depart from the officer who had just received the Tomsk dispatch. But the latter maintained his silence. After studying the telegram, his expression grew even more troubled than before. He unconsciously reached for his sword hilt, then quickly shielded his eyes with his hand, as if the room's bright lights were overwhelming and he needed to focus his thoughts more clearly.

"Tell me," he said, pulling General Kissoff to a window for privacy, his boots making no sound on the polished parquet floor. The winter frost had traced delicate patterns on the windowpanes, offering them a natural screen from curious onlookers. "Have we received any word from the Grand Duke since yesterday?"

"Nothing at all, Your Majesty. I fear soon we won't be able to receive any messages across the Siberian border." Kissoff's voice was above a whisper, his weathered face betraying a deep concern that matched his superior's troubled demeanor. The sounds of the continuing celebration seemed to grow more distant as the weight of their conversation settled between them.

"What about the military units from Amoor and Irkutsk provinces, and those from the Trans-Balkan region? Were they instructed to advance toward Irkutsk?" The Czar's fingers drummed against the window frame as he spoke, his breath fogging the frosted glass.

"Yes, we transmitted those instructions in our final telegram before the communications lines beyond Lake Baikal were severed."

"And what's the status of our contact with Yeniseisk, Omsk, Semipolatinsk, and Tobolsk? Can we still communicate with these governments as we did before the uprising?"

"Our messages have made it through, and I can confirm the Tartar forces haven't moved past the Irtish and Obi rivers," the officer reported. "Though I fear this situation may change at any moment."

"What news of Ivan Ogareff, the traitor?" The Czar's voice hardened at the mention of the name, his reflection in the window growing tenser.

"Nothing yet," General Kissoff answered, clasping his hands behind his back. "Even our police chief can't determine if he's crossed our borders. He seems to have vanished like smoke in the wind."

"Send his description to all our telegraph stations still operating, Nijni-Novgorod, Perm, Ekaterenburg, Kasirnov, Tioumen, Ishim, Omsk, Tomsk, every single one. We do not want him slipping through our network undetected."

"It will be done at once, Your Majesty. I'll have our most trusted operators handle the transmissions."

"And remember, absolute secrecy about this matter. Not a whisper of this must reach beyond these walls."

The General gave a deferential bow of agreement and slipped into the crowd, departing such that no one noticed him leave, his polished boots making not the slightest sound on the marble floor.

Lost in contemplation, the officer stood motionless for several moments, his mind wrestling with the gravity of the situation and its potential consequences for the Empire. Then, composing himself with practiced discipline, he moved among the gathered clusters of people in the ballroom, his face once again showing its usual serenity after that brief moment of disquiet.

The incident that sparked this quick exchange wasn't as secret as General Kissoff and the chasseur officer might have believed. Despite restrictions on open discussion and the lack of official announcements, a select few high-ranking officials received varying degrees of accurate information about the developments beyond the border. At the New Palace reception, civilians without military uniforms or medals, were discussing something that was undisclosed and not even whispered among diplomatic circles. They seemed well-informed about the situation. They stood apart from the glittering crowd, their subdued attire a stark contrast to the ornate military dress and jeweled finery surrounding them. Their hushed conversation, punctuated by meaningful glances and subtle gestures, would have appeared innocuous to casual observers, yet their precise knowledge of classified details suggested connections to sources far more privileged than their modest appearance implied.

How had these two unremarkable individuals discovered what even many distinguished and powerful people suspected? Were they blessed with prophetic abilities that transcended ordinary human limitations? Did they possess some additional sense that let them peer beyond normal human perception, reaching into realms where secrets lay bare? Had they developed a special talent for uncovering hidden truths, honed through years of patient observation and careful analysis? Perhaps their constant immersion in gathering intelligence had altered how their minds worked, reshaping neural pathways until intuition became indistinguishable from fact. This explanation seemed hard to dismiss, especially given how naturally they moved through the corridors of power while remaining invisible to those who wielded it.

An Englishman and a Frenchman, both tall and lean, made up the pair. The Frenchman possessed the characteristic olive complexion of southern Provence, while the Englishman displayed the rosy cheeks typical of Lancashire nobility. The English-Norman moved with calculated precision, his demeanor cool and solemn, dispensing words and movements as if governed by clockwork. His French companion, however, was the embodiment of animation and vigor, conveying his thoughts through a symphony of facial expressions, hand gestures, and verbal flourishes. While the Frenchman expressed a single idea in twenty different ways, the Englishman seemed limited to one unchanging method, as if permanently etched into his mind. Their contrasting natures extended even to their attire, the Englishman favoring pressed wool suits in subdued grays and browns, while his Mediterranean counterpart embraced a wardrobe that spoke of careful attention to current continental fashions. Yet despite their apparent differences, or perhaps because of them, they moved through their work with an almost supernatural synchronicity, each man's qualities complementing the other's shortcomings.

The two men's stark differences would have been apparent to even a casual onlooker. Yet someone skilled in reading faces would have noted their most defining traits differently; the Frenchman lived through his eyes, while the Englishman existed through his ears.

Years of use honed the Frenchman's vision to remarkable precision. His eyes could process information as swiftly as those magicians who can identify a playing card from the briefest glimpse during a shuffle, or spot tiny marks others would miss. Indeed, his "visual memory" had reached an extraordinary level of development. He could reconstruct entire crime scenes from memory days later, sketching out the smallest details with uncanny accuracy, from the precise angle of an overturned chair to the subtle pattern of dust disturbed on a windowsill. This gift had proven invaluable countless times, allowing him to notice crucial discrepancies that others had overlooked in the heat of the investigation.

Unlike his companion, the Englishman seemed gifted in the art of listening. Once he heard someone's voice, it remained etched in his memory. He could identify it among countless others even after a decade or two. Though his ears lacked the mobility of animals with their flexible ear flaps, scientists acknowledge human ears have limited movement capabilities. One might observe, with some amusement, that this Englishman's ears appeared to pivot and adjust in all directions to capture sounds, a phenomenon only a trained naturalist might appreciate. He could discern the subtlest variations in tone and inflection, picking up on the microscopic tremors in a person's voice that might betray deception or distress. Even in a crowded room full of overlapping conversations, he possessed the remarkable ability to focus on a single voice and follow it with laser-like precision, filtering out all other ambient noise as if adjusting an invisible dial. This auditory prowess had proven especially valuable during witness interviews, where the slightest quaver or hesitation in testimony could point toward hidden truths.

These exceptional sensory abilities served both men well in their professions. The Englishman worked as a Daily Telegraph correspondent, while his French companion maintained an air of mystery about his journalistic affiliations. When questioned, he would jest about "corresponding with cousin Madeleine," a response that never failed to elicit knowing smiles from those who asked. Yet beneath this casual exterior, the Frenchman possessed remarkable wit and perception that manifested in unexpected ways. His casual chatter disguised his keen observation skills; he gathered intelligence through aimless, but calculated, meandering conversations. His apparent openness often masked a discretion that perhaps exceeded that of his British colleague, who tended toward more straightforward methods of information gathering. Both men attended the New Palace celebration on July 15th in their capacity as reporters, though their true purposes that evening may have run deeper than mere journalism.

These two individuals showed unwavering dedication to their life's work, pursuing every lead that emerged, no matter how unexpected. Nothing could frighten or deter them from achieving their goals, whether facing physical danger or social ostracism. They possessed the unshakeable composure and authentic courage typical of their profession, maintaining their poise even in the most challenging circumstances. Like passionate riders in a steeplechase racing for information, they bounded over hedges, forded rivers, and cleared fences with the fierce determination of thoroughbred horses willing to either win or perish in the attempt, their resolve never wavering even when the path ahead seemed treacherous.

The newspapers gave them unlimited financial resources, still recognized today as the most reliable, quickest, and most comprehensive way to gather information. Their expense accounts allowed them to travel first-class across continents, book rooms at premier hotels, and maintain the appearances expected of gentlemen in high society. It should also be noted that neither journalist, to their credit, ever spied or eavesdropped on invading personal privacy, but only pursued stories related to political or social issues. They maintained strict ethical standards even when competing papers might have stooped to less savory methods. They specialized in what we now call "major political and military journalism," focusing their considerable talents on matters of international significance rather than society gossip or local scandals.

As becomes clear when studying their work, they maintained distinct perspectives on events and their implications, each bringing his own unique analytical approach and interpretative style. While one might focus on the broader geopolitical ramifications, the other often delved into the nuanced cultural effects of major developments.

During a lavish celebration held within the opulent halls of the constructed palace, two journalists, unacquainted, encountered one another. Their respective newspapers had tasked the Frenchman, Alcide Jolivet, and to cover the event. Though their contrasting personalities and professional rivalry might have kept them apart, they chose instead to engage with one another. As fellow newsmen working the same territory, they recognized the practical benefits of cooperation. One might catch details the other missed, making their interaction helpful. Like hunters sharing the same grounds, they found it wise to exchange information and maintain open communication. Their initial wariness of each other gave way to a grudging respect, as each recognized in the other a dedication to journalistic excellence that transcended national loyalties. Despite representing competing publications, they discovered that collaboration often yielded richer, more nuanced coverage of complex events.

The anticipation was palpable that evening as both kept watchful eyes, sensing something significant was about to unfold in the crowded gathering. The air seemed charged with unspoken possibilities, and both men leaned forward in their seats.

"Even if it turns out to be nothing," Alcide Jolivet mused to himself, running a thoughtful finger along the rim of his untouched glass, "the possibility alone makes it worth investigating." His instincts, honed by years of chasing stories, had never led him astray.

With careful deliberation, the two journalists began testing the waters with one another, each weighing their words like merchants assessing valuable goods. The conversation started as they circled around their shared suspicions.

"I must say," Alcide Jolivet remarked with calculated cheerfulness, falling back on his French manner, gesturing at the assembled crowd, "this gathering is delightful!" His eyes, however, remained sharp and observant beneath his jovial exterior.

"I already sent a telegram saying 'splendid!'" Harry Blount replied with typical British composure, using that English word of praise. He adjusted his cravat around his neck with practiced precision, his expression neutral.

Despite his previous statements, Alcide Jolivet, leaning closer and lowering his voice to a confidential murmur, continued by saying that he felt obligated to inform his cousin about the matter.

"Your cousin?" Harry Blount cut in, his voice revealing his surprise, one eyebrow arching above his wire-rimmed spectacles.

"Indeed," Alcide Jolivet confirmed, adjusting the cuff of his well-tailored jacket with practiced nonchalance, "my cousin Madeleine. She's the one I correspond with, and she appreciates prompt and detailed updates. So I informed her that during the celebration, the sovereign appeared to have a shadow of concern across his face, like a cloud passing over the sun on an otherwise bright day."

"In my eyes, it was quite radiant," Harry Blount responded, attempting to mask his true thoughts on the matter, his fingers drumming an irregular pattern against his leather-bound notebook.

"And I assume you portrayed it as 'radiant' in your Daily Telegraph piece?" Jolivet pressed, a knowing glint in his eye.

"Precisely." Blount's clipped response carried the weight of unspoken reservations.

"Tell me, Mr. Blount, can you recall the events at Zakret in 1812?" Jolivet's tone shifted, taking on an air of scholarly inquiry.

"As clearly as if I'd witnessed them firsthand, sir," the English journalist replied, his shoulders stiffening almost imperceptibly at the historical reference.

Alcide Jolivet went on, leaning forward in his chair with the practiced air of a seasoned storyteller, "Emperor Alexander was attending a celebration held in his honor when news arrived that Napoleon and his advance forces had crossed the Niemen River. Yet the Emperor remained at the festivities, and despite receiving information that could lead to his empire's downfall, he maintained his composure with remarkable self-possession."

"Much like how our host stayed calm when General Kissoff reported the severing of telegraph lines between the frontier and Irkutsk's government," Blount observed, adjusting his cravat with deliberate precision.

"Are you aware of that?" Jolivet's eyes narrowed as he studied his colleague's face.

"Indeed I am!" Blount shot back, his chin lifting with concealed defensiveness.

"Well, I would know about it, as my telegram made it all the way to Udinsk," said Alcide Jolivet with a hint of pride, smoothing the front of his waistcoat as he savored this insignificant victory over his British counterpart.

"Mine only reached Krasnoiarsk," Harry Blount replied, sounding pleased with himself, though his fingers had resumed their nervous tapping against his notebook.

"Then you must also know about the orders sent to the Nikolaevsk troops?" Jolivet pressed, his voice dropping to just above a whisper, as if sharing a sensitive piece of intelligence.

"I do indeed. And I know that the Tobolsk government ordered their Cossacks to gather their forces," Blount declared with an air of professional satisfaction.

"Indeed, Mr. Blount, your statement is quite accurate."

"Just as the Daily Telegraph readers will know it," said M. Jolivet, his eyes glinting with competitive spirit.

"Well, considering everything happening..." Blount muttered, glancing around the crowded room.

"And all the talk going around..." Jolivet added, matching his colleague's conspiratorial tone.

"This should be quite the campaign to cover, Mr. Blount," he continued, drumming his fingers against his glass.

"And I intend to cover it, M. Jolivet!" Blount proclaimed.

"Then we might find ourselves in places far more dangerous than this ballroom floor," Jolivet observed, eyeing the polished parquet beneath their feet.

"More dangerous, true, but..." Blount began, taking an unsteady step backward.

"But with better footing," Alcide Jolivet quipped, reaching out to catch his companion who had lost his balance while stepping backward on the slick floor.

The two journalists parted ways with cordial nods, each satisfied that neither had gained an unfair advantage over the other, though both were already plotting their next moves in their perpetual game of journalistic one-upmanship.

The doors leading to the rooms next to the grand reception hall swung open with a dignified creak, revealing several massive tables set with exquisite china and golden tableware. For this occasion, they imported a magnificent, priceless centerpiece from London, which they placed on the center table reserved for royalty and diplomatic corps members. Surrounding this masterpiece of gold craftsmanship, illuminated by crystal chandeliers that cast dancing reflections across the room, were countless pieces of fine porcelain from the prestigious Sevres Shops, each plate and cup positioned with meticulous precision.

The dinner guests made their way to the dining halls of the New Palace, their shoes clicking against the marble floors as they moved in a choreographed dance of social hierarchy, each person knowing their designated place in the order of precedence. Ladies' silk gowns rustled and gentlemen's medals clinked as they filed through the doorways.

Just then, General Kissoff returned, his face flushed with urgency, and hurried over to the chasseur officer.

"Any news?" the officer demanded, as before, his fingers drumming against his sword hilt.

"Sire, the telegraph lines to Tomsk are now down. We've tried every connection through Kolyvan, but there's nothing but silence."

"Send a courier at once!" The command rang through the air with unmistakable authority.

The officer strode out into a spacious antechamber connected to the hall, his boots echoing against the parquet flooring. This oak-furnished study, nestled in a corner of the New Palace, featured several paintings adorning its walls, including works by the renowned Horace Vernet. The collection featured military scenes, their gilt frames catching the warm lamplight; someone had arranged maps and dispatches on a massive desk beneath them. The air carried the distinct scent of beeswax and leather that permeated all such official chambers.

The sentinel threw open a window with urgency, craving fresh air, and ventured onto a balcony to inhale the crisp atmosphere of a serene July evening. Below him, illuminated by moonlight, stretched a fortified compound featuring two cathedrals, three palaces, and an arsenal. Surrounding this stronghold lay three distinct districts: Kitai-Gorod, Beloi-Gorod, and Zemlianai-Gorod, representing European, Tartar, and Chinese quarters, each sprawling. Three hundred churches, with green cupolas crowned with gleaming silver crosses, along with towers, belfries, and minarets, punctuated the districts. A serpentine river meandered through the landscape, its waters catching and reflecting the moon's gentle glow, while the distant barking of dogs and muffled sounds of nighttime activity drifted up from the streets below.

This meandering waterway was the Moskowa; the grand city was Moscow; the fortified compound was the Kremlin; and the guard officer, who stood with crossed arms and furrowed brow, lost in contemplation as he listened to the distant sounds drifting from the New Palace across the ancient Muscovite city, was none other than the Czar himself. His imposing figure cast a long shadow across the balcony's stone floor as he gazed out over his capital, his military uniform adorned with medals that glinted in the moonlight, while a cool breeze stirred the epaulettes on his shoulders.

Chapter Two

RUSSIANS AND TARTARS

News of grave developments beyond the Ural frontier had compelled the Czar to make an abrupt departure from the magnificent ball at the New Palace, where Moscow's elite, both civil and military, had gathered for a lavish celebration. Intelligence reports showed that a powerful uprising was brewing, one that threatened to tear the Siberian territories away from Russian control. The whispers among the gathered nobility spoke of tribal alliances forming in the east, and of foreign powers, stoking the flames of rebellion.

Siberia, also known as Asiatic Russia, is a vast territory spanning 1,790,208 square miles with a population of two million people. This enormous region stretches from the Ural Mountains in the west, which marks the boundary with European Russia, to the Pacific Ocean in the east. Its borders include Turkestan and the Chinese Empire to the south, while the Arctic Ocean forms its northern boundary from the Sea of Kara to the Bering Strait. The terrain varies from endless frozen tundra and dense taiga forests to rolling steppes and towering mountain ranges, making it as challenging to govern as it is to traverse. Its rich mineral deposits and fur-bearing animals have long made it a source of tremendous wealth for the Russian Empire, despite its harsh climate and sparse population.

Administrators divided the territory into several provinces and governments, including Tobolsk, Yeniseysk, Irkutsk, Omsk, and Yakutsk. It also encompasses two districts, Okhotsk and Kamtschatka, as well as two regions under Russian control: the land of the Kirghiz and that of the Tshouktshes. This expansive territory, extending over one hundred and ten degrees from west to east, serves as a destination for both criminal and political exiles under Russian authority, with many forced to work in the region's many mines and labor camps.

Administering this immense territory falls under two governor-generals, who act as the Czar's highest representatives. The more senior of these officials maintains his seat in Irkutsk, which serves as the distant capital of Eastern Siberia. Between the two Siberian regions flows the Tchouna River, marking their boundary. These governor-generals wield considerable autonomy because of the vast distances separating them from St. Petersburg, though they must still answer to the imperial bureaucracy through regular dispatches and reports detailing their governance of these far-flung lands.

The expansive plains, some fertile, remain untouched by railroad tracks. No iron rails connect to the valuable mines that make Siberia's underground wealth far exceed its surface riches. Travelers must rely on traditional means. In the warmer months, they use kibicks or telgas (horse-drawn carriages), while winter journeys require sleighs. These primitive transportation methods often mean journeys that would take days by rail instead stretch into weeks or months, testing both human and animal endurance against Siberia's harsh elements.

A solitary electric telegraph line, stretching over eight thousand miles with a single wire, provides the only connection between Siberia's eastern and western boundaries. After leaving the Ural, the line travels through many cities: Ekaterenburg, Kasirnov, Tioumen, Ishim, Omsk, Elamsk,

Kolyvan, Tomsk, Krasnoiarsk, Nijni-Udinsk, Irkutsk, Verkne-Nertschink, Strelink, Albazine, Blagowstenks, Radde, Orlomskaya, Alexandrowskoe, and Nikolaevsk. Sending a message from one end to the other costs six roubles and nineteen copecks per word. A branch line from Irkutsk to Kiatka on the Mongolian border forwards messages to Peking within two weeks at a rate of thirty copecks per word. This remarkable feat of engineering requires constant maintenance, with teams of workers stationed at intervals along its length to repair breaks caused by storms, frost, and falling trees or vandalism.

Someone severed the telegraph line running from Ekaterenburg to Nikolaevsk in two places, first past Tomsk, and again between Tomsk and Kolyvan. The damage appeared deliberate, with the copper wires cut and several support poles toppled.

This explained why, when General Kissoff delivered his second report, the Czar had commanded, "Send a courier at once!" His voice had carried the weight of urgency that only a ruler responsible for such vast territories could understand.

The Czar stood silently by the window for several moments, his reflection ghostlike against the palace glass as he contemplated the gravity of the situation. Then the door opened once more, and the chief of police appeared in the doorway, his brass buttons gleaming in the lamplight.

"Come in, General," the Czar said. "Tell me everything you know about Ivan Ogareff."

"He's dangerous, Your Majesty," the police chief responded, his weathered face betraying genuine concern.

"He held the rank of colonel, didn't he?"

"Yes, Your Majesty."

"Was he a capable officer?"

"Capable, but uncontrollable. His boundless ambition led him to pursue any means necessary. He became entangled in covert plots until His Highness, the Grand Duke, stripped him of his rank and banished him to Siberia." The police chief's fingers traced the edge of his uniform as he spoke of the disgraced officer's misdeeds.

"When did this occur?"

"Two years ago. After six months in exile, he returned to Russia, pardoned by Your Majesty's grace. He seemed repentant."

"Has he been back in Siberia since then?"

"Indeed, sire, though he returned of his own accord," the police chief responded, his voice dropping to a near whisper as he added, "There was an era, sire, when no one ever came back from Siberia. The frozen wastes claimed too many souls to count."

"As long as I draw breath, Siberia shall remain a place from which return is possible. Those who show genuine remorse deserve the chance for redemption."

The Czar could speak these words with genuine pride, for he had showed, through his acts of mercy, that Russian justice could be capable of forgiveness. His reforms, though debated, showed a judicious balance of compassion and justice.

The police chief remained silent at this remark, though his disapproval of such lenient policies was clear. He believed police should allow no one they had escorted across the Ural Mountains to return. These new governmental practices troubled him. The very notion that people could face punishment for non-political crimes without permanent exile seemed preposterous to him. Even more shocking was the fact that political prisoners were being permitted to come back from places like Tobolsk, Yakutsk, and Irkutsk. The police chief, who had grown accustomed to the unyielding imperial decrees that never granted pardons, found this fresh approach to governance incomprehensible. His weathered face, lined with decades of service enforcing the old ways, betrayed a mixture of confusion and quiet frustration. The reforms challenged everything he believed about justice and order in the empire. However, he held his tongue, awaiting further questions from the Czar, which soon followed.

"Has Ivan Ogareff made another trip back to Russia since his mysterious journey through Siberia?" the Czar inquired, his penetrating gaze fixed upon the chief's face.

"Yes, he has."

"And have our authorities lost track of him?"

"No, Your Majesty. In fact, a criminal becomes most threatening only after receiving your pardon," the chief replied, his weathered hands clasped behind his back.

Shadows fell across the Czar's noble features, darkening his expression. The police chief may have realized he'd spoken impolitely, despite his unwavering loyalty matching his stubborn convictions. The Czar, choosing to ignore these subtle criticisms of his decisions, pressed on with his questioning, each word measured and deliberate. "What was Ogareff's last known location?"

"Whereabouts was he last seen?" he demanded, leaning forward in his chair.

"Someone spotted him in Perm province, Your Majesty," the chief responded, his voice steady despite the tension in the room.

"Which specific town?"

"The city of Perm itself, sire. Along the banks of the Kama River."

"What were his activities there?"

"He seemed to live quietly, nothing aroused suspicion. He kept to himself, frequenting only a few local establishments."

"Was he being watched by our agents?" the Czar's fingers drummed on the armrest.

"No, Your Majesty," the chief admitted, a bead of sweat forming on his brow.

"When did he depart from Perm?"

"In March, as far as we know. The snow was thawing."

"His destination?"

"That remains unknown, Your Majesty. He vanished like morning mist."

"And his current location?"

"We've lost all trace of him, Your Majesty," the chief concluded, his voice heavy with the weight of this admission.

"In that case, I can tell you myself," the Czar declared, rising from his seat with a grim expression. "I've gotten secret messages that bypassed the police channels. Given what's happening at our borders, I have good reason to trust their accuracy."

"Your Majesty," the police chief exclaimed, his face blanching at the implications, "are you suggesting that Ivan Ogareff is involved in the Tartar uprising?"

Ivan Ogareff's path after departing Perm took him across the treacherous Ural mountains into Siberia. In the windswept Kirghiz steppes, he stirred up unrest among the wandering tribes, exploiting ancient grievances and promising riches from conquest. His journey then led him southward into free Turkestan, where through cunning manipulation and false promises, he convinced leaders in Bokhara, Khokhand, and Koondooz to commit their Tartar forces to invade Siberia. This brewing conflict has now erupted, like a powder keg ignited, severing all links between Eastern and Western Siberia. Also, Ogareff, driven by a consuming thirst for revenge that has festered for years, now seeks to end my brother's life.

The Czar was agitated as he spoke, walking back and forth across the room with rapid footsteps, his polished boots clicking against the marble floor. Though the police chief remained silent, his weathered face betraying nothing, his thoughts turned to earlier times when Russian emperors never granted pardons to exiles, times when plots like Ivan Ogareff's would have been impossible to execute. The very notion seemed to pain him. Moving closer to where the Czar had settled into an ornate armchair, its gilded arms gleaming in the lamplight, he inquired, 'Has Your Majesty issued the necessary orders to crush this uprising without delay?'"

"Indeed," replied the Czar, his fingers drumming on the chair's arm. "The most recent dispatch to Nijni-Udinsk has mobilized forces across multiple regions: the Yenisei, Irkutsk, and Yakutsk governments, plus the territories surrounding the Amoor and Lake Baikal. The entire eastern frontier is being fortified. Meanwhile, regiments from Perm and Nijni-Novgorod, along with frontier Cossacks, their horses already saddled and ready, are conducting rapid marches toward the Ural Mountains. However," he added with a grimace of frustration, "it will take several weeks before they can engage the Tartar forces in combat."

"Is your majesty's brother, the Grand Duke, isolated within Irkutsk's government, with no means of communication with Moscow?" asked the general, his brow furrowed with concern.

"Yes, that's correct," the Czar replied.

"But the recent dispatches must have informed him of your majesty's planned measures, and what help he can expect from the neighboring governments around Irkutsk?" the general persisted, leaning forward in his chair.

"The Czar is aware of that," he replied, his face darkening with worry, "but what remains unknown to him is that Ivan Ogareff isn't just a rebel, he's also a traitor and harbors deep personal hatred toward him. The Grand Duke handled Ogareff's initial fall from grace, but more crucially, he cannot recognize this man. Thus, Ogareff intends to enter Irkutsk under a false identity and pledge his services to the Grand Duke. After winning his trust, he'll wait until the Tartars surround Irkutsk before betraying both the city and my brother, whose death he seeks. I've discovered this through my confidential sources, reliable agents who've infiltrated Ogareff's inner circle. The Grand Duke remains unaware of these facts, but he must be informed before it's too late!"

"Your Majesty, we need a messenger who's both clever and brave, someone who can navigate the treacherous terrain and evade detection..."

"I'm expecting such a person any minute now," the Czar replied with quiet confidence.

"Let's hope they move quickly," the police chief continued, adjusting his collar. "If I may say so, Your Majesty, Siberia provides fertile ground for uprisings. The vast wilderness makes it difficult to maintain order."

"Are you suggesting, General, that the exiled prisoners might join forces with the insurgents?" the Czar demanded, his eyes narrowing.

"My deepest apologies, Your Majesty," the police chief muttered, realizing he had indeed revealed his own paranoid suspicions. His face reddened with embarrassment.

"I trust in their loyalty to our nation," the Czar declared, rising from his chair to emphasize his point.

"Siberia holds more than just political prisoners, Your Majesty," the police chief pointed out, trying to recover his position.

"Those criminals? General, they're all yours!" he declared with a dismissive wave of his hand. "I'll be the first to admit they're the worst humanity has to offer. They have no homeland to call their own. But this uprising, no, this rebellion, isn't directed at the emperor. Its target is Russia itself, the motherland these exiles still dream of returning to someday, and mark my words, they will return. Never would a true Russian join forces with a Tartar, not even for a moment, to undermine Muscovite power! The very suggestion is an insult to their honor!"

The Czar showed wisdom in placing his faith in the loyalty of those alienated by his policies. His tendency toward mercy, which guided his sense of justice when he could oversee matters, along with his softening of the harsh imperial decrees, suggested his judgment was sound. The emperor's instinct to temper justice with compassion had served him well in other delicate situations throughout his reign, earning him both respect and gratitude from those who might otherwise have turned against the crown. However, even without considering how this merciful approach might help quell the Tartar uprising, the situation remained concerning, as there was a significant risk that many Kirghiz people would throw their support behind the rebels. Their nomadic traditions and complex web of tribal alliances made them susceptible to the rebels' promises of autonomy and self-governance.

The greater, lesser, and middle hordes comprise the three distinct groups that organize the Kirghiz people, numbering around four hundred thousand (400,000) "tents" or two million individuals. Some tribes maintain independence, while others pledge allegiance to either Russian authority or the powerful Khans of Khiva, Khokhand, and Bokhara, who rule over Turkestan. The middle horde, being both the wealthiest and largest, controls vast territories between the Sara Sou, Irtish, and Upper Ishim rivers, as well as Lakes Saisang and Aksakal. The greater horde extends eastward from the middle horde's territory, reaching the Omsk and Tobolsk governments. Should the Kirghiz people revolt, it would mean an uprising in Asiatic Russia, with the likely consequence of Siberia breaking away east of the Yenisei River, destabilizing trade routes and diplomatic relations that had taken decades to establish.

The Kirghiz, inexperienced in formal warfare, excel more at nighttime raids and caravan robberies than traditional military engagements. According to M. Levchine's assessment, "a well-organized infantry formation or square could overcome a Kirghiz force ten times its size, while a single piece of artillery could inflict devastating casualties." Their military weakness stems from their nomadic lifestyle, which prioritizes mobility and quick strikes over sustained combat operations. Despite their tactical limitations, their intimate knowledge of the harsh terrain and ability to survive in extreme conditions make them formidable opponents in their native steppes, where conventional armies often struggle to maintain supply lines and cohesion.

While this observation may be accurate, it overlooks a crucial detail: such infantry formations must first traverse the vast distances to reach the insurgent territory, and someone must transport artillery pieces from Russian provincial arsenals, often located two or three thousand miles away. The journey is challenging since, apart from the primary route connecting Ekaterenburg to Irkutsk, the marshy steppes prove difficult to cross. This means Russian forces would require several weeks to engage the Tartar forces in their territory. During this extended march, supply wagons become mired in boggy ground, horses succumb to exhaustion, and soldiers battle both the elements and disease. The native insurgents, meanwhile, can monitor these slow-moving columns from the surrounding highlands, choosing the optimal moment to harass their flanks or cut off isolated units. Even when Russian forces arrive at their destination, they often find their opponents have long since dispersed into the wilderness, leaving behind little more than cold campfires and trampled grass.

Omsk serves as the military headquarters of Western Siberia, established to maintain control over the Kirghiz people. The boundaries, which the semi-independent nomads have crossed multiple times, were under threat, and evidence suggested that Omsk itself faced imminent danger. Multiple breaches likely occurred in the defensive network of military outposts, Cossack stations positioned between Omsk and Semipolatinsk. People worried that the "Grand Sultans," ruling the Kirghiz territories, might submit to, or be forced into, Tartar rule. The Tartars, sharing the Muslim faith with the Kirghiz, might unite two powerful forces: the resentment born from slavery and the religious conflict between Greek Orthodox Christianity and Islam. The Tartars of Turkestan had already been working to bring the Kirghiz hordes under their control, using both military force and diplomatic persuasion. Reports from merchants and travelers spoke of increased activity among the nomadic tribes, with large gatherings occurring on traditional meeting grounds and an unusual number of messengers moving between camps. Russian intelligence suggested that weapons and horses were being stockpiled, while tribal elders held frequent councils under the cover of darkness. The dire situation forced abandoning several frontier settlements, with their inhabitants seeking refuge behind Omsk's fortified walls.

The Tartars' ancestry comes from two distinct ethnic groups: Caucasians and Mongolians. Renowned orientalist Abel de Remusat identifies the Caucasian branch, which includes Turkish and Persian populations and many smaller Central Asian ethnic groups, as the ancestor of European peoples and the archetype of Western beauty. Three principal groups, nomadic steppe Mongols, the Manchu who would rule China, and the Tibetan mountain-dwellers, comprise the Mongolian lineage, distinguished by its unique physical traits.

Primarily Caucasian, the Tartars who threatened Russia's imperial ambitions during this period hailed from the vast expanse of Turkestan. A system known as Khanates divided this territory into several semi-autonomous states, each ruled by a Khan. The major khanats included Bokhara, with its ancient cities and trade routes, Khokhand, controlling the fertile Fergana Valley, and Koondooz, dominating the southern mountain passes. Among these, Bokhara emerged as the most formidable power, its military might and strategic location making it threatening to Russian interests. Russian forces had engaged in many bloody conflicts with Bokhara's successive rulers, who provided military support and sanctuary to Kirghiz rebels fighting against Russian dominion. This support was part of a calculated strategy to maintain a buffer zone between their territory and the expanding Russian Empire. The present ruler, Feofar-Khan, known for his tactical acumen and fierce independence, continued this long-standing policy of aggressive resistance to Russian encroachment.

The Khanate of Bokhara boasts a diverse and thriving population of two and a half million people, drawn from various ethnic groups, including Uzbeks, Tajiks, and Persian merchants. Its military might include sixty thousand soldiers during peacetime, which can triple during wartime, plus thirty thousand cavalry trained in the traditional mounted warfare tactics of the steppes. This wealthy region's resources span animal life, from prized Turkmen horses to fat-tailed sheep, plant varieties including cotton and fruits, and abundant mineral deposits of copper and precious stones. Its territory has grown through acquiring Balkh, Aukoi, and Meimaneh, and now encompasses nineteen major urban centers connected by well-traveled caravan routes.

The capital, Bokhara, stands as a magnificent city encircled by towers and walls extending over eight English miles, with many gates guarded day and night by the khan's most trusted warriors. Made famous by Avicenna and other tenth-century scholars, it serves as the intellectual heart of Muslim learning, with its countless madrasas and mosques drawing students from as far as India and Arabia, and stands among Central Asia's most renowned cities. Samarcand, another notable city, houses Tamerlane's tomb with its ribbed azure dome and the celebrated palace containing the blue stone, a crucial element in each new khan's coronation ceremony, believed to carry the blessing of ancient rulers. An impressive fortress, its massive walls rising from living rock and featuring sophisticated defensive works that have repelled countless would-be invaders, protects the city.

Karschi, with its three-layered defenses and towering watchtowers, sits in an oasis surrounded by treacherous marshlands teeming with tortoises, lizards, and venomous snakes, making it unconquerable. Is-chardjoui maintains its security through a substantial population of twenty thousand inhabitants, its streets bustling with armed merchants and skilled warriors. The khanate's natural defenses, including snow-capped mountains, treacherous passes, and vast windswept steppes that stretch to the horizon, make it a formidable state that would require significant Russian forces to overcome.

The ruthless and power-hungry Feofar, known for his piercing gaze and swift justice, now controlled this region of Tartary with an iron grip. He had formed blood-sworn alliances with other khans, those of Khokhand and Koondooz, savage and greedy warriors eager to join any cause that appealed to Tartar sensibilities and promised plunder. With growing support from Central Asian tribal leaders, who supplied him with horses and weaponry, he emerged as the rebellion's supreme commander, following the intricate schemes of Ivan Ogareff. This traitor, driven by both mad ambition and a rooted hatred born of past humiliations, had orchestrated an ambitious assault on Siberia, believing he could fracture the mighty Muscovite Empire at its eastern frontier.

Following Ogareff's masterful guidance, the Emir (the title claimed by Bokhara's khans since ancient times) had unleashed his vast armies across Russian borders with devastating efficiency. After invading Semipolatinsk province, he forced the outnumbered Cossacks to retreat in disarray, their defensive lines crumbling before his superior numbers. His relentless advance reached beyond Lake Balkhash, where he won over the nomadic Kirghiz people with promises of autonomy and shared spoils. His brutal campaign left a trail of unspeakable destruction in its wake, he plundered villages, devastated entire regions, conscripted those who yielded to his authority, and imprisoned or executed those who dared fight back. He moved from town to town, accompanied by his massive entourage of wives, concubines, slaves, and sycophantic courtiers, all the traditional trappings of Oriental power and wealth, displaying the brazen confidence and ruthless determination of a modern-day Genghis Khan, whose legendary conquests he sought to emulate.

His current location remained unknown, as did the size of his army's advance before Moscow learned of the uprising, and the positions to which Russian forces had withdrawn. All communications had ceased. Questions remained unanswered: Had Tartar scouts severed the wire between Kolyvan and Tomsk? Had the Emir reached Yeniseisk? Was Western Siberia in chaos? Had the uprising spread eastward? The electric current, the only messenger immune to winter's cold and summer's heat, capable of lightning-speed transmission, could no longer cross the steppes. Therefore, Ivan Ogareff's treachery prevented anyone from warning the Grand Duke in Irkutsk of the impending danger.

The only solution was to send a messenger in place of the disrupted telegraph line. Such a person would need considerable time to cover the vast distance of five thousand two hundred miles separating Moscow from Irkutsk. Getting past the rebel forces and invaders would demand extraordinary bravery and wit. Yet with sharp intelligence and unwavering determination, such feats were possible. The journey would require traversing treacherous mountain passes, crossing raging rivers, and enduring the harsh Siberian elements that had broken countless men before.

"But where can I find someone with such qualities?" the Czar pondered to himself, his fingers drumming on the ornate arm of his chair. The fate of his empire might well rest upon this single decision, and the clock was ticking against him. Every hour of delay gave the Emir's forces more time to merge their gains and push deeper into Russian territory.

© 01/01/2025
QuantumDigitalPublishing.io
Michael Strogoff or, The Courier of the Czar
Book 1 - Chapter III

Chapter Three

MICHAEL STROGOFF MEETS THE CZAR

The heavy door to the imperial cabinet swung open once more with a resonant creak of ancient hinges, and a herald in his crimson livery announced General Kissoff.

"What of the courier?" the Czar demanded, leaning forward in his ornate chair with contained anticipation, his fingers drumming against the polished armrest.

"He awaits outside, Your Majesty," General Kissoff responded with a slight bow, his decorated uniform catching the afternoon light streaming through the tall windows.

"Have you selected someone suitable for this task?"

"I stake my reputation on this man's abilities, sire. My word and honor stand behind this choice."

"Has he served within the Palace walls?"

"Indeed, he has, Your Majesty. For several years with distinction."

"You're familiar with him?"

"I know him, sire. He has proven himself repeatedly, completing challenging assignments with remarkable efficiency and discretion. His loyalty is beyond reproach."

"Has he worked beyond our borders?"

"As far as Siberia's depths, through the harshest winters and most treacherous conditions."

"From where does he hail?"

"He is Siberian-born, from Omsk. A loyal son of the frozen north."

"Does he possess the necessary traits, levelheadedness, wit, and valor?"

"Without question, Your Majesty. He embodies all these qualities and more. Where others might falter, he will persevere. His resolve is as solid as the Ural Mountains themselves."

"His age?"

"Thirty years, sire. Old enough for wisdom, young enough for vigor."

"And his physical condition? Is he robust and healthy?"

"Your Majesty, he's able to endure freezing temperatures, starvation, dehydration, and exhaustion to their absolute limits. I've witnessed him traverse hundred-mile stretches through blizzards that would kill lesser men."

"He must possess incredible strength."

"Indeed, he does, Your Majesty. He can wrestle a bear and climb sheer cliffs with nothing but his bare hands. His endurance is legendary among our couriers."

"What of his character?"

"He has the noblest spirit. Never once has he wavered from his duty or compromised his principles, even when faced with temptation or threat."

"Tell me his name."

"Michael Strogoff," the general replied with clear pride.

"Is he prepared to depart?"

"He's waiting for your commands in the antechamber, fully equipped and ready to move at a moment's notice."

"Send him in," commanded the Czar, leaning forward in his ornate chair.

The imperial library doors opened to admit Michael Strogoff, the courier. A tall and robust figure, with broad shoulders and a muscular chest, commanded attention, suggesting great strength. His facial features reflected his Caucasian heritage. His physique suggested a man was impossible to move against his will; when he planted his feet, they seemed to merge with the ground beneath them, as immovable as ancient oak roots. Upon removing his Muscovite cap, thick curls of dark hair cascaded over his expansive forehead like a warrior's crown. His complexion remained pale, showing color only when his heart quickened its pace, a trait common among those born to the northern reaches. Clear, direct blue eyes gazed out from his face with unwavering confidence, scanning the room with the practiced efficiency of one accustomed to assessing his surroundings. His furrowed brow hinted at a heroic spirit, what physiologists would call "the hero's cool courage", that rare quality that allows a man to think clearly even during danger. A well-proportioned nose with wide nostrils complemented his mouth, whose protruding lips revealed the generous and noble spirit within. His clean-shaven face bore the weathered marks of one who spent countless hours in the saddle, exposed to both bitter winds and scorching sun.

Michael had all the qualities of a man who takes action rather than lingers in hesitation. He moved with purpose, wasting no energy on needless gestures or idle chatter. When standing, he maintained the disciplined stillness of a soldier at attention, his spine straight as a ramrod, his shoulders squared with military precision. Yet when he moved, each step revealed a self-assured grace that reflected his sharp, agile mind, like a leopard padding through its territory.

His attire was that of a distinguished military officer, styled after a light cavalry dress uniform. He cut an impressive figure in his fur-trimmed brown jacket 20adorned with yellow braiding on the fabric, showing just enough wear to suggest regular use rather than mere ceremonial display. His form-fitting trousers, pressed to razor-sharp creases, tapered into gleaming cavalry boots, complete with spurs that clinked with each measured step. His chest bore the distinguished marks of service, a cross and several military decorations, their polished surfaces catching the light and speaking silently of battles fought and victories won in service to his country.

A member of the Czar's elite courier corps, Michael Strogoff held officer rank among these selected individuals, each handpicked for their exceptional abilities and unshakeable loyalty to the crown. His defining trait, clear in the way he walks, countenance, and entire bearing, which caught the Czar's attention, was his unwavering dedication to executing commands. This quality, which the renowned author Tourgueneff noted could "elevate one to the highest positions in the Muscovite empire," proved especially valuable in Russia, where absolute fidelity to duty often meant the difference between an empire's triumph and its collapse.

If anyone could successfully undertake the perilous journey from Moscow to Irkutsk through hostile territory, overcoming obstacles and facing many dangers, Michael Strogoff was that person. His reputation for completing impossible missions preceded him, and his fellow officers spoke in hushed tones of his remarkable ability to navigate treacherous situations with both cunning and honor. Years of service had honed his instincts to near perfection, making him as comfortable reading terrain as most men were reading books.

He possessed a major advantage that would help his plan succeed: his deep familiarity with both the region's geography and its various local languages. This knowledge came not only from his previous travels through the area but also from being a native Siberian himself, having learned to read the land's moods like most men read faces.

Peter Strogoff, who passed away a decade ago, made his home in Omsk, a town in the province bearing the same name. His widow, Marfa Strogoff, continues to live there, maintaining the family's modest but well-respected homestead. It was in this region, among the untamed steppes of Omsk and Tobolsk provinces, that the renowned hunter raised his son Michael to be resilient, teaching him the ways of survival that would later prove invaluable.

As a professional huntsman, Peter Strogoff braved all seasons. Whether in scorching summer heat or bitter winter cold, sometimes facing temperatures plunging to fifty degrees below zero, he roamed the ice-covered plains and navigated through birch, larch, and pine woodlands. He set traps, pursued small game with his rifle, and tackled larger prey with spear or knife, passing these ancestral skills to his son with the patience and precision that only a lifetime of experience could provide.

The most formidable of his quarry was the Siberian bear, a fierce creature rivaling the polar bear in size and known for its exceptional aggression during the harsh winter months. Throughout his career, Peter Strogoff had felled thirty-nine of these fearsome beasts, the fortieth becoming his ultimate conquest. According to Russian folklore, hunters fortunate enough to survive encounters with thirty-nine bears often meet their fate at the claws of the fortieth. a superstition whispered around campfires that proved prophetic for the elder Strogoff.

From an early age, Michael Strogoff showed exceptional courage and strength, inheriting his father's steadfast nerves and hunter's instincts. He began joining his father Peter on bear hunts when he was just eleven, serving as his father's spear-bearer while Peter carried only a knife, a testament to both the father's skill and his trust in his young son's reliability. At fourteen, Michael achieved a remarkable feat by single-handedly killing his first bear, using the very techniques his father had drilled into him since childhood. Even more impressive was the young boy's display of extraordinary physical prowess when he dragged the massive bear's hide several miles back to their home, a distance that would challenge even grown men, refusing all offers of help from passing woodsmen along the way.

The rigorous lifestyle shaped him into a resilient man, capable of enduring extreme conditions that would break others. He could withstand intense cold and heat, go without food for twenty-four hours, and stay awake for ten nights straight. Like the hardy Yakout people of the north, his constitution seemed forged from iron. When others would perish from exposure on the open steppe, he could craft shelter and survive, fashioning windbreaks from the sparsest materials and finding sustenance where others saw only barren ground.

His senses were sharp, rivaling those of the Delaware tribes of North America. He could navigate through white-out conditions when fog obscured all landmarks and even find his way during the extended darkness of polar nights. His father had passed down an intimate knowledge of nature's subtle signs, the shape of ice formations, positioning tree branches, distant mists on the horizon, faint sounds carried on the wind, far-off noises, and the movement of birds through heavy fog. These minute details formed a language he could read, a secret code written in nature's own hand that revealed itself to those patient enough to learn its ways. Even in the depths of winter, when the very air seemed frozen despite that, he could detect existing game or approaching weather changes by observing the subtle alterations in the surrounding environment.

The harsh winter conditions had tempered his body like a Damascus steel blade in Syrian waters, giving him, as General Kissoff noted, the strength of iron. Yet remarkable was his heart of gold, making him as noble in character as he was tough in the constitution. Those who knew him well often remarked that his resilience seemed supernatural, though he dismissed such claims with characteristic modesty.

Michael Strogoff's heart knew only one true love: his mother, Marfa. She remained in their family home in Omsk, situated along the Irtish river, where she had spent countless years with her husband, the old huntsman. Each time Michael departed, his heart grew heavy, though he vowed to visit whenever circumstances allowed, a promise he honored without fail. Despite the vast distances and treacherous conditions that often separated them, their bond remained unshakeable, strengthened by the shared memories of his childhood years spent learning the ways of survival in the unforgiving Siberian wilderness.

In his twentieth year, Michael earned a coveted position among the Russian Emperor's select group of imperial messengers. The youthful courier from Siberia showed his exceptional capabilities, showing remarkable physical prowess, sharp intellect, unwavering commitment, and strict adherence to duty. His first major accomplishment occurred while traversing the treacherous Caucasus territories, where he maneuvered through areas disrupted by Schamyl's insurgent forces, navigating perilous mountain passes and evading hostile patrols with an instinct that seemed almost supernatural. He later garnered additional recognition during a vital mission to Petropolowski in Kamtschatka, at the easternmost edge of Russia's Asian dominion, where he braved fierce storms and treacherous seas to deliver crucial diplomatic dispatches. Throughout his extensive journeys, Michael maintained exceptional poise, demonstrated sound judgment, and displayed unwavering courage, leading his commanders to advance him to higher positions. Because he was so reliable, people entrusted him with even the most sensitive messages; his fellow couriers spoke of his achievements with admiration and awe.

During his breaks from far-off assignments, he always made time to visit his elderly mother. His extensive work in the empire's southern regions had kept him away from old Marfa for an unprecedented three years, the longest separation they had ever endured. Though they exchanged letters when possible, the written word was a poor substitute for the warmth of her embrace and her home-cooked meals that reminded him of simpler days. He had been planning to use his upcoming leave to journey to Omsk within days when circumstances changed. As a result, Michael Strogoff stood before the Czar with no hunch of what his ruler might require of him.

The Czar stared at him in complete silence, while Michael remained as still as a statue, his military bearing perfect, his eyes focused straight ahead as protocol demanded.

Content with his examination, the Czar gestured for the police chief to take a seat and dictated a brief letter, his voice barely above a whisper to ensure absolute privacy.

After writing the letter, the Czar carefully reviewed it before signing with his characteristic flourish. Above his signature, he wrote "Byt po semou", written in Russian and translates to "Nothing to report here" or "All is quiet here" the traditional authoritative phrase used by Russian emperors since Peter the Great's time.

Someone put the letter in an envelope marked with the imperial seal and sealed it.

The Czar rose from behind his ornate desk and beckoned Michael Strogoff forward with a commanding gesture.

Michael took several measured steps across the plush carpet and halted with military precision, standing ramrod straight at attention, his shoulders squared and chin lifted, prepared to respond to whatever his emperor might ask.

The Czar's penetrating gaze, sharp and analytical, met Michael's eyes once more, studying him with imperial scrutiny. "Your name?" he demanded, his voice carrying the weight of absolute authority.

"Michael Strogoff, sire," came the clear, unwavering response.

"Your rank?"

"Captain in the Czar's courier corps, at your service."

"Are you familiar with Siberia?" The question carried particular emphasis.

"I am Siberian born, sire," Michael answered with quiet pride.

"From where?"

"Omsk, sire," he replied, naming the fortress city.

"Do you have family there?" The Czar's questioning grew more personal.

"Yes, sire," Michael responded, his voice softening.

"What family?"

"My elderly mother," he answered, a hint of warmth breaking through his professional demeanor.

The Emperor paused his interrogation, his fingers tightening around the sealed document. Then, gesturing with the letter, he said, "Michael Strogoff, I entrust you with this letter; deliver it only to the Grand Duke, no one else."

"I shall deliver it, your majesty," Strogoff replied with unwavering conviction.

"You'll find the Grand Duke in Irkutsk," the Czar continued, his eyes never leaving his courier's face.

"Then to Irkutsk I shall go," came the resolute response.

"You must cross through territories in rebellion, now overrun with Tartars who would steal this letter. They are ruthless, and their spies are everywhere."

"I shall cross through them," Strogoff answered, his jaw set with determination.

"Most importantly, guard yourself against Ivan Ogareff, the betrayer whom you might encounter during your journey. He knows our ways, our methods. He is as cunning as he is dangerous."

"I shall be on guard against him," declared Strogoff, his voice hardening at the mention of the traitor's name.

"Will your path take you through+

Omsk?" The Czar's tone grew gentler, almost paternal.

"Indeed, your majesty, that lies along my route," Strogoff answered, sensing the weight of what would follow.

"If you see your mother, you risk being recognized. You must not see her!" The command was absolute, though tinged with sympathy.

Michael Strogoff hesitated for a moment, the first crack in his steadfast demeanor showing at the mention of his mother.

"I will not see her," he said, his voice firm despite the pain showing in his eyes.

"Swear to me that nothing will make you reveal who you are or where you're going. Not torture, not threats, not even the pleading of those you hold dear."

"I swear it," Strogoff responded without hesitation, his right hand moving to his heart.

"Michael Strogoff," continued the Czar, handing the letter to the young courier with deliberate solemnity, "take this letter; the safety of all Siberia depends on it, and perhaps the life of my brother, the Grand Duke. Guard it with your very life."

Strogoff declared, "Someone will deliver this letter to His Highness the Grand Duke," securing the document within his uniform.

"Then you will get through, no matter what happens? No matter what obstacles you face?"

"I will get through, or they will kill me," he stated with unwavering conviction.

"I want you to live," the Czar insisted, placing a paternal hand on Strogoff's shoulder.

"I will live, and I will get through," answered Michael Strogoff, his eyes meeting his sovereigns with steadfast determination.

The Emperor nodded, appearing content with Strogoff's straightforward response, seeing in the young courier's bearing all the resolution he had hoped for.

"Proceed then, Michael Strogoff," he declared, drawing himself up to his full height, "go forth in service of God, Russia, my brother, and myself! Let nothing deter you from your sacred duty."

The messenger bowed to his ruler and departed, his footsteps echoing with purpose as he exited the New Palace moments later into the gathering dusk.

"You've selected well, General," the Emperor remarked, watching the door through which his chosen courier had disappeared. "Very well indeed."

"I believe so, Your Majesty," General Kissoff responded, clasping his hands behind his back with quiet confidence. "You can rest assured that Michael Strogoff will accomplish everything humanly possible. His record of service speaks for itself."

"Indeed, he is the epitome of capability," the Emperor affirmed, turning from the doorway to face his general. "There is something in his manner that inspires absolute trust, a quality most rare and valuable in these uncertain times."

Chapter Four

FROM MOSCOW TO NIJNI-NOVGOROD

The journey between Moscow and Irkutsk, which Michael Strogoff was about to undertake, covered a vast distance of three thousand four hundred miles. In the days before telegraph lines stretched from the Urals to Siberia's eastern border, courier services carried messages. The fastest riders could make the Moscow-to-Irkutsk trip in eighteen days, though this was rare. More typically, even with access to the best transportation options available to the Czar's messengers, the journey across Asiatic Russia took between four and five weeks, with many stops at posting stations to change horses and rest.

Michael Strogoff was someone who could withstand the harshest cold weather, having been born and raised in the severe climate of Siberia. He preferred to make his journeys in the depths of winter, as it allowed him to travel the entire route by sleigh. Winter travel offered distinct advantages, as the vast steppes became smooth under their blanket of snow, and rivers transformed into frozen highways of ice, perfect for swift and effortless sleigh travel. The bitter cold also kept bandits and marauders at bay, making the journey safer for those hardy enough to brave the elements. In these conditions, a skilled driver could cover fifty or sixty miles in a day, provided the weather remained clear, and the horses stayed strong.

The winter season brought its own perils, like thick, persistent fogs, bitter cold spells, and devastating blizzards powerful enough to bury and destroy entire caravans. The plains also teemed with thousands of ravenous wolves that roamed in massive packs, their haunting howls echoing across the frozen landscape. Yet Michael Strogoff would have preferred these natural dangers, as winter's harsh conditions would have confined the Tartar invaders to their urban strongholds, making troop movements impossible and his journey easier. The deep snows and frozen ground would have prevented their swift horses from covering any meaningful distance, halting their expansion. However, he had no choice in the timing or conditions, he had to accept whatever challenges lay ahead and begin his journey.

Michael Strogoff stood ready to face these daunting challenges head-on, his resolve as firm as the frozen earth beneath his feet. His years of experience traversing these routes had taught him that hesitation only bred doubt, and doubt could be fatal in such unforgiving terrain.

His first task was to avoid any appearance of being an imperial courier. In these rebellion-torn lands, where spies lurked at every corner, the slightest hint of his true identity could doom his mission. General Kissoff had provided him with ample funds to ease his journey. He deliberately withheld any official documents that would mark Strogoff as an imperial agent, such papers being the most valuable form of safe passage. Instead, the General gave him only a simple travel permit, a "podorojna."

The authorities issued the travel permit under the name Nicholas Korpanoff, identifying him as a merchant from Irkutsk. The document granted Korpanoff permission to travel with companions and included a special provision allowing him to leave Russia even if the Moscow government banned foreign nationals from departing the country. Strogoff had memorized every detail of his cover story, practicing the mannerisms and speech patterns of a seasoned merchant until they became second nature. He had worn clothes that showed signs of wear from long trading journeys, complete with subtle stains from marketplace haggling and the dust of caravan trails. Such attention to detail could mean the difference between life and death in territories where rebel sympathizers scrutinized every traveler with suspicion.

The podorojna granted authorization to use post-horses, though Michael Strogoff could only use it when certain it wouldn't raise questions about his mission, while in European territory. As a result, when crossing through rebellious Siberian provinces, he would have no special privileges at relay stations, neither in selecting preferred horses nor in requesting personal transportation. Michael Strogoff had to remember his cover identity: he was no longer a courier but an ordinary merchant named Nicholas Korpanoff, traveling between Moscow and Irkutsk, and thus subject to all the usual delays and difficulties of regular travel.

To move through undetected, quickly if possible, but at any pace necessary, these were his instructions. He understood that maintaining his merchant facade meant accepting the frustrations of waiting for fresh horses alongside common travelers, haggling over prices like any cost-conscious trader would, and showing neither impatience nor urgency when faced with the inevitable delays that plagued Siberian travel. Such restraint would prove challenging given the vital nature of his mission, but appearing too eager to proceed could draw unwanted attention from those who watched the roads.

Three decades earlier, when an important dignitary traveled, their entourage required two hundred Cossacks on horseback, two hundred infantry soldiers, twenty-five mounted Baskirs, three hundred camels, four hundred horses, twenty-five wagons, a pair of portable vessels, and two cannons. Such was the massive convoy needed for any Siberian expedition of significance, a small moving city that wound its way across the vast steppes like a great serpent, visible for miles around.

Michael Strogoff traveled light, with no military equipment or support, no artillery, cavalry, infantry, or pack animals. He would travel by whatever means were available: carriages or horses when possible, and on foot when necessary. This simplicity was both his greatest vulnerability and his strongest defense, allowing him to blend with the merchants and travelers who traversed these routes.

From Moscow to Russia's border, the first thousand miles would be fairly straightforward. The route was well-served by modern transportation, railways, postal coaches, steam-powered vessels, and horse relay stations were available to all travelers, including a courier serving the Czar. The infrastructure here represented the height of Russian civilization, a far cry from what lay ahead in the wilderness beyond.

On July 16th, Michael Strogoff arrived at the station in traditional Russian attire, having traded his uniform to catch the first train. He wore a close-fitting tunic, the characteristic peasant belt, loose trousers tucked into high boots, and carried a knapsack. Though unarmed in appearance, he had concealed a revolver beneath his belt and tucked a substantial knife away in his pocket; the blade, part cutlass and part yataghan, was of a type Siberian hunter used to gut bears while preserving their valuable pelts. He had adjusted his practiced stance and military bearing to mirror the casual slouch of a merchant or tradesman heading east, completing his transformation from imperial courier to common traveler.

At Russian railway stations, a diverse mix of people often congregates, creating bustling social hubs. These stations serve not just passengers embarking on journeys, but also friends and family who come to bid them farewell, merchants hawking their wares, and peasants seeking day labor. The lively atmosphere and varied crowd of characters, from noblemen in fine coats to bedraggled pilgrims clutching holy icons, make these stations feel like miniature public squares where news and gossip flow among the constant din of arrivals and departures.

Michael boarded a train bound for Nijni-Novgorod, where the railway line connecting Moscow and St. Petersburg ended, though it would later extend to Russia's border with the expanding network of iron rails. The trip covered less than three hundred miles through the heart of European Russia, with the journey taking ten hours to complete across the sprawling plains and scattered woodlands. Upon reaching Nijni-Novgorod, Michael Strogoff planned to continue his journey either by land or by taking a Volga riverboat, whichever would get him to the rugged peaks of the Ural Mountains fastest, knowing that speed was essential to his mission.

The vigilant Strogoff settled into his compartment corner, adopting the demeanor of a content businessman trying to pass time with slumber. But Strogoff maintained a watchful rest; one eye stayed alert, both ears attentive to his surroundings, prepared to spring into action at the first hint of danger or useful information.

Whispers of the Kirghiz uprising and Tartar incursion had circulated through the populace, carried along the railway like autumn leaves in the wind. His fellow passengers, thrust together by circumstance, discussed these developments, though with the characteristic restraint of Russians well aware that informants might be listening for any hint of seditious talk.

The journey included merchants heading to the renowned Nijni-Novgorod fair, along with many other passengers seeking fortune or fleeing troubles. This diverse group comprised Jews, Turks, Cossacks, Russians, Georgians, Kalmucks, and various others, their traditional garments and mannerisms, creating a vibrant tapestry of Imperial Russian society. Despite their different backgrounds, most of them communicated in the common Russian language, though breaking into their native tongues when emotion got the better of them. The rhythmic clicking of the rails provided a steady backbeat to their multilingual murmurings.

The merchants debated how the grave situation unfolding east of the Ural Mountains might affect them. Their primary worry centered on potential government restrictions, especially in provinces near the border, that could harm their commercial interests. They viewed the entire conflict purely through the lens of how it might damage their business ventures. Had a uniformed soldier been present, and uniforms commanded great respect in Russia, these merchants would have held their tongues. However, no one in Michael Strogoff's train compartment appeared to be military personnel, and the Czar's courier was careful not to reveal his true identity. He sat quietly and listened, his weathered hands folded calmly in his lap.

A man wearing an Astrakhan fur cap and a well-worn brown robe, marking him as Persian, spoke up, stroking his graying beard. "Word is that caravan tea prices are rising. The routes through Kashgar have become treacherous."

"Tea prices won't drop anytime soon," replied a grim-faced elderly Jewish merchant, adjusting the worn leather ledger on his knee. "The Western markets will snap up everything available at the Nijni-Novgorod fair. But Bokhara carpets, that's another story altogether. The warehouses in Moscow are already overflowing with last season's inventory."

"Do you source your merchandise from Bokhara?" asked the Persian merchant, adjusting his cap as a gust of wind swept through the gathering.

"No, we import from Samarcand, which carries even greater risks. It's practically impossible to rely on trade from those territories, there's unrest among the khans stretching from Khiva all the way to the Chinese frontier. Three of my caravans have already been delayed this season alone."

"Ah," the Persian responded with a knowing smile, stroking his beard, "I suppose if the carpets cannot arrive, we won't have to worry about settling the payments either."

"But think of the potential earnings, blessed Abraham!" the diminutive Jewish trader interjected, clutching his ledger tighter. "Surely that counts for something? The profits from a single successful shipment could offset a dozen losses!"

"You make a valid point," another merchant chimed in, his silk kaftan rustling as he leaned forward. "Though any goods coming through Central

Asia face significant market uncertainties, the same applies to the tallow and shawls from the eastern regions. We've all felt the sting of those risks."

"Hey, watch yourself, dear sir," called out the Russian journeyman with a teasing smile, his weathered face crinkling with amusement. "You'll end up soaking those fine shawls of yours if you let them get too close to the tallow."

The merchant, clearly irritated by the mockery, snapped back, his face flushing red beneath his turban, "You find that entertaining, do you?"

"Come now," the traveler continued, spreading his calloused hands in a placating gesture, "whether you pull at your hair or cover yourself in ashes, will it make any difference to what's happening? Only it would affect the stock market. Better to laugh than weep over matters beyond our control."

"It's quite obvious you're not in trade yourself," the diminutive Jewish merchant pointed out, adjusting the silver chain of his pocket watch with nervous fingers.

"Indeed not, esteemed child of Abraham!" he declared, puffing up his chest. "You won't find me dealing in any of those goods, not hops, goose down, honey, beeswax, hemp seeds, cured meats, caviar, timber, wool, decorative ribbons, hemp fiber, flax, leather, or fur pelts. Though I must say, the market for such items never ceases to fascinate."

"Do you purchase these items?" the Persian interjected, cutting off the traveler's enumeration, his dark eyes narrowing with suspicion.

"Sparingly, and for personal consumption," replied the other man with a knowing look, drumming his fingers against his knee. "A man must live, after all."

"He's quite the jester," the Jew remarked to the Persian, keeping his voice low and measured.

"Or perhaps an informant," the Persian whispered, leaning closer to his companion. "We should exercise discretion and limit our conversation. The authorities are especially vigilant these days. One never knows who might share our journey. These walls have ears, as they say."

Elsewhere in the train car, the discussion had shifted from business matters to concerns about the Tartar invasion and its troublesome effects. The air grew heavy with worried murmurs.

"They're going to take all the horses in Siberia," one traveler remarked, his weathered face etched with concern. "Moving between the regions of Central Asia will become challenging. The trade routes we've relied upon for generations may soon be lost to us."

"Have you heard if it's correct," the person next to him inquired, leaning in closer with furrowed brows, "that the middle horde Kirghiz has sided with the Tartars?"

"That's what they're saying," the traveler replied in hushed tones, nervously glancing around the compartment. "But in this country, who can claim to know what's really happening? The stories change with each passing village."

"Word has reached me about military forces massing near the border. The Don Cossacks have taken positions along the Volga River, preparing to confront the rebellious Kirghiz tribes. Their cavalry units have been mobilizing day and night, from what I understand."

"Should the Kirghiz move down the Irtish, travel to Irkutsk would become perilous," the other person noted, wiping perspiration from his forehead. "Also, my attempt to send a telegram to Krasnoiarsk yesterday failed. The operator couldn't even establish a connection. I fear it won't be long before Tartar forces cut off all contact with Eastern Siberia."

"Look here, my friend," the first man went on, his voice trembling with contained anxiety, "the merchants are right to worry about their business dealings. First, they'll take the horses, then the boats and wagons, every way of getting around, until no one in the entire empire will move an inch. We'll all be trapped like rats."

"I have a bad feeling the Nijni-Novgorod fair won't finish as successfully as it started," the other man replied with a worried shake of his head, drumming his fingers nervously on his knee. "But protecting Russia's borders must come first. Business concerns are secondary. God help us all if the empire's frontiers fall."

Throughout the train compartment, and indeed the other cars as well, passengers discussed the same topics, but with notable caution in their manner. While they spoke of actual events, they avoided speculating about Moscow's motives or passing judgment on the government's decisions. The tension was palpable as voices dropped to hushed tones whenever official matters arose.

A curious passenger seated in the front carriage drew particular attention to himself. This foreigner seemed determined to absorb every detail of the journey, peppering others with questions that were met with vague replies and uncomfortable shifting in seats. Much to his fellow travelers' annoyance, he kept his window lowered throughout the trip, frequently leaning out to study the passing landscape on the right side, letting in clouds of dust and soot from the locomotive. With meticulous attention, he jotted down in his already well-filled notebook details about each town they passed, asking about their names, geographic location, economic activities, population figures, and even mortality rates. His pen moved swiftly across the pages, recording every scrap of information he could glean from the reluctant responses of his fellow passengers, who exchanged knowing glances at his persistent inquiries.

The journalist Alcide Jolivet peppered people with trivial questions, hoping that amid the responses he might uncover a newsworthy detail "for his cousin," a phrase he repeated so often it had become something of a running joke among the other passengers. However, his persistent inquiries aroused suspicion, and those around him, believing him to be a spy, carefully avoided any discussion of current events in his presence, their conversations dropping to whispers whenever he approached.

Frustrated by his inability to gather any information about the Tartar incursion, he made a wry note in his journal: "Travelers of great discretion. Very close as to political matters." He underlined these words twice, then added with a touch of sarcasm, "One might think the fate of the empire hangs upon their silence." Closing his notebook with an audible snap, he turned his attention back to the dusty landscape rushing past his window.

Harry Blount and Alcide Jolivet, both journalists traveling on the same train to cover the war, were unaware of each other's presence since their morning departure from Moscow station. While Jolivet recorded his observations in his leather-bound notebook, drawing suspicious glances from fellow passengers who shifted in their seats, Blount took a different approach. His quiet, observant demeanor and minimal conversation helped him blend in with his compartment companions, offering only a polite nod or brief comment about the weather. Unlike Jolivet, whose constant scribbling marked him as an outsider, no one suspected Blount of being a spy, which proved helpful. His fellow travelers spoke freely around him, often revealing more than their usual cautiousness would permit, their voices carrying across the rhythmic clatter of wheels on rails. As a result, the Daily Telegraph correspondent gained valuable insights into how deeply recent events had affected Nijni-Novgorod's merchants, who spoke of empty warehouses and canceled shipments, and the growing threats to Central Asian trade routes, where caravans now traveled in heavily armed convoys, if they dared to travel at all.

"The surrounding passengers were on edge, their faces drawn and voices hushed. War was the only topic of conversation, and they discussed it with surprising openness, treating the conflict between the Volga and Vistula as if it were already underway," he documented in his journal, noting how even the wealthiest merchants spoke of abandoning their trading posts.

The Daily Telegraph's readership would be just as well-informed as Alcide Jolivet's "cousin." Harry Blount, however, positioned on the train's left side, only observed the rolling hills while ignoring the expansive plains on the right, his notebook balanced on his knee. With typical British self-assurance, he wrote, "The terrain between Moscow and Wladimir is mountainous," a description that would have amused any local familiar with the region's gentle topography.

The Kremlin leadership was preparing strict measures to prevent potential disturbances throughout Russia's heartland, dispatching additional troops to key cities and strengthening border patrols. While the uprising hadn't penetrated Siberia's borders, there were concerns about possible unrest spreading to the Volga regions, which lay dangerously close to Kirghiz territory. Military checkpoints had appeared at major crossroads, and telegraph operators reported increased surveillance of communications.

The authorities had yet to uncover any sign of Ivan Ogareff. No one knew if the traitor had joined forces with Feofar-Khan, seeking foreign help to satisfy his personal vendetta, or if he was trying to incite rebellion in Nijni-Novgorod. The city's great market attracted a diverse mix of Persians, Armenians, and Kalmucks at this time of year, and Ogareff might have planted agents among them to spark an uprising. Such schemes were possible in Russia, given the empire's vast complexity and the relative ease with which conspirators could disappear into its sprawling territories.

Indeed, this enormous nation, spanning 4,000,000 square miles, bore little resemblance to the more uniform states of Western Europe. Its territory, stretching across Europe and Asia, contained over seventy million people speaking thirty different languages, with dialects and sub-dialects multiplying that number several times over. While the Slavic peoples formed the majority, the empire encompassed Russians, Poles, Lithuanians, and Courlanders, each maintaining their distinct cultural traditions and social hierarchies. Beyond these were the Finns, Laplanders, and Estonians, along with many northern tribes whose names defied pronunciation by even the most learned scholars. The population also included Permiaks, Germans, Greeks, Tartars, various Caucasian peoples, as well as Mongol, Kalmuck, Samoid, Kamtschatkan, and Aleutian groups, each with their own customs, religious practices, and ancestral territories. Given such diversity, maintaining unity across this vast state was an immense challenge, one that required time and the careful governance of multiple generations of rulers, whose policies had to balance central authority with local autonomy to prevent the empire from fracturing under its own weight.

With relentless determination, Ivan Ogareff continued to evade capture, likely making his way toward the Tartar forces. At each railway stop, vigilant inspectors would board the train, examining every passenger under direct orders from police command to locate Ogareff. The authorities remained convinced that the betrayer was still within Russia's European territories. Any passenger who aroused suspicion found themselves detained at local police stations for questioning, while the train continued its journey without delay, the fate of those left behind of little concern to their fellow travelers.

Arguing with the Russian police is futile, as they operate with complete arbitrariness and military discipline, being organized as a military force. Their unquestioning obedience is not surprising, given that they answer to a monarch whose official title alone shows his vast authority, a ruler who commands an empire stretching from Poland to Siberia, from the Arctic to Armenia, whose symbol is a double-headed eagle grasping the scepter and globe of absolute power, whose crest bears the emblems of ancient kingdoms, and whose authority is ordained as Emperor and Autocrat of All the Russias. Such extensive dominion and claims to power translate into an enforcement arm that brooks no opposition. The police carried out their duties with mechanical efficiency, their faces stern and impassive as they moved through the carriages. Their dark uniforms and gleaming badges served as constant reminders of state authority, while their practiced movements spoke of years spent perfecting the art of intimidation. Those passengers wise enough to travel with impeccable documentation found the inspections merely inconvenient; those less fortunate discovered how swiftly suspicion could turn to detention.

Michael Strogoff had his documentation in perfect order, which meant he could travel with no interference from law enforcement. His papers bore all the necessary stamps and seals, each carefully maintained and protected within a leather folder that showed signs of frequent use but meticulous care.

When they reached Wladimir station, the train paused long enough for the Daily Telegraph's reporter to both observe and contemplate this historic Russian capital, forming a thorough impression of the city. The ancient churches with their distinctive onion domes pierced the sky, while the weathered stone walls of the Kremlin spoke of centuries of turbulent history.

As the train halted at Wladimir station, new passengers boarded, including a young woman who stepped into Michael Strogoff's compartment. Finding an empty seat across from the courier, she settled in, placing beside her a simple red leather traveling bag that appeared to be her only possession. The bag, though well-worn at the corners, was of good quality leather and bore no identifying marks or tags. She sat with her eyes lowered, avoiding any contact with her chance companions, and readied herself for the hours of travel still ahead. Her dark traveling dress, modest but well-tailored, suggested someone accustomed to moving in respectable circles, though her demeanor spoke of someone wishing to pass unnoticed.

Michael Strogoff found himself studying his new traveling companion with keen interest. He politely offered to switch seats with her, because he noticed she was facing away from the engine and thought she would be more comfortable in his seat. She declined his offer with a graceful nod.

The teenager appeared to be in her mid-teens, perhaps sixteen or seventeen. Her striking features embodied the classic Slavic beauty, with a hint of severity that promised to mature into true elegance rather than simple attractiveness. Light golden hair flowed from beneath the kerchief covering her head, the fine strands catching the late afternoon sunlight filtering through the compartment window. Her brown eyes radiated gentleness and warmth, while her straight nose connected to pale, slender cheeks through delicate, responsive nostrils. Despite her perfectly shaped lips, she seemed to have forgotten how to smile long ago. The overall impression was of youth touched too early by life's harsher realities, though her inherent grace remained undiminished.

The traveler stood tall and graceful, her posture clear despite the loose, flowing dress +

draping her form. Though still in her youth, her prominent forehead and sharp features suggested maturity beyond her years, in the depth of her moral conviction, a quality that caught Michael Strogoff's keen eye. Life had left its mark on this young woman; past hardships had shaped her, and her future path seemed uncertain. Yet she possessed an unmistakable resilience, facing life's challenges with unwavering determination. Her strength of character showed itself in both quick decisive action and steady perseverance, maintaining a composure that would impress even the most steadfast men in times of crisis. Her hands, though delicate, bore slight calluses that hinted at a life of practical necessity rather than idle comfort, and the way she carried herself spoke of someone accustomed to shouldering responsibility alone. Even the modest simplicity of her traveling attire seemed a conscious choice rather than mere circumstance, reflecting an inner dignity that transcended outward appearances.

The first impression she made was striking. Her distinctive features attracted Michael Strogoff, a man of powerful character. While avoiding any uncomfortable staring, he studied his fellow passenger with genuine curiosity. The young woman's attire was modest, yet suited to travel. Though clearly not without means, as was clear at a glance, her clothing showed meticulous care and thoughtful selection. She carried all her belongings in a single well-worn leather bag which, because of the cramped space, rested on her knees, its brass buckles dulled from years of faithful service.

An elegant dark pelisse, its neckline adorned with a pressed blue ribbon despite the rigors of travel, comprised the woman's attire. Beneath it, she wore layered dark garments, a short skirt over a longer robe that extended to her ankles, both pieces cut from sturdy wool that would withstand the harsh demands of long-distance journeying. Sturdy leather half-boots protected her petite feet with thick soles, suggesting preparation for extensive travel, their careful polish at odds with the obvious miles they had already covered. The practical ensemble spoke of someone who understood the balance between maintaining appearances and facing the realities of life on the road.

Something about her clothing style struck Michael Strogoff as distinctly Livonian. The subtle details of her ensemble, from the precise cut of her wool garments to the particular way she wore her layers, led him to conclude she likely hailed from the Baltic provinces, where such practical yet refined fashion was common among the merchant class.

Where was this solitary young woman headed, traveling by herself at a time in life when most would consider paternal guidance or brotherly guardianship essential? Was she perhaps arriving from somewhere in Western Russia after a lengthy voyage across the empire's vast expanses? Could Nijni-Novgorod be her final destination, or did her journey extend past the empire's eastern borders into territories less hospitable to lone travelers? Would she find familiar faces, family members or acquaintances, waiting with open arms when her train arrived? Or was it more likely that she would be just as alone in the bustling city as she was in this train car? The latter seemed more likely, given her composed but isolated demeanor.

Her solitary lifestyle was clear in her every movement and gesture, each one practiced and precise. As she boarded the carriage and settled in for the trip, she moved with a self-contained efficiency that spoke of long practice navigating unfamiliar spaces alone. She did not disturb her fellow passengers, taking great care to minimize her presence and avoid causing any inconvenience, her movements almost ghost-like in their consideration. Everything about her behavior revealed someone who had grown used to standing alone, relying on her own resources and judgment, having learned the delicate art of existing in public spaces without drawing undue attention to herself.

In the carriage, Michael Strogoff watched the young woman, though he maintained his distance and made no attempt to speak with her. There was only one moment when he intervened, her fellow passenger, a merchant who had earlier made those tactless comments about tallow and shawls, had dozed off and his heavy head was lolling close to her, swaying back and forth between his shoulders like a mounted pendulum. Strogoff gave him a firm shake awake and conveyed that he needed to sit upright.

The trader, ill-mannered, muttered complaints about "nosy people sticking their noses where they don't belong," and shifted uncomfortably in his seat. But when Michael Strogoff fixed him with a severe look, one that carried all the authority of a man accustomed to being obeyed, the drowsy man shifted to lean the other way, sparing the young passenger from his unwelcome presence.

In a fleeting glance, the passenger caught Strogoff's eye, expressing gratitude, before resuming her composure. A subtle exchange, lasting only a heartbeat, revealed much about her reserved nature.

The train lurched violently as it navigated a sharp bend of twelve miles before reaching Nijni-Novgorod. The jarring impact sent it climbing up an embankment's slope, wheels screeching against the iron rails as they fought for purchase. This incident revealed to Strogoff the true nature of the young woman's character, a revelation that would later prove significant.

The erupting chaos inside the train cars tossed the frightened passengers around. Shouts and clamor filled the air while confusion spread through every compartment, luggage tumbling from overhead racks and tea cups shattering on the wooden floors. The commotion suggested a severe incident had occurred, with some passengers crying out about derailment or worse. Before the train could even come to a halt, doors flew open as terrified travelers rushed to escape their carriages, fearing the worst, their faces masks of panic in the afternoon light.

A sudden thought of the young girl crossed Michael Strogoff's mind amid the pandemonium. As the other passengers in her compartment rushed out in panic, screaming and pushing, nearly trampling one another in their haste to reach the exits, she stayed in her seat, composed nevertheless, hands folded in her lap. Only a hint of paleness betrayed any emotion on her face, and her eyes remained steady, focused on some distant point through the window as if the surrounding chaos was a minor inconvenience.

She made no move to leave, and neither did Michael Strogoff.

They both remained motionless, like two islands of calm in a sea of panic and confusion.

"What remarkable composure," Michael Strogoff mused to himself, finding himself oddly impressed by the young woman's steadfast demeanor in the face of apparent danger.

The frightening incident turned out to be harmless. The luggage car's coupling had broken, which caused the initial jolt and brought the train to a halt. Had this not happened, the train would have plunged off the elevated track into marshy ground below. Though the accident delayed them for an hour while workers cleared the track and secured the wayward car, the train continued on its way, the rhythmic clacking of wheels on rails resuming their familiar cadence. They pulled into Nijni-Novgorod station at 8:30 in the evening, the platform lights casting long shadows across the worn wooden boards.

The police inspectors, stern-faced men in dark uniforms, positioned themselves at the carriage doors before any passengers could disembark, checking each person with methodical precision. Their presence created a bottleneck as the inspectors forced weary travelers to submit to their scrutiny.

When Michael Strogoff presented his podorojna papers under the name Nicholas Korpanoff, they quickly waved him through, not even glancing at the official documents bearing the imperial seal. The other passengers sharing his compartment, who were traveling to Nijni-Novgorod, also passed inspection without issue since none of them raised any suspicions in the watchful eyes of the authorities.

Instead of a passport, which had become obsolete in Russia, the young woman presented an unusual document, a permit bearing a distinctive private seal that shimmered in the lamplight. The inspector studied it carefully, turning the paper this way and that, before looking up to scrutinize her appearance against the description provided. His weathered face betraying nothing.

"Your origin is Riga?" he inquired.

"Indeed," she confirmed with quiet confidence.

"Your destination, Irkutsk?" he continued, making a small notation in his ledger.

"Correct," she replied, standing straight under his examination.

"Which path will you take?" His pen hovered above the page.

"Through Perm," she stated without hesitation, her fingers unconsciously adjusting the hem of her traveling coat.

"Excellent!" the inspector declared, closing his ledger with a sharp snap. "Be sure to have your permit stamped at the Nijni-Novgorod police station before continuing your journey."

The young girl nodded her head in agreement.

As Michael Strogoff listened to this exchange, he felt both astonished and concerned, his weathered brow furrowing beneath the brim of his cap. This young girl was traveling alone to distant Siberia at such a dangerous time? The usual hazards of the journey were now compounded by the risks of an invaded land during rebellion. Bandits and deserters prowled the roads while entire villages lay abandoned. How would she make it? What fate awaited her in those vast, unforgiving territories where even armed men feared to venture alone?

Once the inspection concluded, they unlatched the carriage doors with a metallic clang that echoed through the compartment. However, before

Michael Strogoff could make his way to her, perhaps to offer help or guidance, the young Livonian woman had already slipped into the bustling crowd that filled the railway station's platforms, her slender figure weaving between merchants, travelers, and porters. She became the first passenger to exit and vanishing from sight, leaving behind only questions in Strogoff's troubled mind.

© 01/01/2025
QuantumDigitalPublishing.io
Michael Strogoff or, The Courier of the Czar
Book I - Chapter V

Chapter Five

THE TWO ANNOUNCEMENTS

Situated where the Volga and Oka rivers meet, NIJNI-NOVGOROD (also known as Lower Novgorod) serves as the principal city of its namesake district. At this point, Michael Strogoff had no choice but to abandon his railway journey, as the tracks extended no further. From here onward, his travel would become increasingly slow and dangerous, forcing him to rely on more traditional means of transportation through the vast Russian terrain.

The city of Nijni-Novgorod, though home to around thirty-five thousand (35,000), residents, swelled to over three hundred thousand (300,000), people during its renowned three-week fair. This massive influx of traders and visitors increased the city's population by ten times its normal size, transforming the quiet streets into bustling thoroughfares filled with merchants, performers, and travelers from across Europe and Asia. Before 1817, these commercial gatherings had taken place in Makariew, but thereafter Nijni-Novgorod became the fair's permanent home, its strategic location at merging two major rivers, making it an ideal center for trade and commerce. The city's architecture reflected this dual nature, with its ancient kremlin overlooking the modern commercial districts that had sprung up to accommodate the fair's enormous activity.

Despite the lateness of Michael Strogoff's departure, both sections of Nijni-Novgorod remained bustling with activity. The city, divided by the Volga River into two distinct parts, featured an upper town perched atop a precipitous cliff, where a Russian fortress known as a "Kreml" stood guard, its ancient stone walls a testament to centuries of history and conflict.

Michael Strogoff struggled to locate suitable accommodations in the area. Though not in an immediate rush since he planned to travel by steamboat, he still needed to secure lodging. Before settling that matter, however, he confirmed the steamer's departure time. Upon visiting the office of the steamship company operating between Nijni-Novgorod and Perm, he received unwelcome news. The next boat wouldn't depart until noon the following day. A seventeen-hour delay frustrated someone on such a time-sensitive journey. Yet he remained composed, knowing that no alternative transport could match the steamer's speed to either Perm or Kasan. He reasoned it would be prudent to wait, as the steamboat's speed would help make up for lost time, even considering the crowds of merchants and travelers, who would compete for passage along the same route.

Wandering the streets of Nijni-Novgorod, Michael Strogoff searched for lodging, though finding a place to sleep wasn't his primary concern. His growling stomach drove him. Had he not been famished, he would have continued roaming the city streets until dawn. Fortune smiled upon him at the City of Constantinople inn, where he discovered both food and shelter. The establishment's proprietor, a stout man with ruddy cheeks, showed him to a modest room which, despite its sparse furnishings, featured a Virgin Mary icon and several saints' images adorned in yellow gauze frames. The flickering light of an oil lamp cast dancing shadows across their solemn faces.

Laid out before him was a feast: a goose stuffed with tangy filling floating in rich cream, accompanied by hearty barley bread and fresh curds. Steam rose from the browned bird. A sweet mixture of powdered sugar and cinnamon sat nearby, along with a pitcher of kwass beer, Russia's traditional fermented beverage, its distinctive aroma filling the air. He ate, savoring each bite with the appreciation of a hungry traveler, unlike his table companion, a devout member of the Raskalnik sect of Old Believers, who, bound by strict religious abstinence, wouldn't touch the potatoes served to him and drank his tea without sugar. The man's weathered face remained stern as he sipped his plain beverage.

After completing his evening meal, Michael Strogoff opted not to return to his quarters, choosing instead to wander through the streets of Nizhny Novgorod. Though daylight still illuminated the sky with streaks of amber and purple, the townspeople were heading home, their shadows lengthening as they hurried along. The wooden shutters creaked shut one by one, leaving the thoroughfares deserted until all inhabitants had retreated to their homes, save for a few stray dogs skulking in the gathering darkness.

What prevented Michael Strogoff from retiring to his bed, which would have been the sensible choice after such an extensive train journey across the Russian countryside? Was his mind occupied with thoughts of the young Livonian lady who had shared his travels, her quiet dignity and self-possession making a lasting impression? Indeed, having no other pressing matters, she occupied his thoughts, though he tried to dismiss such distractions. Was he concerned she might face harassment in this bustling metropolis, where merchants and travelers from all corners of the empire mingled? Such worries weren't unfounded, and he had good cause for concern, given the rough characters he'd observed in the taverns and marketplaces. Did he harbor hopes of encountering her again, perhaps to offer his guardianship through the city's winding streets? No, such a meeting seemed improbable in the sprawling town. And as for protection, what authority did he possess, being another traveler himself?

Whispering in solitude, he reflected on his isolation among the nomadic peoples surrounding him. Yet his own perils seemed insignificant when measured against what awaited her. The vast expanse of Siberia and the distant city of Irkutsk loomed ahead. While he faced these dangers for his homeland and his Emperor, her motives remained a mystery. What drove her? Who had granted her permission to cross these contested borders? Beyond lay territories in open rebellion, with Tartar raiders swarming across the steppes, burning villages and slaughtering those who resisted their advance.

Michael Strogoff gathered his thoughts, his hand unconsciously tightening on the leather strap of his travel pack as his mind wrestled with these troubling questions. The wind whistled through the tall grass around him, carrying with it the faint scent of wood-smoke from distant camps.

"Surely," he reasoned, "she must have planned this journey before the invasion began. Yet perhaps she remains unaware of current events. No, that's impossible. Nadia was present when the merchants discussed the Siberian unrest and showed no sign of surprise. She didn't even ask questions. She must have known what was happening and still proceeded. Poor girl! Her reasons for traveling must be compelling! But despite her clear courage, her physical strength will fail her. Even setting aside the dangers and obstacles, such a grueling journey will prove too much for her endurance. The harsh terrain and unforgiving climate would test even the hardiest traveler. She'll never make it as far as Irkutsk!"

Lost in thought, Michael Strogoff meandered through the streets, confident in his ability to find his way back, thanks to his thorough knowledge of the town. The evening shadows lengthened around him as he walked, and the sounds of merchants closing their shops for the day echoed off the weathered buildings.

After roaming for about an hour, he found rest on a bench beside a spacious wooden house, one of many surrounding an expansive clearing. The worn planks of the bench creaked beneath him as he sat, and the sweet scent of pine from the freshly cut lumber stacked nearby filled his nostrils. He had settled in when he felt the sudden weight of someone's hand press on his shoulder, the grip strong and purposeful.

"What do you think you're doing there?" barked a burly man who had materialized behind him, his shadow falling across the bench like a dark curtain.

"Taking a rest," Michael Strogoff said, keeping his voice steady despite the unexpected confrontation.

"Planning to spend the entire night on that bench, are you?" The man's gravelly voice carried an unmistakable note of suspicion.

"Perhaps I am," Michael Strogoff shot back, his tone sharper than befitted the humble merchant he was pretending to be. He regretted the slip in his crafted demeanor.

"Step into the light where I can get a look at you," the man commanded, shifting his weight forward with the practiced stance of someone used to confrontation.

Michael Strogoff, mindful that caution was paramount, recoiled. "That won't be necessary," he replied, taking ten measured steps backward, his boots scraping against the packed earth.

As Michael studied the stranger, he noted the man's nomadic appearance, the kind associated with wandering fair folk whose presence often made others uncomfortable. The man's clothes were well worn but maintained, speaking of a life lived on the move. Peering through the growing darkness, Michael spotted what confirmed his suspicions: a sizeable wagon-home parked near the small house, its wooden sides weathered by countless miles of travel, the sort of mobile dwelling favored by the Roma travelers who could be found throughout Russia, setting up wherever they might earn even the most modest living. The wagon's small windows glowed with warm lamplight, suggesting others were inside.

When the gypsy moved forward a few steps, intending to question Michael Strogoff further, the cottage door opened. A woman appeared, her dark silhouette framed by the warm light behind her, speaking in a dialect that Michael Strogoff recognized as a blend of Mongol and Siberian languages, the harsh consonants rolling off her tongue with practiced ease.

"Not another spy! Leave him be and come eat. Your papluka is getting cold." Her voice carried both authority and irritation as she gestured at the man.

Despite his deep aversion to spies, Michael Strogoff couldn't suppress a smile at being labeled as one. Although he maintained his neutral expression, he recognized the absurdity of the situation.

Using the same language but with a distinct accent, the Bohemian answered, his tone carrying a hint of deference mixed with amusement, "Your observation is correct, Sangarre! And also, our departure is set for tomorrow."

"Tomorrow?" Sangarre echoed, clearly taken aback, her figure stiffening in the doorway as she processed this unexpected news.

"Indeed, Sangarre," the Bohemian confirmed, spreading his arms in an expansive gesture. "Tomorrow we leave, and it's by the Father's own command that we journey to our destination! The stars themselves align for our departure."

Following this exchange, both individuals stepped inside their cottage, making sure to secure the door behind them with a heavy wooden latch that scraped against its metal housing. The sound of their continuing conversation became muffled behind the thick walls.

"Excellent!" Michael Strogoff thought to himself, a slight smirk playing at the corners of his mouth. "If these nomads want their conversations to remain private in my presence, they should consider speaking in a different tongue. Their carelessness serves me well enough."

Being of Siberian descent and having spent his early years in the Steppes, where language was as vital as breath itself, Michael Strogoff could comprehend every dialect spoken between Tartary and the Sea of Ice. The countless hours spent among traders, travelers, and tribesmen had honed this skill to near perfection. Yet he paid little attention to the precise meaning of their words, letting them wash over him like wind across the plains. After all, what reason did he have to care about the schemes of wandering Bohemians?

He headed back to his lodgings for some rest as night had fallen. On his way, he walked alongside the Volga River, its surface visible beneath the multitude of vessels that crowded its waters. The gentle lapping of waves against wooden hulls and the distant calls of night watchmen provided a soothing backdrop to his thoughts.

Within an hour, Michael Strogoff had fallen into a deep sleep on one of those firm Russian mattresses that foreigners often find uncomfortable. The bed, stuffed with dense horsehair and covered by rough-woven sheets, felt like home to his travel-hardened body. He woke at dawn the next morning, July 17th.

With five hours remaining in Nijni-Novgorod, Michael Strogoff faced what felt like an eternity. The prospect of another morning wandering the streets, as he had done the previous evening, seemed his only option. His scheduled tasks, eating breakfast, securing his bag, and having his podorojna checked at the police station, would occupy only a fraction of his wait. He calculated that even if he performed each task with deliberate slowness, he would still have three hours of idle time to endure.

Being someone who never lingered in bed after sunrise, he rose and dressed, his military habits serving him well, even in civilian life. He took special care to secure the imperial-sealed letter in its hidden pocket within his coat's lining, fastening his belt over it with practiced precision. After shouldering his packed bag, its leather worn smooth from his travels, he decided against returning to the City of Constantinople inn. Instead, planning to breakfast along the Volga's bank near the wharf where merchants were already setting up their morning trade, he settled his bill and departed.

Taking no chances, Strogoff first visited the steam-packet company's office to confirm the Caucasus would depart on schedule, finding comfort in the clerk's assured nod. There, a new thought struck him. Since the young Livonian girl was bound for Perm, she might also take passage on the Caucasus. This meant they might be travel companions, though he remained uncertain whether this prospect pleased or concerned him.

The upper town and its fortress-like kremlin, stretching two miles around and bearing similarities to Moscow's own citadel, stood deserted, its stone walls catching the early morning light. Not even the governor maintained residence there, having long since moved to more comfortable quarters in the lower town. Yet while the upper town lay lifeless as a cemetery, its empty windows staring across the landscape, the lower section bustled with activity, already alive with traders, laborers, and the daily commerce of river life.

After traversing the Volga via a pontoon bridge under Cossack horsemen's watch, Michael Strogoff arrived at the open area where he had encountered the gypsy encampment the previous evening. Near: Near the Nijni-Novgorod fairgrounds, on the outskirts, lay the location of the governor-general's makeshift residence; imperial decree required his presence throughout the fair, as the diverse crowd demanded constant vigilance.

The field was covered with stalls, set up in neat rows that created wide pathways where people could move without getting jammed together. Planners' experience in managing large gatherings was clear in the careful organization, with designated routes for foot traffic and horse-drawn carts marked by colored flags and wooden signs in multiple languages.

People organized these trading districts into distinct sections, each devoted to specific types of goods. You could find separate areas for ironwork, fur trading, wool merchants, timber sellers, textile makers, and preserved fish vendors, among others. Some creative merchants constructed their stalls using the very products they sold, building walls from tea bricks or stacks of cured meat. This unique and somewhat American-style marketing approach used the actual merchandise as both storefront and advertisement. Leather, spices, smoked fish, and fresh timber filled the air, their mingled scents accompanied by the peculiar music of haggling in dozens of languages.

A diverse crowd of Europeans and Asians filled the bustling marketplace, their voices a lively mix of negotiations and discussions as the sun rose. Goods from across the world overflowed the square in astonishing variety. Luxurious furs and glittering precious stones lay alongside delicate silks and intricate Cashmere shawls. Turkish carpets competed for attention with weapons from the Caucasus and gossamer-light gauzes from Smyrna and Ispahan. Tiflis armor stood near aromatic caravan teas, while European bronzes and precise Swiss timepieces shared space with fine Lyon velvets and sturdy English cottons. The marketplace showcased everything from practical harness to fresh produce, Ural minerals including malachite and lapis-lazuli, an array of spices and perfumes, medicinal herbs, and basic commodities like wood, tar, rope, and horn. Plump pumpkins and juicy watermelons added splashes of color to this remarkable bazaar, which seemed to gather all the treasures of India, China, Persia, the Caspian and Black Sea regions, and even goods from as far as America and Europe, all converging at this remarkable trading hub. Merchants in colorful robes and Western suits alike gestured as they bartered, their practiced hands weighing silver coins and examining goods with expert precision. The more established traders had erected semi-permanent structures with intricate wooden carvings and brass fittings, while others made do with simple canvas awnings that snapped in the morning breeze, their shadows dancing across the cobblestones below.

The scene defied description, a massive tide of humanity ebbing and flowing in all directions amid chaotic energy and clamor. While the local people and working classes displayed great animation, they were far surpassed by the visitors in their fervor. Among them were traders who had journeyed for twelve months across the expansive steppes of Central

Asia with their goods, knowing another year would pass before they saw their businesses again. The Nijni-Novgorod fair held such commercial significance that its yearly transactions reached the staggering sum of one hundred million dollars, a testament to its position as one of the world's great marketplaces.

In the open spaces between districts of this makeshift town, various entertainers gathered: mountain-dwelling gypsies read palms for gullible visitors who always frequent such gatherings, their weathered hands tracing life lines with practiced mysticism; Zingaris or Tsiganes (as Russians call these descendants of ancient Copts) performed their exotic songs and traditional dances, their colorful skirts whirling in mesmerizing patterns; foreign theater troupes presented Shakespeare adaptations to eager crowds, their makeshift stages adorned with tattered velvet curtains. Along the wide pathways, handlers led their performing bears, their massive beasts shuffling to primitive drum beats, while animal tamers in menageries wielded whips and heated irons, drawing harsh cries from their subjects that echoed through the bustling marketplace. In the central plaza's middle, surrounded by four rows of enthusiastic onlookers, "Volga sailors" sat on the ground as if aboard their vessel, mimicking rowing movements under directing their conductor's baton, he being the metaphorical helmsman of this imaginary boat, his commands carrying across the plaza like those of a true river captain. What a peculiar tradition, one that spoke to the deep connection between the Russian people and their mighty rivers!

At that moment, following an age-old tradition at the Nijni-Novgorod fair, hundreds of caged birds were released into the air above the massive crowd. Having: Having collected a few copecks from onlookers, the bird sellers unlatched their cages and freed their birds. A great flock of birds soared skyward, filling the air with cheerful songs, their wings catching the sunlight as they dispersed in all directions like scattered jewels against the azure sky.

That year, the prominent Nijni-Novgorod trade fair attracted two respected Western European journalists, Harry Blount from England and Alcide Jolivet from France. Jolivet, ever the optimist, found himself quite satisfied with the local accommodations and cuisine, leading him to write glowing reviews about Nijni-Novgorod in his journal, praising the hearty stews and fresh-baked bread served at local taverns. Blount's experience proved different, unable to secure either a meal or proper lodging, he was forced to sleep outdoors beneath the stars, with only his traveling cloak for warmth. This unfortunate situation prompted him to draft a scathing critique of the town, condemning innkeepers who turned away travelers willing to pay for even basic hospitality and shelter, noting in his dispatches how such treatment reflected on a city that prided itself on its international commerce.

With one hand tucked in his pocket and the other gripping a cherry-stemmed pipe, Michael Strogoff gave the impression of being calm and unruffled. However, anyone watching would have noticed the occasional tensing of his eyebrows, betraying his intense eagerness to depart. His fingers drummed an unconscious rhythm against the smooth wood of the pipe stem, another subtle tell that belied his outward composure.

For two hours, he wandered through the streets, finding himself drawn back to the marketplace. As he moved among the merchants and shoppers, he noticed the traders from Asia's borderlands showing clear signs of distress. Their business was declining, with many merchants whispering among themselves in their native tongues while casting furtive glances at their dwindling stocks of silk, spice, and leather goods. Another detail caught his attention. In Russia, you find military personnel everywhere. However, today was different. The soldiers, Cossacks, and other military forces were absent from the bustling market, leaving an unsettling void in the usual rhythm of commerce and surveillance. Most likely, they were confined to their barracks, anticipating imminent deployment orders, their absence speaking volumes about the gravity of the situation developing beyond the city's walls.

A flurry of military activity was clear, though not from the common soldiers. Since the previous evening, officers and aides had been rushing to and from the governor's residence on horseback in all directions, their mounts' hooves clattering against the cobblestones as they carried dispatches with increasing urgency. The heightened activity suggested something of grave importance was unfolding. Messengers traveled along the routes to both Wladimir and the Ural Mountains, their horses lathered with sweat from the relentless pace, while telegraph lines to Moscow buzzed with non-stop communications, the operators working in shifts to handle the volume of encrypted messages.

The news of the police chief's urgent summons to the governor-general's palace spread through the central square where Michael Strogoff stood, passed from merchant to merchant in hurried whispers. Word had it that a crucial message from Moscow had arrived, carried by a special courier who had ridden through the night.

"They're shutting down the fair," someone called out, the announcement sending ripples of concern through the gathered crowd.

"The Nijni-Novgorod regiment has been given marching orders," another voice announced, triggering a wave of murmurs and worried exchanges among the merchants who had traveled so far to attend the fair.

"I hear the Tartars are threatening Tomsk!" The words rang out like a gunshot, causing nearby merchants to grab at their purses and goods.

The crowd erupted with shouts of "The head of police is here!" Thunderous applause broke out across the gathering, dying down until complete stillness fell over the assembly. Women pulled their children closer, and merchants ceased their haggling mid-sentence. As the police chief made his way to the center of the square, everyone could see he was clutching an official document, its imperial seal glinting in the morning sun.

Breaking the silence, he proclaimed in commanding tones, his voice carrying to every corner of the hushed marketplace: By a decree of the Governor of Nijni-Novgorod:

First, the government prohibits all Russian citizens from leaving the province for any reason; immediate arrest will follow.

"Second: All persons of Asian descent must vacate the province within twenty-four hours, taking with them only what they can carry."

Chapter Six

BROTHER AND SISTER

These restrictions caused significant hardship for individuals and disrupted countless lives and livelihoods, the volatile political situation left no other reasonable choice for maintaining security.

The order prohibiting all Russian subjects from leaving the province served a crucial purpose; if Ivan Ogareff remained, it would make it difficult for him to join Feofar-Khan and assume a dangerous leadership role in the Tartar forces. The military authorities understood that restricting movement was essential to containing potential threats, even at the cost of civilian inconvenience.

The decree mandated that any person of Asian descent must depart from the province within twenty-four hours, allowing just enough time to gather essential belongings and make hurried travel arrangements. This sweeping order would expel all merchants from Central Asia, along with various nomadic groups like the Bohemians and gypsies, whom they suspected of having ties to the Tartars. Russian authorities viewed these diverse populations as potential security risks, each individual serving as an informant or spy in the growing network of insurgency, making their removal a matter of urgent necessity. Harsh measures reflected the administration's growing anxiety about the deteriorating situation along the frontier.

The town of Nijni-Novgorod, bustling with visitors and boasting of Russia's most vibrant commercial center, reeled from the impact of these dual proclamations. Local merchants whose ventures extended beyond Siberia found themselves stranded within the province. The first declaration was unambiguous and absolute, brooking no exceptions, individual concerns had to bow before public necessity. The second proclamation, while targeting only foreign traders of Asian descent, left them no choice but to gather their wares and retrace their journey homeward. Perhaps most severely affected were the traveling performers and entertainers, who faced an arduous journey of a thousand miles to reach the closest border, a predicament that spelled genuine hardship for these wandering artists. As vendors dismantled their stalls and packed away their goods, the bustling marketplace fell into an eerie quiet. The air was thick with whispered conversations and hurried negotiations as merchants attempted to salvage what business they could before their forced departure. Even the local taverns and inns, usually teeming with traders sharing tales over steaming cups of tea, took on a somber atmosphere as their regular patrons made preparations to leave.

Objections and cries of anguish arose in response to this extraordinary order, but the watchful Cossacks silenced these protests with

law enforcement officers, their stern faces betraying no sympathy for the desperate pleas. The massive evacuation of the sprawling grounds begun without delay, proceeding with mechanical efficiency. Vendors collapsed their canopy covers with trembling hands, theatrical structures dismantled board by board. The campfires extinguished, leaving trails of acrid smoke, and circus performers took down their rigging with practiced but heavy movements. The weary, wheezing horses that pulled the traveling wagons emerged from their temporary shelters, their hooves clattering against the worn cobblestones. Officers and military personnel, wielding whips and batons, hurried along with those who lingered, showing no hesitation in destroying the shelters even while the unfortunate nomads still occupied them, sending splinters of wood and shreds of canvas flying through the air.

Vigorous actions clarified that Nijni-Novgorod's square would become empty by nightfall, with the bustling marketplace's noise giving way to an eerie stillness that seemed to echo off the surrounding buildings like a ghostly reminder of what once was.

Nomadic tribes faced an even harsher reality beyond the initial expulsion order. Authorities prevented them from returning to their homes and from seeking refuge in Siberia's vast steppes, where generations of their ancestors had roamed across the snow-dusted plains. Their only options lay southward, toward Persia, Turkey, or Turkestan plains near the Caspian Sea, territories that promised uncertain welcome at best. The Russian authorities had established strict boundaries with unwavering severity: these displaced people could not cross the Ural River post or the mountain range that extended along Russia's frontier, creating an impenetrable wall of bureaucracy and military might. This meant they had no choice but to embark on an arduous journey of six hundred miles, traversing treacherous terrain and hostile weather, before reaching any territory where they could settle, assuming they survived the grueling exodus with their families and meager possessions intact.

As the police chief concluded reading the proclamation, a thought struck Michael Strogoff. He found it strange how the proclamation's order to expel all foreigners of Asian descent coincided with the previous evening's conversation between the two Zingari gypsies. He recalled the old man's words: "The Father himself sends us where we wish to go." Everyone knew that "the Father" was how common people referred to the emperor. This raised troubling questions in Strogoff's mind: How had these gypsies expected this decree? What prior knowledge did they possess? Where were they planning to go? Something felt amiss about these individuals, and Strogoff suspected that rather than hindering them, the government's proclamation might serve their purposes. The timing was too precise to be mere coincidence, and their confident demeanor suggested they had been preparing for this very moment.

These thoughts vanished as another consideration consumed Michael's attention. The Zingaris, their cryptic remarks, and the peculiar timing of the proclamation all faded from his mind. Instead, his thoughts turned to the young Livonian girl. "Poor child," he mused. "The border is now closed to her." He could picture her delicate features twisted with worry, her hopes of reaching her destination now dashed by the stern words of bureaucracy. The thought of her alone and stranded in this hostile environment weighed heavily on his conscience.

The Livonian maiden, who hailed from Riga, found herself in a precarious position. Being a Russian subject by virtue of her birthplace in the Baltic province, she was now bound by law to remain within Russian borders, trapped by circumstances beyond her control. Her previous travel permit, got through proper channels and at considerable expense, had become nothing more than worthless paper considering enacted regulations. With Siberian routes now closed off and military checkpoints multiplying by the day, she could not pursue her journey to Irkutsk, regardless of how urgent or important her reasons might be for wanting to reach that distant city nestled in the heart of Siberia.

Michael Strogoff pondered on this matter, his brow furrowed in concentration. He reasoned that while staying true to his crucial mission, he might find ways to assist this courageous young woman, an idea that resonated with his sense of duty and honor. Having a clear understanding of the severe risks that he, as a strong and capable man well-versed in the ways of rough travel, would face, he realized the dangers would be far more threatening for an unaccompanied young woman in these turbulent times. Her journey to Irkutsk would follow his same route through the vast Siberian wilderness, requiring her to navigate through hostile invading forces just as he planned to do. Even if she had sufficient funds for normal travel conditions, which seemed unlikely given her modest appearance, how could she manage a journey that had become both treacherous and costly, with prices for safe passage rising as dangers increased?

"Well then," he mused, "should she journey toward Perm, it's almost certain our paths will cross. I can keep a protective eye on her without her knowledge, and since she seems just as eager as I am to reach Irkutsk, she won't slow my progress. Perhaps fate has arranged this meeting for a purpose."

But thoughts have a way of flowing into one another, like tributaries joining a mighty river. Until now, Michael Strogoff had considered his actions charitable, but a new perspective dawned on him, casting the situation in an different light, one that made his pulse quicken with revelation.

He pondered, muttering to himself, his fingers drumming against the window sill. "I require her help far more than she could ever need mine. With her by my side, I'll draw less unwanted attention. A solitary traveler crossing the steppe might be suspected of being the Czar's messenger. However, if this young woman travels with me, I'll match the Nicholas Korpanoff described in my podorojna, just another ordinary merchant making his way east with a companion. She must join me. There's no other way. I must track her down, whatever it takes. She hasn't found transportation to leave Nijni-Novgorod since last evening, not with the current chaos in the city. I must search for her now. Heaven, help me find her!"

Standing amid the chaos of Nijni-Novgorod's main square, Michael scanned the crowd for any sign of the girl. The scene before him was one of utter confusion, expelled foreigners protesting their treatment, while Cossacks and government agents herded them away, creating a deafening din. Merchants packed their stalls, fearful of the growing unrest, while bewildered travelers clutched their papers close. He knew she wouldn't be found in this mayhem. The morning was still young, just past nine, and with the steamboat's departure not until noon, he had two precious hours to locate her and convince her to join him as his fellow traveler.

He made his way back across the Volga and searched through the neighborhoods beyond, finding them much less crowded. The narrow streets offered a stark contrast to the square's pandemonium, with only the occasional sound of shutters being drawn or hushed conversations behind closed doors. He visited the churches, those sanctuaries that draw in all who grieve and suffer, their ancient stone walls offering solace to the desperate and displaced. But the young Livonian woman was nowhere to be found among the scattered worshippers kneeling in prayer.

He insisted to himself that she was still in Nijni-Novgorod, and he refused to believe otherwise. He spent two more hours wandering the streets, driven by a powerful inner force left no room for weariness or conscious thought. The afternoon sun cast long shadows across the cobblestones as he checked every alley and courtyard. Yet despite his relentless efforts, he found no trace of her.

A thought came to him. Could the girl be unaware of the decree? Though he dismissed this as unlikely, since such a momentous announcement would have reached everyone's ears by now, rippling through the city like waves on the Volga. Given her keen interest in even the tiniest updates from Siberia, her constant vigilance for news of any kind, it seemed impossible that she wouldn't know about the governor's proclamation, especially since it affected her.

However, if she remained unaware, she would arrive at the quay within the hour, joining the crowd of hopeful travelers, only to have some heartless official deny her passage and dash her hopes to pieces! He had to find her before then and prevent such a cruel rejection, no matter what it took. The thought of her facing such disappointment spurred him to quicken his pace once more.

Try as he might, his search proved futile, and he lost hope of locating her. As the clock struck eleven, Michael considered showing his podorojna papers from the Czar at the police chief's office. While the proclamation didn't apply to him, since his situation had been expected, he wanted to ensure there would be no obstacles to his departure from the town.

Michael crossed back over the Volga to the district where the police chief's headquarters were located. Despite orders for all foreigners to leave the province, they still had to complete mandatory paperwork before departing, which had drawn a massive throng of people to the area. The crowd stretched down several blocks, with anxious faces peering out from beneath parasols and hat brims as they waited in the summer heat.

To prevent Russian sympathizers of the Tartar cause from sneaking across the border in disguise, strict security measures were enforced. Anyone seeking to leave required official authorization, even if turned away. Guards scrutinized documents with painstaking attention to detail, comparing signatures and seals against reference materials while questioning travelers about their destinations and purposes. The process was slow and methodical, causing tempers to flare among those who had already spent hours waiting their turn.

The police station bustled with a diverse crowd, traveling performers, Roma people, and wandering tribes mixed with traders from across Asia, including merchants from Persia, Turkey, India, Turkestan, and China, all crowding the courtyard and administrative offices. Their colorful attire and varied languages created a tapestry of cultures beneath the stern institutional walls.

The masses rushed, knowing transportation would be scarce for the throng of exiled citizens. Those who delayed risked being stranded in the city past the deadline, leaving them vulnerable to harsh treatment by the governor's officers, who were already beginning to show less patience with each passing hour.

Through his powerful arm strength, Michael managed to make his way across the courthouse, shouldering past the press of bodies and ducking under extended arms clutching papers. Getting to the clerk's window inside the office proved far more challenging, with the crush of humanity bottlenecking at the narrow doorway. Yet, with a whispered word to an inspector and the strategic placement of some roubles, he secured his passage. After escorting Michael to the waiting area, a quiet alcove away from the main crowd, the inspector left to summon a senior clerk. Michael Strogoff felt confident he would soon resolve matters with the authorities and regain his freedom of movement, though he kept his expression neutral as other waiting travelers cast curious glances his way.

As he waited, his eyes wandered around until they landed on a striking sight. A young woman slumped on a bench caught his eye; her body language betrayed deep anguish, although her face was hidden, only her profile visible against the whitewashed wall. Michael Strogoff recognized her. It was the young Livonian girl, her delicate features as memorable as they had been during their brief encounter on the train.

She had visited the police station seeking approval for her travel documents, unaware of the governor's latest directives. The officials declined to allow her papers, their bureaucratic refusal delivered with cold indifference to her obvious distress. While she had permission to travel to Irkutsk, the new mandate was absolute. It superseded all prior approvals and blocked any civilian passage into Siberian territory. Michael, thrilled to have crossed paths with her again in such an unlikely place, made his way toward the young woman, weaving between the wooden benches and scattered travelers.

Her eyes lifted, and a smile spread across her features as she recognized the familiar face of her fellow traveler. The shadow of despair that had clouded her countenance moments before gave way to a glimmer of hope. She stood up, desperate hope filling her chest as she prepared to beg for his assistance, like someone flailing in deep water, reaching for anything that might save them. Her trembling hands clasped together as she waited for him to approach.

Just then, the agent's hand landed on Michael's shoulder, his fingers pressing into the fabric of his coat. "The police chief is ready for you now," he announced in a clipped, official tone.

"Excellent," said Michael with practiced neutrality. Without acknowledging the person he'd spent the entire day searching for, without even the slightest nod or fleeting glance of comfort that might put either of them at risk, he turned and followed his guide down the crowded corridor.

The young Livonian woman slumped back onto her weathered wooden bench, watching as the only person she could turn to for help vanished into the maze of administrative offices. Her shoulders sagged with the weight of renewed despair.

Michael Strogoff returned in less than three minutes, with the agent striding by his side. He was clutching his podorojna, the document that would grant him passage through Siberia, with an air of quiet triumph. Without breaking stride, he walked over to the young Livonian woman and extended his hand toward her, his expression neutral but his eyes conveying silent reassurance.

"Sister," he said, the single word carrying the weight of a sacred promise.

The word struck her with immediate understanding, resonating through her like a bell's obvious tone. She stood up at once, as though moved by an unexpected divine insight that left no room for doubt, her previous despair melting away like morning frost in sunlight.

"Sister," Michael Strogoff said again, his voice gentle but firm, "they have given us permission to carry on our journey to Irkutsk. Would you like to accompany me?" His steady gaze conveyed the depth of protection this offer entailed.

"I'll come with you, brother," the young woman answered without hesitation, slipping her hand into Michael Strogoff's with the trust of a lifelong sibling. Her fingers trembled, but her grip was sure. Together, they stepped out of the police station and into the crisp air, leaving behind the suffocating bureaucracy that had threatened to derail both their journeys.

Chapter Seven

GOING DOWN THE VOLGA

Just before noon, the steamboat's bell called a sizeable crowd to the Volga wharf. The gathering included not just willing passengers, but also many who were traveling under duress, their faces drawn with resignation and worry. The Caucasus stood ready for departure, its boilers operating at maximum pressure, the metal sides of the vessel vibrating with contained energy. Wisps of smoke drifted from the funnel, while white vapor crowned both the escape-pipe's end and valve covers, creating a hazy curtain against the late summer sky. The police maintained a strict surveillance over the Caucasus's departure,

interrogating travelers and turning away any whose responses they found unsatisfactory, their stern faces brooking no argument.

On the quay, many Cossacks stood ready to support the agents if needed, their sabers glinting in the midday sun and their horses pawing at the wooden planks, though their intervention proved unnecessary as everyone complied without protest. At the appointed time, when the final bell tolled its deep, resonant note across the water, the steamboat's mighty engines churned the water into a frothy wake, and the Caucasus navigated between the twin sections that made up Nijni-Novgorod, leaving behind a collection of waving handkerchiefs and worried faces on the shore.

With little trouble, Michael Strogoff and his young Livonian companion secured passage aboard the Caucasus. The podorojna document, issued in the name of Nicholas Korpanoff, permitted this supposed merchant to travel through Siberia with company. They appeared as siblings journeying under official protection, their matching dark attire and reserved demeanor lending credence to the deception. Side by side at the ship's stern, they watched the troubled city grow smaller, still in upheaval from the governor's proclamation. The afternoon sun cast long shadows across the deck as smoke billowed from the steamboat's twin stacks overhead. Michael maintained his silence, asking the girl nothing, waiting for her to speak when she felt the need. Eager to flee the town where she would have remained captive if not for her unexpected guardian's timely aid, she too stayed quiet, her delicate hands gripping the ship's railing as she gazed at the receding shoreline. Yet her grateful glances spoke volumes, and the slight trembling of her shoulders betrayed the emotion she struggled to contain.

The majestic Volga River, known to ancient civilizations as the Rha, stretches three thousand miles, making it Europe's longest waterway. While its upper reaches contain somewhat unhealthy waters, they become cleaner after merging with the swift-flowing Oka River at Nijni-Novgorod, which originates in Russia's central regions. Russia's intricate network of rivers and canals resembles an enormous tree, with waterways branching throughout the empire. At the heart of this system stands the Volga as the main trunk, culminating in seventy distinct channels that empty into the Caspian Sea. Ships can travel the river from its delta all the way to Rjef, a settlement in Tver province, covering most of its impressive length. Along its banks, countless villages and towns have flourished for centuries, their church spires and wooden houses dotting the landscape like pearls on a string. The river's might has shaped not only Russia's geography but also its culture, commerce, and very identity, earning it the cherished nickname "Mother Volga" among the Russian people who depend upon its waters for sustenance and trade.

The steamboats traveling between Perm and Nijni-Novgorod cover the 250-mile journey to Kasan. These vessels benefit from the Volga's current, which adds two miles per hour to their speed, allowing passengers to watch the rolling countryside and riverside settlements glide past at a satisfying pace. However, upon reaching the junction with the Kama River just below Kasan, the boats must leave the Volga and navigate upstream on the smaller Kama to reach Perm. Even with its powerful engines, the Caucasus could only achieve ten miles per hour against the Kama's current, its paddle wheels churning against the resistant waters. With a one-hour stop in Kasan, where passengers could stretch their legs and purchase refreshments from local vendors, the complete journey from Nijni-Novgorod to Perm takes between 60 and 62 hours.

The steamship featured an excellent layout with three separate passenger classes based on social standing and wealth, each deck maintained to meet the expectations of its occupants. Having booked two premium cabins in first class, with their polished brass fittings and plush velvet furnishings, Michael Strogoff ensured his young traveling companion could withdraw to her private quarters whenever she desired, away from the curious glances of fellow passengers.

The steamship Caucasus carried a diverse array of travelers; its decks vibrated with the diverse cultures that defined trade along the great waterways. Several merchants from Asia had departed Nijni-Novgorod without delay, eager to resume their business dealings before winter's approach. The first-class section hosted an eclectic mix of passengers: Armenian traders in flowing robes and distinctive miters, their animated conversations filling the air; Jewish merchants identifiable by their pointed caps, reviewing their ledgers; wealthy Chinese passengers in their traditional attire of loose-fitting robes in blue, violet, or black silk, moving with measured grace; Turkish travelers sporting their customary turbans of finest cotton; Indian traders wearing square caps and simple cord belts, some of whom controlled much of Central Asia's commerce through ancient family networks; and Tartar merchants in braided boots and embroidered shirts that sparkled with metallic thread. They forced these traders to stow their many trunks and packages both below deck and on the main deck, creating narrow passages between towering stacks of cargo. The transportation costs for their belongings would be substantial, as regulations permitted only twenty pounds of luggage per passenger, a restriction that caused no small amount of grumbling among those whose livelihoods depended on their wares.

Aboard the Caucasus, clusters of passengers gathered near the bow, including both foreigners and Russians who had permission to return to their provincial towns. Among them were mujiks wearing their traditional caps and checked shirts beneath flowing pelisses, their weathered faces bearing witness to lives spent working the land. Volga peasants stood out in their distinctive attire: blue trousers tucked into well-worn boots, rose-colored cotton shirts cinched with cords, and felt caps pulled low against the sun. Several women dotted the crowd, dressed in floral cotton garments, colorful aprons, and vibrant headscarves that fluttered in the river breeze. These passengers, traveling third-class, seemed untroubled by their lengthy journey home, sharing bread and stories as they watched the shoreline drift past.

As the Caucasus sailed on, it passed countless vessels being towed upstream, all bound for Nijni-Novgorod with their cargo. A endless procession of wooden rafts drifted by, their rough-hewn logs lashed together with heavy rope, followed by barges so laden their sides dipped beneath the water's surface. The bargemen called out to each other across the water, their voices carrying news and greetings. However, their journey was futile because the large fair they were headed to shut down at the beginning, causing significant losses for merchants and traders.

The steamer's wake sent waves crashing against the shoreline, startling clusters of wild ducks into flight with a cacophony of alarmed calls. A few herons, disturbed by the commotion, lifted from the shallows on wide gray wings. Beyond the water's edge, sparse herds of cattle, sheep, and pigs dotted the parched pastures, which were fringed by drooping willows and trembling aspens. Here and there, weathered wooden fences marked property boundaries, their posts listing at odd angles in the dry earth. The land stretched outward in a patchwork of meager buckwheat and rye fields, rising gradually toward distant hills that lay half-tamed by cultivation. A few isolated farmhouses stood like lonely sentinels amid the crops, their chimneys sending thin wisps of smoke into the cloudless sky. The entire vista possessed a stark simplicity that would have left even the most determined landscape artist wanting, its unadorned features offering little to capture on canvas.

"We've been on the Caucasus for two hours now," said the young Livonian woman, adjusting her shawl against the river breeze as she turned to Michael. "Tell me, brother, is Irkutsk your destination?"

"Indeed it is, sister," Michael replied with a gentle nod, his eyes scanning the distant horizon. "Since we share the same path, wherever my journey takes me, you'll be welcome to follow."

"Tomorrow, brother, I'll explain why I've traveled so far from the Baltic shores, venturing beyond the Urals," she said, her voice carrying a hint of weariness that matched the pallor of her face.

"There's no need for explanations, sister," he responded, noting how her shoulders seemed to sag with an invisible burden.

"I will tell you everything," the girl said, managing a weak smile that didn't quite reach her eyes. "Sisters shouldn't keep secrets from their brothers. But I can't do it today. I'm too exhausted and heartbroken."

"Would you like to retire to your cabin to rest?" Michael Strogoff asked, concern clear in his tone as he observed her growing fatigue.

"Yes, yes; tomorrow," she murmured, her words trailing off like leaves caught in the river's current.

"Let's go then..."

He stopped mid-sentence, wanting to add his companion's name at the end, but couldn't since he still didn't know it. The omission hung between them like an unfinished bridge, reminding him how much remained unknown about his newfound traveling companion.

"Nadia," she said, extending her hand in greeting, her voice soft but steady despite her obvious exhaustion.

"Please, Nadia," Michael responded with gentle warmth, "feel free to rely on your brother Nicholas Korpanoff." With that, he guided her through the narrow corridor to the private cabin he had arranged for her, located just beyond the saloon's polished wooden doors. The small room wasn't luxurious, but it would provide the sanctuary she needed.

Michael Strogoff made his way back to the ship's deck, breathing in the crisp evening air. Keen to gather any information that might affect his travels, he positioned himself among clusters of talking passengers, his back against a weathered railing. He remained silent, not wishing to join their discussions, but his ears caught every snippet of conversation carried on the breeze. If anyone questioned him, he planned to identify himself as Nicholas Korpanoff, a merchant returning to the border region for business matters. He was determined to keep secret his special authorization to journey into Siberia, knowing that even the slightest slip could jeopardize his crucial mission.

Passengers aboard the steamer, all of them from foreign lands, seemed consumed by the day's events and the implications of the new decree. These weary travelers, still recovering from their arduous trek through Central Asia, now faced the grim reality of turning back. Though seething with frustration and dismay, they kept their emotions in check, their voices hushed. A potent mixture of reverence and dread held their tongues. Rumors circulated around that police spies might be among them on the

Caucasus, monitoring their every word. Most deemed it wiser to maintain silence, recognizing that deportation, however unpleasant, was far better than languishing in a fortress prison. As a result, the men either remained quiet or spoke in such guarded whispers that gleaning any worthwhile information proved impossible. Even those who had journeyed together for weeks now kept their distance from one another, their previous camaraderie dissolved by suspicion. The deck's atmosphere grew heavy with unspoken fears as the sun was setting, casting long shadows that seemed to mirror the dark mood of its occupants. Several merchants who had invested in their planned ventures stood apart, their faces drawn with worry as they calculated their mounting losses.

A voice caught Michael Strogoff's attention, though he had gathered no useful information from the other passengers, who grew silent when he approached. The booming voice belonged to someone speaking Russian with a distinct French accent, addressing another passenger that seemed out-of-place amid the tense atmosphere on deck.

"Well, what a surprise!" the French-accented voice exclaimed, carrying across the deck with theatrical flair. "I didn't expect to see you here on this vessel. Weren't you at that grand imperial celebration in Moscow? I believe I also spotted you in Nijni-Novgorod. The world grows smaller by the day!"

"Indeed, it is I," the second person replied, their tone suggesting they wished the conversation hadn't begun at all.

"I must say, I hadn't expected such close pursuit," the Frenchman continued, oblivious to his companion's reticence.

"I'm not pursuing you, sir; I'm moving ahead of you," came the clipped response, tinged with concealed irritation.

"Moving ahead! Moving ahead!" the Frenchman chortled with exaggerated amusement. "Let's walk side by side instead, in perfect sync, like soldiers on parade. For now, at least, shall we agree that neither of us will overtake the other? It would make our journey far more pleasant, wouldn't you say?"

"I intend to pass you," the traveler stated, brooking no argument.

"That remains to be seen when we reach the battlefield. Until then, why not travel together? We'll have plenty of time and opportunity for rivalry later," the Frenchman offered with a conciliatory gesture.

"You mean enmity," came the cold correction.

"Enemies then, if you prefer. I must say, I appreciate your precise choice of words, my dear fellow. One always knows where they stand with you," he replied with an appreciative smile that went unacknowledged.

"How could it hurt?" The words carried a note of resigned acceptance.

"It wouldn't hurt at all. If I may, I'd like to outline where we both stand in this matter," the Frenchman pressed, seizing upon this slight opening.

"Go right ahead," came the weary permission.

"You're headed to Perm just as I am?"

"Just as you are," the companion confirmed.

"And I assume you'll continue from Perm to Ekaterenburg, as that's the most secure and reliable path across the Ural Mountains?" The Frenchman's tone grew animated.

"Most likely," was the noncommittal response.

"After crossing the border, we'll find ourselves in Siberia, right in the middle of the invasion," the Frenchman concluded, his voice taking on a more serious edge.

"Indeed, we will," came the flat acknowledgment, heavy with unspoken implications.

"Well then, only at that point should we say, every man for himself, and God for..." The Frenchman left the familiar phrase unfinished.

"For me." The words came out like ice chips.

"For you alone! Fine! But since we have seven neutral days ahead of us, and since we won't be getting any news updates during our journey across this desolate stretch, why not be friends until we become competitors again?" He spread his hands in an expansive gesture of reconciliation.

"Adversaries." The correction was swift and cutting.

"Yes, that's better, adversaries. But until then, let's work together instead of trying to sabotage each other. Though I promise to keep any observations, I make to myself." His tone carried a hint of wry amusement at their verbal sparring.

"I can hear everything." The companion's words held a warning edge that suggested both awareness and suspicion.

"Do we agree?" The Frenchman persisted, undaunted by the other's coolness.

"Yes, we do." The words came, as if dragged from unwilling lips.

"May I have your hand on it?" The Frenchman's eyes sparkled with genuine warmth.

"Of course."

"Adjusting his collar, the first man stated, "I sent the order's exact wording to my cousin at 10:17 this morning."

"And I dispatched it to the Daily Telegraph at 10:13." The response was cool and precise.

"Well done, Mr. Blount!" He gave a slight bow of acknowledgment.

"Mr. Jolivet, your work is impressive."

"I'll do my best to top that!" Jolivet's characteristic enthusiasm bubbled through.

"It is challenging." Blount's mouth twitched in what might have been the ghost of a smile.

"Nevertheless, I'll make the attempt." He squared his shoulders with determination, ready for whatever lay ahead.

The two journalists exchanged greetings, the Frenchman with casual warmth and an expansive gesture, the Englishman with formal reserve and a perceptible nod. Though the governor's decree didn't apply to either of them, since they were Western Europeans with proper documentation and credentials, their shared professional instincts had led them both to depart from Nijni-Novgorod at the same time. It made sense that they would choose the same transportation and route across the vast, unforgiving Siberian plains. Whether as rivals or reluctant allies, they would travel companions for the next week until their proper work began, the race to deliver the most compelling news to their respective papers. After that, may the better reporter prevail! It was Alcide Jolivet who had reached out in friendship, extending his hand with characteristic Gallic charm, which Harry Blount had acknowledged, albeit with noticeable coolness and the stiff propriety typical of his countrymen.

At dinner that very evening, the chatty Frenchman and the reserved, stern Englishman were spotted sharing a table and engaging in conversation while enjoying authentic Cliquot, priced at six roubles per bottle and crafted from local birch sap. Their unlikely camaraderie drew curious glances from other diners, who found the contrast between Jolivet's expansive gestures and Blount's measured nods rather amusing. Upon observing their animated discussion, which drifted into heated debates about European politics and the merits of their respective journalistic methods, Michael Strogoff thought to himself, "These men seem rather nosy and intrusive, I'll cross paths with them again during my journey. I'd be wise to maintain my distance." He noticed how they scrutinized each new arrival in the dining room, their practiced eyes betraying their profession's inherent curiosity.

Between dinner and evening, the young Livonian woman remained in her cabin, sound asleep. Michael chose not to disturb her rest, knowing the rigors of travel could be especially taxing on someone in her delicate state. When she emerged onto the Caucasus' deck, the day was waning, her face showing the benefits of her extended repose. The extended dusk brought welcome relief from the day's oppressive heat, and passengers embraced the cooler air, their spirits lifting as the temperature dropped. As night approached, most preferred to stay on deck rather than retreat to the saloon below, seeking escape from the stuffiness of the interior cabins. They reclined on benches, savoring the gentle breeze created by the steamer's movement through the water, their conversations growing softer as evening settled in. During this season and at this latitude, true darkness never descended, the sky maintained a perpetual twilight between sunset and sunrise, bathing the river in an ethereal blue-gray light that seemed to hover between day and night, providing enough light for the helmsman to navigate the Caucasus among the many vessels traveling the Volga's waters, from small fishing boats to other grand steamers making their way along the great river's course.

The darkness was complete between eleven and two, with only a new moon in the sky, its faint presence discernible through wisps of passing clouds. Most travelers had drifted off to slumber on the deck, and the rhythmic splash of paddles against water was the sole sound breaking the quiet, punctuated by the distant cry of a night bird along the shoreline. Michael Strogoff, kept from resting by his worries, paced back and forth near the stern, his footsteps careful and measured on the wooden planks. At one point, he wandered past the engine-room, where the muted throb of machinery provided a steady heartbeat to the night, and into the section where second and third-class passengers were quartered.

Deep in slumber, passengers sprawled across every available surface, on benches, on cargo bales, and on the deck planks, their forms visible in the dim glow of the few remaining lit oil lamps. One had to step to avoid disturbing the sleeping forms that covered every inch of space, creating a maze of humanity that required careful navigation. Most were peasant workers, their bodies hardened by years of rough living, finding adequate rest even on the unyielding wooden deck, their weather-worn faces relaxed in sleep beneath rough wool caps and shawls. Yet despite their tolerance for discomfort, they would unleash a torrent of harsh words at any careless person who kicked them awake, their rural dialects making their complaints all the more colorful.

Michael Strogoff moved to avoid waking his fellow travelers, placing each foot with deliberate care between the sleeping forms. His stroll to the boat's edge was an attempt to ward off drowsiness through gentle exercise, though the late hour made even this simple task feel clandestine. As he approached the forward deck and began ascending the forecastle steps, voices caught his attention, hushed but animated tones that carried in the still night air. He paused, noting they emanated from a cluster of passengers bundled in heavy cloaks against the river's chill. The darkness concealed their identities, though the steamer's chimney would erupt in crimson flames, sending sparks cascading over the group like a shower of glittering sequins brought to life, illuminating the outlines of their hunched forms.

Just as Michael prepared to climb the ladder, his ears caught fragments of conversation in the peculiar language he'd encountered earlier at the nighttime fair, those same harsh consonants and rolling syllables that had struck him as so foreign before. Acting on instinct, he froze in place to listen more carefully, daring to breathe lest he give himself away. The darkness beneath the forecastle concealed his presence like a protective cloak, though he couldn't make out the speakers themselves through the deep shadows. He would have to rely on what he could hear, straining his ears to catch every whispered word floating down from above.

He caught snatches of conversation that seemed trivial at first, yet they enabled him to identify the male and female voices he'd encountered earlier in Nijni-Novgorod. The distinctive cadence and pitch were unmistakable, sending a chill down his spine. This discovery heightened his vigilance, as there was a distinct possibility that these same Tsiganes, now exiled, had managed to secure passage aboard the Caucasus, perhaps with motives as dark as the shadows concealing them.

The traveler's attentiveness proved fortunate, as he caught a conversation in Tartar between two speakers, their words cutting through the ambient sounds of creaking wood and lapping waves:

"Word has it that Moscow has dispatched a messenger to Irkutsk," said one voice, the words thick with significance and contained satisfaction.

"Indeed," replied Sangarre, her tone carrying a deadly certainty that made the hidden listener's blood run cold, "but this messenger's journey will be futile, he'll either reach his destination when it's too late, or never make it there at all."

Michael Strogoff flinched upon hearing these words that were clear about him, his muscles tensing beneath his travel-worn clothes. He peered through the gathering darkness, trying to confirm whether the speaking couple were indeed the ones he had in mind, but his efforts proved futile in the ship's deep shadows.

Michael Strogoff made his way back to the vessel's stern, his footsteps careful and measured on the damp planks, choosing an isolated spot where he sat alone, his face concealed behind his weathered hands. Though he appeared to be sleeping to any who might glance his way, his mind was far from resting. Instead, he wrestled with troubling thoughts that churned like the river waters below: "Who could have discovered my journey, and what do they stand to gain from this knowledge? How many other eyes might watch my every move?" The weight of his mission seemed to press even heavier upon his shoulders with each passing moment.

© 01/01/2025
QuantumDigitalPublishing.io
Book I – Chapter VIII

Chapter Eight

GOING UP THE KAMA

On July 18th, at 6:40 AM, the Caucasus docked at the Kasan quay, which lay seven miles from the city.

Located where the Volga and Kasanka rivers meet, Kasan serves as the region's primary administrative center, hosting both a Greek archbishopric and a prestigious university. The city's diverse inhabitants maintain strong ties to their Asian heritage, clear in the colorful minarets that pierce the skyline alongside Orthodox church domes. Despite the considerable distance from the docking area, throngs of people gathered at the waterfront, eager for information about events further east. The morning sun cast long shadows across the crowd as they pressed forward, their worried murmurs carrying across the water. The provincial governor had enacted regulations matching those in Nijni-Novgorod, with stringent controls on movement. A contingent of police officers and Cossacks maintained order among the masses, their uniforms stark against the civilian clothing as they facilitated movement for both arriving and departing passengers of the Caucasus while conducting thorough inspections of papers and belongings. Two distinct groups emerged on the quay: the departing Asiatic peoples facing expulsion, their faces drawn with concern as they clutched their possessions, and the mujiks whose journey ended in Kasan, relief visible in their weathered features.

Standing at the quay, Michael Strogoff observed with detachment the typical commotion that accompanies a steamship's arrival, his trained eyes scanning the organized chaos below. Dock workers scurried about with practiced efficiency, while merchants hawked their wares to weary travelers. With the Caucasus scheduled for a one-hour stopover to replenish its coal supplies, Michael remained on board, positioning himself near the ship's railing. Concern influenced his decision for the young Livonian girl, who had yet to emerge on deck, and he was reluctant to leave her unattended, given the uncertain climate that seemed to pervade the port.

The early morning sun had crept over the horizon, casting long shadows across the weathered planks of the dock, when the pair of reporters began their day, following the time-honored tradition of hunters everywhere. Upon reaching the shore, they immersed themselves in the bustling throng, each pursuing his distinct investigative style with professional determination. Harry Blount captured the scene through detailed sketches and careful observations in his leather-bound notebook, his pencil moving with precise strokes as he documented the unfolding drama at the port. Meanwhile, Alcide Jolivet relied on his razor-sharp memory as he moved through the crowd with casual grace, gathering information through countless conversations, his cheerful demeanor and quick wit drawing out details from even the most reticent sources.

Reports circulated throughout the frontier about the growing scale of both the rebellion and invasion. Getting messages from Siberia and the empire had become challenging, with many couriers disappearing along the established routes. Michael Strogoff learned all these details from travelers who had just arrived, their faces drawn with concern as they shared their accounts. Such troubling news heightened his anxiety and strengthened his desire to cross the Ural Mountains, where the vast mountain range stood as both barrier and gateway to the heart of the conflict. Once there, he could assess the validity of these rumors and prepare for any developments. Considering how he might gather more specific information from a Kasan local, something unexpected caught his attention, drawing his gaze toward the crowded docks.

The band of Tsiganes that Michael had spotted at the Nijni-Novgorod fair the previous day was now among those departing the Caucasus, their distinctive presence impossible to miss in the morning light. He watched as the elderly Bohemian and his female companion directed their troupe of performers, twenty dancers and singers between fifteen and twenty years old, as they disembarked with practiced efficiency. The young artists wore weathered cloaks draped over their sequined costumes, the fabric telling stories of countless performances and long journeys across the countryside. As the morning sun caught their garments, casting prismatic reflections across the dock, Michael realized these were the same sparkles he had noticed in the night, glinting in the firelight from the steamboat's chimney like scattered stars against the darkness.

Michael muttered under his breath, "Strange, these Romani travelers stayed hidden below deck all day, then huddled beneath the forecastle after nightfall. This secretive behavior isn't typical of their people at all." He furrowed his brow, recalling how performing troupes reveled in attention, practicing their routines on deck to draw curious onlookers.

He was now certain that the whispered conversation he'd overheard had come from that swarthy group, between the elderly Romani man and the woman he'd called Sangarre, a Mongolian name. Almost unconsciously, Michael found himself drifting toward the gangplank as the nomadic band began departing the vessel, his footsteps matching their measured pace.

The elderly gypsy man sat there, his demeanor modest for someone of his bold heritage. He seemed to shrink from noticing rather than seek it out, as if trying to fade into the weathered planks of the dock itself. The countless seasons darkened his weathered hat, which he pulled low to shade his lined features, casting deep shadows across his face. Despite the warmth, he hunched beneath an old cape that wrapped around his frame, concealing his build like armor against prying eyes. His shabby attire made it impossible to discern his physical characteristics, though occasional tremors betrayed his advanced age. Beside him stood Sangarre, a Romani woman of about thirty years. She cut an impressive figure, tall and shapely, with a dusky complexion, striking eyes that seemed to pierce through anyone who dared meet her gaze, and hair the color of honey that cascaded past her shoulders in wild waves.

The young gypsy dancers were beautiful, each displaying the distinctive facial characteristics of their heritage, high cheekbones, olive skin, and eyes that sparkled with an ancient wisdom. Among the Tsiganes, such natural beauty is common, so much so that several prominent Russian aristocrats, in their attempts to match British nobility's unconventional ways, have taken Tsigane brides from among these dancers, scandalizing Moscow's more traditional social circles. One dancer's voice carried a haunting melody with an exotic rhythm, her words flowing with the practiced ease of generations of storytellers:

"Golden strands shimmer bright
Through my dark tresses, flowing
While crimson gems shine,
Round my neck softly glowing.
Free as winds in the sky
Through vast lands I must fly"

The song continued flowing from the girl's merry lips, her bare feet moving in perfect rhythm across the worn wooden floor, but Michael Strogoff's attention had wandered elsewhere. He noticed the Tsigane woman, Sangarre, studying his face with unsettling intensity as if attempting to burn his features into her mind. Her unwavering stare made him uncomfortable, though he refused to show it.

The moment lasted only before Sangarre departed, trailing after the elderly man and his group as they disembarked, her colorful skirts swishing against the weathered planks. "That gypsy has nerve," Michael thought to himself, his jaw tightening. "I wonder, could she have recognized me from

Nijni-Novgorod? These Tsiganes possess uncanny vision, like cats peering through darkness, their eyes missing nothing of importance. Perhaps that woman identified me beneath this merchant's guise..."

Strogoff considered pursuing Sangarre and her fellow travelers, but hesitated, his hand touching the papers hidden within his coat. "Better not," he reasoned to himself, forcing his muscles to relax. "Acting rashly by confronting the elderly fortune teller and his group could expose my true identity. They've only just come ashore, and I'll be well past the border before they can cross it. True, they might travel the Kasan-Ishim route, but that path offers little comfort to travelers, with its rough terrain and sparse settlements. And my tarantass, with its sturdy Siberian steeds, will outpace any gypsy wagon on those challenging roads! Relax, Korpanoff, all is well." Yet even as he reassured himself, a shadow of doubt lingered in his mind.

By then, both the man and Sangarre had vanished from sight, melting into the bustling crowd like shadows at midday.

Kazan serves as a well-deserved gateway to Asia and functions as a vital hub for trade between Siberia and Bokhara, with two major routes starting here that traverse the Ural Mountains. Michael Strogoff made a wise decision to select the path through Perm and Ekaterinburg. This principal thoroughfare, maintained with government-funded relay stations, extends from Ishim all the way to Irkutsk, offering travelers regular opportunities for rest and fresh horses at established posts along its length.

There is another path linking Kasan to Ishim, the very one Michael had mentioned, which bypasses Perm's minor diversion. While this alternative route might be shorter, several drawbacks: the complete lack of post stations, maintained roads, and scarce settlements along the way offset its benefits. The path winds through desolate stretches where travelers must fend for themselves, often going days without encountering another soul. Michael Strogoff had chosen; assuming the gypsies would take this second route between Kasan and Ishim, as seemed likely, he stood an excellent chance of reaching the destination ahead of them, given his superior means of transport and intimate knowledge of the terrain.

As the clock struck the hour, the Caucasus' bell echoed across the water, summoning fresh travelers and alerting those already aboard. Dawn had broken at seven, and the ship, supplied with fuel, hummed with anticipation. The vessel's frame quivered as steam coursed through its pipes, signaling its readiness to depart. The deck grew busy with travelers bound for Perm from Kasan, their luggage creating a maze of trunks and bags that the crew navigated.

Scanning the crowd, Michael observed that among the two journalists, only Blount had returned to the ship. He wondered if Alcide Jolivet would appear before departure, noting how the Englishman stood apart from the other passengers, writing in his ever-present notebook with his characteristic stern expression.

Just as they were about to cast off, Jolivet came rushing up to the ship, his coat flapping behind him as he sprinted along the dock. Though the Caucasus had already begun pulling away and the gangway had been removed, such obstacles didn't deter Alcide Jolivet. With an acrobatic leap worthy of a circus performer, he landed on the vessel's deck, colliding with his competitor, who stepped aside with a disapproving grunt while maintaining his writing stance.

"For a moment there, I thought you'd miss the boat," his rival remarked, glancing up from his notebook.

"Nonsense!" Jolivet retorted, brushing off his coat and straightening his cravat with practiced flair. "I would have caught up to you, either by hiring a boat and charging it to my cousin, or by paying twenty copecks per mile to travel by post and horse. What else could I do? The telegraph office was quite a trek from the waterfront, especially in this dreadful heat."

"Did you visit the telegraph office?" Harry Blount inquired, his lips tensing as his pen stopped mid-sentence.

"That's precisely where I went!" Jolivet replied with a beaming smile, delighting in his competitor's concealed interest.

"And is it still working for Kolyvan?" Blount's voice carried a hint of urgency now.

"I can't say for certain, but I can tell you one thing: the line between Kasan and Paris is operational." Jolivet leaned against the ship's railing, savoring the moment.

"Did you manage to send a message to your cousin?" The Englishman's stern demeanor cracked.

"Most eagerly." Jolivet's eyes twinkled with mischief.

"So you'd discovered...?" Blount's notebook now hung forgotten at his side.

"Listen here, my friend, as they say in Russia," Alcide Jolivet responded with a theatrical flourish, "I'm an honest man and won't hide anything from you. The Tartars, led by Feofar-Khan, have moved past Semipolatinsk and are following the Irtish downstream. Make what you will of that information!" He punctuated his revelation with a satisfied grin.

"By Jove!" Harry Blount fumed, his jaw clenching with suppressed frustration. His rival had scooped him on crucial intelligence, likely gathered from a Kasan local, and already dispatched it to Paris. The London papers would be playing catch-up, and his editors would be livid. Without a word, Blount crossed his arms behind his back, strode away with measured steps, and dropped heavily into a seat at the vessel's stern, where he stared at the churning wake below.

The morning sun had climbed to mid-height, casting dancing reflections off the river's surface, when the Livonian girl emerged from below deck, squinting in the bright light. Michael Strogoff moved to her side and grasped her hand with brotherly tenderness. "Sister, come look at this," he said, guiding her toward the Caucasus' bow where the magnificent riverscape stretched before them.

The travelers reached the meeting point of the Volga and Kama rivers in the Caucasus region, where the waters merged in a vast confluence that had guided merchants and travelers for centuries. After following the Volga downstream for three hundred miles through the heart of Russia, they would now change course to journey upstream along the Kama for an equal distance, fighting against the river's persistent current.

The Kama River stretched wide before them, its banks adorned with lush forests that swayed in the morning breeze. The water sparkled in the sunlight, dotted here and there with white sails of merchant vessels and fishing boats plying their ancient trade. Rolling hills formed the horizon, their slopes covered with aspens, alders, and majestic oaks whose branches reached toward the cloudless sky. Gaps in the treeline revealed small villages, their wooden houses and church spires, a testament to human persistence in this wild landscape.

Yet the young Livonian woman remained unmoved by this natural splendor, her thoughts fixed on matters beyond the scenic vista. Her hand still rested in her companion's, and she turned to him with a single question, her eyes reflecting determination rather than wonder: "How far are we from Moscow?"

"Nine hundred miles," Michael stated, his voice carrying the certainty of someone well-versed in Russia's vast distances.

"Only nine hundred covered, with seven thousand still ahead," Nadia whispered, her voice tinged with concern as she contemplated the enormous journey that still lay before them. The magnitude of their undertaking seemed to weigh on her slender shoulders.

The dining bell's clear ring interrupted their exchange, its resonant tone carrying across the deck. Nadia walked alongside Michael Strogoff toward the restaurant car, their footsteps echoing on the wooden planks. She ate, choosing modest portions fitting for someone of limited means, a small bowl of soup and a crust of dark bread. Observing her restraint, Michael chose a simple meal like hers, though his physique suggested a preference for richer food. Within twenty minutes, they had returned to the deck, settling themselves at the stern where the churning wake provided both spectacle and privacy. Without hesitation, Nadia leaned close to Michael and began speaking in hushed tones meant for his ears alone, her words lost in the steady thrum of the ship's engines.

"I am an exile's daughter," she said, her fingers twisting the worn fabric of her dress. "My name is Nadia Fedor. Just a month ago I lost my mother in Riga, and now I journey to Irkutsk to be with my father in his exile." Her voice carried the weight of recent grief.

"As it happens, Irkutsk is my destination too," Michael replied, his expression softening with genuine concern. "I would be grateful to Providence if I can deliver Nadia Fedor to her father's care."

"You are kind, brother," Nadia answered, the familial term carrying a note of trust.

Michael Strogoff mentioned he had secured a special travel permit for Siberia, and that no Russian official could interfere with his journey. The document bore the imperial seal itself, though he did not elaborate on how he had obtained such a privilege.

Nadia didn't press for more details. She viewed this chance encounter with Michael to reach her father more quickly, a stroke of fortune in otherwise dark times.

'I had a permit to travel to Irkutsk,' she explained, brushing a strand of dark hair from her face, 'but the new regulations canceled it. If not for you, brother, the town would have trapped me, and I would have died there.

'And you were willing, Nadia,' Michael asked, studying her with newfound respect, 'to brave the Siberian steppes all by yourself?'

"I hadn't heard about the Tartar invasion before leaving Riga. The news only reached me when I arrived in Moscow." Her voice remained steady, though her fingers twisted in her lap.

"Yet you chose to press on?"

"I had no choice. It was my duty." The words fell from her lips like stones, heavy with conviction.

Those simple words revealed everything about her courage and determination. In them, Michael recognized the same unwavering sense of purpose that drove his own journey across the vast Russian empire.

She went on to tell them about her father, Wassili Fedor, a respected doctor in Riga whose gentle hands had healed countless patients over the years. After authorities accused him of belonging to a secret organization, charges he vehemently denied until the end, they ordered him to relocate to Irkutsk. The police who delivered this decree had escorted him across the border, giving him no chance to put his affairs in order.

With only moments to spare, Wassili Fedor hugged his ailing wife and daughter before being dragged away in tears, his medical bag left forgotten by the door. Eighteen months later, his wife passed away while being cradled by their daughter, her final whispered words a plea to find him. Young Nadia Fedor found herself without parents and destitute, their modest savings depleted by her mother's lengthy illness. She requested permission from Russian authorities to reunite with her father in Irkutsk, which they granted, perhaps seeing no threat in a lone girl's journey. She informed him of her plans by letter, choosing words that would both comfort and prepare him for her arrival. Though her funds covered the extensive journey ahead, she remained resolute, selling what few family possessions remained to gather enough rubles for the first leg of travel. She would contribute whatever effort she could muster, taking odd jobs along the way if necessary, trusting divine providence to handle the rest.

Chapter Nine

DAY AND NIGHT IN A TARANTASS

On July 19th, the steamship Caucasus made its last stop along the Kama River at Perm. This bustling provincial capital governed one of Russia's most expansive regions, with territory stretching across the Ural Mountains into Siberia. The area was rich in natural resources, with extensive mining operations extracting marble, salt, platinum, gold, and coal. Despite its strategic importance as a gateway city, Perm itself was rather unsightly and lacking in amenities, with muddy unpaved streets and simple wooden buildings dominating the landscape. However, this mattered little to Siberia-bound travelers, who came prepared from more developed regions with all their essential supplies, from preserved foods to warm clothing and medical necessities.

In Perm, Siberian travelers sell their vehicles, which often show wear and tear from the extensive journey across the plains. The city's markets buzz with activity as merchants haggle over the price of well-used carriages and worn wheels. This city also serves as a key trading point where people journeying between Europe and Asia purchase carriages, or when winter comes, sleighs. Local craftsmen maintain busy workshops, repairing and outfitting these conveyances with the sturdy features needed for the harsh terrain ahead.

Michael Strogoff had planned his route. Though a mail carrier operated across the Ural Mountains, this service was no longer running. However, even if it had been available, Strogoff would have declined it, as he wanted complete control over his travel speed without relying on others. He made the prudent decision to gain his own carriage and travel in stages, knowing that self-sufficiency would be crucial for the challenging journey ahead.

Because of strict policies targeting Asian foreigners, many visitors had already departed Perm, making transportation scarce. Michael had no choice but to use whatever means of travel others had passed over, often settling for vehicles that were serviceable but far from ideal. While still in European territory, he could show his podorojna as the Czar's messenger, which gave him priority access to horses from the postmasters and allowed him to bypass the usual waiting periods at way stations. However, once he crossed into Siberia, he would have to rely on the purchasing power of his Russian currency, a prospect that demanded careful management of his financial resources. He knew prices often doubled or tripled beyond the Urals, where the harsh conditions and limited supply networks drove up costs for even the most basic necessities.

Deciding between transportation options, the traveler had to choose between a telga and a tarantass horse drawn carriage. The telga was a basic four-wheeled wooden cart, with its components held together by sturdy ropes. Despite its basic and uncomfortable nature, one significant advantage was its ease of repair should something break down during the journey. The Russian frontier had plenty of fir trees, so people could fashion replacement axles from the forest wood when necessary. The telga was robust enough to carry the "perck-ladnoi" (special express mail service) and could handle any road condition. Though the ropes sometimes broke, causing the back half to get stuck in mud while the front portion reached the post station on just two wheels, such outcomes were acceptable given the vehicle's practical nature. Local craftsmen were well-versed in making quick repairs to these simple conveyances, often using nothing more than rope, wooden pegs, and rough-hewn planks. Even in the most remote villages, local craftsmen could repair a broken telga and make it roadworthy within hours, a crucial consideration for anyone undertaking a long journey through Siberia's unforgiving terrain.

The fortunate discovery of a tarantass saved Michael Strogoff from having to use a telga. Russian coach-builders would do well to improve upon this vehicle's design. Like the telga, the tarantass lacks springs, and wood serves as a substitute for iron throughout its construction. However, its four wheels, set eight or nine feet apart, provide reasonable stability on rough roads. The splash-board protects travelers from mud, and one can draw a sturdy leather hood over the passengers to shield them from intense summer heat and severe storms. The tarantass shares the telga's durability and ease of repair, but proves more reliable in keeping all its parts together during travel. Its wider wheelbase and reinforced axles make it well-suited for the rutted paths and unexpected obstacles common along Siberian routes.

After a meticulous search through Perm, Michael located a tarantass, the only one in the entire city. To maintain his disguise as Nicholas Korpanoff, a humble merchant from Irkutsk, he made a show of lengthy price negotiations. He haggled with the owner, a weathered old man with decades of experience selling carriages, maintaining the demeanor of someone concerned about every kopek spent. The transaction took an hour of back-and-forth bartering, punctuated by dramatic sighs and reluctant counter-offers from both parties.

At his side during the search was Nadia, who shared his determination to find suitable transportation. Though their ultimate destinations differed, both displayed an identical sense of urgency, as if driven by a single, shared purpose. Their quick strides through Perm's dusty streets and focused expressions marked them as travelers who could not afford to waste precious time.

"Michael," Nadia said, wiping perspiration from her brow as they inspected yet another stable, "you needn't worry about my comfort during our journey."

"How can I not, dear sister, when you deserve far better than these harsh traveling conditions?" His voice carried genuine concern as he tested the worn suspension of the tarantass.

"Have you forgotten I would have walked the entire way on foot to reach Father if necessary?" She straightened her shoulders, her chin lifting with determination.

"Your bravery isn't in question, Nadia. I worry some hardships might prove too taxing for a woman." Michael's eyes softened as he regarded her, noting how young she looked despite her fierce demeanor.

"I will bear whatever difficulties come, without fail," she declared, her hands clasped before her. "The day you hear me complain is the day you can abandon me by the roadside and continue on alone." The steel in her voice left no room for argument, and her gray eyes flashed with an intensity that matched her words.

Thirty minutes passed before Michael showed his travel permit, after which they hitched three post-horses to the tarantass. These shaggy beasts, with their thick coats and long legs, resembled small bears. Though not large, the Siberian horses displayed a fierce spirit, pawing at the frozen ground and tossing their heavy manes in anticipation. The iemschik, or carriage driver, followed a distinct harnessing method: he placed the biggest horse between two lengthy shafts, which ended in a decorated hoop adorned with bells and tassels. Because the cold air was filled with the horses' breath, the iemschik used ropes to tie the other two horses to the carriage steps. They completed the setup using basic, smooth string reins for steering.

Neither Michael Strogoff nor his young Livonian companion traveled with any luggage. This benefited them, as the tarantass they rode in could only accommodate two passengers plus the iemschik driver, who displayed remarkable balance on his tiny perch, his weathered hands gripping the reins with practiced ease. Michael's need for swift travel and the girl's limited means made traveling light a necessity rather than a choice, though Nadia seemed unbothered by the sparse arrangements, her earlier determination clear in her straight-backed posture.

As they reached each relay station, a new iemschik took over driving duties. The driver from their first leg of the journey was a true Siberian, as untamed in appearance as his steeds. He had cut his wild hair across his brow, and he wore a hat with upturned edges and a crimson sash. His coat featured distinctive crossed lapels, adorned with buttons bearing the emperor's seal. Upon arriving with his horses, this iemschik cast a scrutinizing look at his tarantass passengers. The complete absence of baggage caught his attention, though, he wondered where any luggage could have fit. Taking in their rather worn appearance, his expression turned to one of obvious disdain.

"Crows," muttered the driver, indifferent to who might hear, "crows, for six copecks per mile!"

"Eagles!" Michael corrected him, well-versed in the driver's coded language. "Eagles, mind you, nine copecks per mile, with extra for your trouble."

The iemschik's weathered face brightened somewhat at this promise of additional payment, though his pride as a driver remained evident in his rigid posture. He clicked his tongue and adjusted his sash, a habitual gesture among the Siberian drivers that spoke of both impatience and acceptance. The distinction between "crows", common travelers who paid the minimum fare, and "eagles", more generous passengers, was one that could differ between a leisurely pace and the swift journey Michael required.

The driver's whip cracked in response, the sharp sound echoing across the station yard as he gathered the reins with practiced efficiency.

In Russian coachman slang, passed down through generations of drivers who plied the Empire's vast network of roads, their spending habits categorized passengers. The "crow" referred to thrifty or poor travelers who paid the bare minimum, just two or three copecks per mile for horse transport at post stations, often haggling over every kopeck. In contrast, the "eagle" described generous travelers who spent and gave substantial tips, earning their preferential treatment and the drivers' genuine respect. As one might expect, the "crow" couldn't hope to travel as swiftly as the noble "eagle," for a driver's enthusiasm often matched the weight of his passenger's purse.

Nadia and Michael settled into their seats in the horse-drawn carriage, testing the worn but sturdy springs beneath them. They stowed a modest supply of food, dried meat, hard bread, and several flasks of water, in the storage compartment, preparing for potential delays between the government-maintained rest stops, which were known for their good accommodations and regular spacing along the route. With the scorching heat bearing down, they raised the carriage's leather cover, adjusting its position to maximize shade while maintaining airflow, and as noon struck, they departed Perm, leaving a dusty trail in their wake as the wheels began their rhythmic turning on the well-worn road.

The coachman's skill at maintaining his team's swift pace would have amazed any foreign travelers unfamiliar with Russian or Siberian customs. The lead horse, more robust than its companions, maintained an unwavering extended trot regardless of the terrain's incline. Its two fellow steeds seemed to know only how to gallop, adding playful bounds to their stride. The coachman never struck them, relying instead on the sharp cracks of his whip to motivate them. He would shower them with colorful phrases and invoke every saint's name when they showed proper obedience. While the simple rope reins offered little control over these spirited animals, they responded to gruffly spoken commands, "na pravo" to turn right and "na levo" to turn left more effectively than any physical guidance.

The iemschik's words shifted between sweet encouragement and harsh scolding. When pleased, he'd call out: "Forward, my precious doves! Soar ahead, my beautiful swallows! Take wing, my darling pigeons! Keep strong, dear cousin on the left! Press on, beloved father on the right!" But when dissatisfied, his tone would turn sharp and biting, unleashing a torrent of creative insults that somehow spurred the horses to even greater speeds. The animals seemed to understand the subtle variations in his voice, responding as much to his melodic intonation as to the actual words themselves. Even during the most challenging stretches of road, where loose stones threatened to upset their rhythm, the horses maintained their pace through this curious dialogue with their master.

But when the horses slowed, his tone turned cutting, each barb striking the sensitive creatures: "Move yourself, you miserable snail! Curse you, you worthless slug! I'll cook you over flames, you wretched tortoise! Your bones will feed the wolves if you don't pick up those hooves!"

The tarantass sped along at twelve to fourteen miles per hour, powered by the iemschiks' forceful shouts rather than their physical strength. Michael Strogoff felt at ease in this style of transport, having grown accustomed to its particular quirks during countless journeys across the empire's vast expanse. The constant bumps and jolts didn't bother him, he well knew Russian drivers did not try to dodge obstacles like stones, ruts, bogs, fallen trees, or ditches in their path. They believed the shortest route was always straight ahead, regardless of terrain. Though his companion risked injury from the violent lurching of the tarantass, which threatened to shake loose every bolt and board, she endured it without complaint, her hands gripping the wooden rail with quiet determination.

Nadia remained quiet for a moment, her mind working through the calculations as the vehicle bounced along the rugged road. Then, focusing on her singular goal of completing their journey, she spoke up with the precise tone of someone who had studied the route. "By my calculations, the distance between Perm and Ekaterenburg is three hundred miles. Have I calculated correctly, brother?"

"Your calculation is accurate, Nadia," Michael confirmed, adjusting his position as the tarantass hit another bump. "Once we arrive in Ekaterenburg, we'll find ourselves at the base of the Ural Mountains, on their far side. The city marks the boundary between European Russia and Siberia."

"What's the duration of the mountain crossing?" she asked, her eyes scanning the horizon as if already searching for the mountain peaks.

"It'll take two days since we won't stop moving. And when I say, Nadia," he emphasized, his voice taking on a more serious tone, "I mean that. I can't afford any delays until I reach Irkutsk. Every hour counts on this journey."

"Don't worry about me, brother," she replied with quiet determination, her chin lifting. "I won't hold you back, not even for a single hour. I'm ready to travel non-stop. The hardships of the road don't frighten me."

"In that case, Nadia," he said, studying her resolute expression, "provided the Tartar invaders haven't blocked our path, we should make it in about twenty days. Though the road ahead won't be easy."

"Have you taken this route before?" Nadia inquired, leaning forward with interest.

"Several times," he answered, his eyes distant with memory. "I remember the path."

"Wouldn't winter conditions have made our journey quicker and more certain?" she asked, considering the alternatives.

"Indeed, you could have traveled faster, but the freezing temperatures and snow would have taken quite a toll on you," Michael replied, his voice tinged with concern. "The Siberian winter shows no mercy to travelers, no matter how determined they might be."

"That's of no concern! Russia thrives in winter conditions. Our people have conquered these lands for generations!"

"Indeed, Nadia! You need extraordinary resilience to withstand such harsh conditions. I've experienced temperatures plummeting beyond forty degrees below zero in the Siberian steppes! Despite wearing my reindeer fur, I felt my heart growing numb, my muscles seizing up, and my feet turning to ice even with three layers of wool socks. I watched as my sleigh horses became encased in frost, their breath freezing at their nostrils, forming delicate crystals that sparkled like diamonds in the pale winter sun. Even my flask of brandy turned solid as stone, so hard that my blade couldn't scratch it. Still, my sleigh raced forward like a gust of wind, the runners creaking against the frozen ground beneath. The vast white plain stretched, without a single hindrance! No rivers blocked our path, just solid ice everywhere, making for clear passage and reliable travel! But the true cost of such journeys, Nadia, can only be told by those who never made it back, their bodies forever lost beneath the blinding snowstorms. I've seen powerful men, veterans of countless winter treks, brought to their knees by nature's merciless grip."

"But you made it back to us, brother," Nadia said, her voice carrying a note of admiration.

"True, though remember I'm Siberian-born. From my earliest years, I would accompany my father hunting through the endless white forests, which toughened me against such harsh conditions. Yet Nadia, when you declared that winter wouldn't have deterred you, that you'd have made the journey alone, prepared to face Siberia's brutal weather, I could only picture you collapsed in the snow, your strength giving out, never to stand again."

"Tell me, how many winters have you spent crossing the steppe?" the young Livonian woman inquired, her eyes bright with determination.

"I've been there three times, Nadia, during my journeys to Omsk," he said, rubbing his hands together as if remembering the bitter cold.

"What business took you to, Omsk?" she inquired, leaning forward.

"I was visiting my mother. She was waiting for me there," he replied, his voice growing quieter with the memory.

"Well, I'm headed to Irkutsk myself, where my father waits," she responded. "I carry my mother's last words for him, words that must not die unspoken in the frost. So you see, brother, nothing could have stopped me from making this journey."

"You possess true courage, Nadia," Michael said, studying her face with newfound respect. "The Lord Himself must be guiding your path through these frozen lands."

The iemschiks took turns throughout the day, driving the tarantass at great speed from station to station. These "highway eagles" proved themselves worthy of their mountain-dwelling namesakes, their skilled hands guiding the troika of horses over rutted paths and through treacherous mountain passes with remarkable precision. The travelers earned special treatment thanks to their generous payment for horses and liberal distribution of tips, which ensured fresh mounts were always ready upon their arrival. While the postmasters might have found it curious that a young Russian man and his sister could traverse the closed territory of Siberia after the recent decree, their documentation was impeccable and their passage rights were legitimate, bearing all the necessary stamps and signatures.

During their journey from Perm to Ekaterenburg, Michael Strogoff and Nadia discovered they weren't traveling alone. The Czar's messenger had noticed another carriage ahead of them in the early parts of their trip, a well-appointed traveling coach that seemed to maintain a consistent lead of several miles but since horses were available at the stations, he wasn't concerned about it. The vast Siberian countryside could accommodate many travelers without their paths crossing.

Travelers would stop only to eat during daylight hours. Post-houses offered both accommodation and meals. Even without an inn nearby, Russian peasant homes proved welcoming. The villages, sharing a similar appearance with their white-walled chapels topped by green roofs, were hospitable. Any traveler could approach any house, and the door would open. The moujik (peasant) would emerge with a warm smile and welcoming hand, offering bread and salt to the visitor. They would light the samovar's coals and make their guest feel at home. The host family would even give up their own space to ensure the traveler's comfort, often insisting on sleeping in the barn or kitchen while giving their best rooms to their guests. In Russian culture, people viewed strangers as relatives, "one sent by God," and even the most modest households honored this sacred obligation of hospitality.

"How long since the last carriage passed through?" Michael asked the postmaster upon arrival that evening, his boots still dusty from the road.

"About two hours, little father," came the reply from the weathered old man.

"Was it a berlin carriage?"

"No, a telga."

"How many were traveling?"

"Two passengers," the postmaster answered, stroking his gray beard.

"Are they moving quickly?"

"Like eagles!" he exclaimed, spreading his arms wide for emphasis.

"Then have fresh horses readied at once," Michael commanded, already reaching for his travel papers.

The two companions maintained their relentless pace through the night, refusing any rest despite their mounting fatigue. While the weather held steady for now, the air grew thick and charged, heavy with foreboding. They hoped to avoid any storms while crossing the treacherous mountain passes, where such weather could prove catastrophic for travelers caught exposed on the winding roads. Drawing on his experience in reading nature's warnings, Michael recognized the telltale signs of an impending clash of the elements, the unnatural stillness, the metallic taste in the air, the way the horses tossed their heads.

The darkness brought with it no disturbances, though every shadow seemed pregnant with possibility. Despite the constant shaking and rattling of the carriage over the rough terrain, Nadia found several hours of fitful rest, her head bumping against the wooden frame. They had lifted the covering to allow what little fresh air they could get in the oppressive atmosphere, though the night breeze offered scant relief from the stifling heat.

Michael remained vigilant throughout the night, his eyes never leaving the road ahead, wary of the drivers who were known to doze while on duty despite the dangers. His hand stayed close to the reins, ready to take control if needed. They maintained excellent time, pushing the horses to their limits and wasting not a moment at the posting stations or during their journey, each delay feeling like an eternity to their urgent mission.

Early in the morning, around eight o'clock on July 20th, they first spotted the Ural Mountains rising on the eastern horizon. The massive mountain range, which forms the natural border between Russia and Siberia, lay far ahead of them, its jagged peaks visible through the morning haze. They realized they wouldn't reach it until nightfall, the daunting distance serving as a stark reminder of the challenging journey still ahead. They would have to traverse the treacherous mountain passes during the darkness of the following night, a prospect that filled them with equal parts determination and unease. Throughout the day, thick clouds rolled in and blanketed the sky, making the temperature more comfortable than the previous days' sweltering heat, though the weather showed ominous signs of becoming stormy, with distant rumbles of thunder echoing across the plains.

Climbing the mountains at night was likely unwise, and Michael would have waited if given the choice. The treacherous paths would be even more dangerous in darkness, with loose stones and sheer drops impossible to spot until it was too late. At the last stop, when the iemschik pointed out thunder echoing through the rocky terrain and gestured at the blackening sky, Michael asked,

"Can you see another telga ahead?"

"Yes."

"What's our distance behind it?"

"About an hour."

"Press on, I'll triple your payment if we reach Ekaterenburg by tomorrow morning." The promise of extra coin seemed to steady the driver's nerves, though his white-knuckled grip on the reins betrayed his lingering anxiety about the journey ahead.

© 01/01/2025
QuantumDigitalPublishing.io

Chapter Ten

A STORM IN THE URAL MOUNTAINS

The imposing Ural Mountains serve as a natural divide between Europe and Asia, stretching over two thousand miles across the continent's heart like a colossal stone wall erected by nature itself. These mountains carry two names with identical meaning, "Urals" in Tartar and "Poyas" in Russian, both translating to "belt," describing their function as a vast mountain chain that cinches the landscape like a giant's belt. This magnificent range begins at the Arctic Sea's coast, where frozen winds howl across barren peaks, and extends all the way to the sun-baked Caspian borders, creating an unbroken barrier of jagged rock and dense forest. For Michael Strogoff, these mountains presented a crucial obstacle he needed to traverse before entering Siberian Russia, a challenge that would test both his resolve and his timing. While the crossing took just one night under normal conditions, moving through well-worn passes and along established routes, the situation now looked ominous. Distant thunder rumbled like artillery fire across the peaks, heralding an approaching storm that promised no mercy. Intense electrical energy charged the atmosphere; only a massive explosion could release it. This unusual atmospheric state promised dangerous conditions, with lightning crackling between clouds and the air vibrating with tension.

To prepare for their journey, Michael secured his young fellow traveler's safety. He reinforced the hood with additional ropes, creating a crisscross pattern above and behind to prevent it from being torn away by the wind. He strengthened the vehicle by doubling the traces and packed the nave-boxes with straw, both to reinforce the wheels and reduce the jarring movements that were inevitable while traveling in darkness. As a final measure, he installed a crossbar with pins and screws to connect the front and back sections of the tarantass, which were held together only by axles to the main body. The modifications, though time-consuming, would prove essential for the treacherous journey ahead.

Nadia climbed back into the cart, and Michael positioned himself next to her. A pair of leather curtains hung from the lowered hood, offering some shelter from the harsh wind and rain. Two large lanterns attached to the iemschik's perch cast a dim glow that illuminated their path, but served as warning beacons to prevent collisions with other vehicles. The flames within the lanterns flickered against the strengthening gusts, their dancing light creating eerie shadows that stretched and wavered across the rough terrain ahead. Despite the reinforcements, the tarantass still creaked with each gust of wind that swept down from the mountains.

Their careful preparations proved wise, as a difficult journey lay ahead. The path climbed toward the thick, menacing clouds overhead. If these clouds didn't break into rain soon, the resulting fog would make it treacherous to guide the tarantass forward, with the constant risk of plunging over one of the steep drops that lined their route. Already, wisps of mist were curling around the wheels like ghostly fingers.

Although modest in elevation, the Ural mountain range's highest peak reaches about five thousand feet. Because the summer sun melts any snow accumulating on the mountains during Siberian winters; therefore, there is no permanent snow cover. The climate supports substantial vegetation, with trees and shrubs growing quite tall, their branches often reaching out over the narrow mountain paths like grasping arms. The region attracts many workers to its abundant mineral resources, including iron, copper, and precious stone mines, their rough-hewn entrances visible as dark mouths in the mountainsides. Small settlements called "gavody" dot the area, their smoke-stained buildings clustered around mine entrances and water sources. Horse-drawn carriages can travel through the well-maintained mountain passes, though the journey is never without risk.

The task may be straightforward in pleasant weather with clear skies, but it becomes treacherous when nature unleashes its fury and the wanderer finds himself caught in its midst. Having faced mountain storms before, Michael Strogoff was well aware of their ferocity, and he suspected this one might rival the brutal winter blizzards that terrorized these peaks, storms that had claimed the lives of many less-prepared travelers.

The clouds held back their rain for now, allowing Michael to lift the leather curtains that shielded the tarantass' cabin. He peered out into the darkness, observing the roadside where strange shadows danced, cast by the flickering glow of the lanterns that swayed from their mounting hooks. In her seat, Nadia remained still with crossed arms, her gaze fixed outward, while beside her, Michael's torso stretched halfway outside the carriage as he studied both the heavens and ground below, his experienced eyes searching for any sign of the impending tempest's arrival.

An eerie stillness hung in the air, like nature itself was holding its breath. Overhead paralyzed and unable to function, dense, dark clouds loomed overhead like lungs. Only their traveling carriage, with its grinding wheels, groaning axles, and snorting horses, broke the suffocating quiet, its iron-shod hooves striking sparks from the stones and echoing like tiny thunderclaps through the desolate landscape.

No one was on the empty thoroughfare. Through the tight mountain passes of the Ural, in the ominous darkness, their carriage passed without meeting anyone, no people on foot, no riders on horseback, not a single other vehicle. The dense woods also showed no signs of life; no charcoal makers had fires glowing in the forest depths, no miners' camps appeared near any excavation sites, and not a single cabin was spotted among the thick undergrowth. Even the nocturnal creatures that filled such wilderness with their calls and rustling seemed to have abandoned their usual haunts, as if warned away by some primal instinct that humans could not perceive.

Given this unusual situation, delaying until daybreak would have been understandable. Yet Michael Strogoff couldn't justify waiting. His duty demanded he press on. Still, a troubling question nagged at him: what could drive those travelers ahead in the telga to take such a reckless risk?

The lightning started flashing across the sky around eleven o'clock as Michael kept watch. The bright flashes revealed and concealed the silhouettes of towering pines, their branches swaying in the strengthening wind. Whenever their tarantass approached the road's edge, the illuminated depths of steep ravines became visible below, yawning like hungry mouths in the darkness. As their vehicle jolted hard, they realized they were crossing crude plank bridges spanning deep chasms, with thunder echoing beneath them, the rotting wood creaking under their weight. A growing roar filled the air as they climbed higher, like the voice of some ancient mountain spirit warning them away. Mixed with these sounds were the iemschik's calls, alternating between harsh reprimands and gentle encouragement to his struggling animals, his voice growing hoarse from the constant effort. The poor beasts, more affected by the heavy air than the rough terrain, stumbled, their flanks heaving with exhaustion, no longer responding even to their shaft bells' familiar jingle, which was lost in the howling wind.

"What time will we get to the ridge's peak?" Michael asked the iemschik or carriage driver, his voice audible over the howling wind.

"If we make it at all, one in the morning," he answered, shaking his head, his weathered face creased with concern.

"Surely you've weathered mountain storms before, my friend?" Michael pressed, trying to sound more confident than he felt.

"Indeed, and God willing, this won't be my final one!" the driver replied with a grim chuckle that seemed to catch in his throat.

"Are you frightened?"

"No, not frightened. But I stand by what I said, setting out was unwise." The iemschik's knuckles whitened as he gripped the reins tighter.

"Staying behind would have been even more unwise," Michael muttered, more to himself than the driver.

"Keep going, my little doves!" the iemschik called out to his horses, his voice carrying a mixture of determination and resignation. His duty was to follow orders, not question them, no matter how treacherous the path ahead might seem.

A piercing sound cut through the tranquil air. Lightning illuminated the scene with brilliant clarity, and before the deafening thunder could finish its roll, Michael glimpsed towering pines swaying atop a distant peak. Though the storm had unleashed its fury, it remained confined to the heights above, where the gale force winds wreaked havoc. The sharp crack of splintering wood echoed as tree after tree succumbed to the hurricane's mighty gusts. A cascade of broken trunks came crashing down, sweeping across the road and plummeting over the cliff's edge two hundred feet ahead of the tarantass.

The carriage lurched to a sudden halt, its wooden frame groaning in protest as the horses stamped at the ground, their breath visible in the chilled mountain air.

"Rise up, my lovely ones!" shouted the coachman, his whip cracking above the rolling thunder. He surveyed the treacherous path ahead, his weathered face etched with concern.

Michael reached for Nadia's hand, feeling her fingers trembling in the darkness. "Sister, have you fallen asleep?"

"No, dear brother," she whispered, her voice steady despite the chaos surrounding them.

"Brace yourself, the storm is almost upon us!" another flash of lightning that cast stark shadows across their faces punctuated Michael's warning, revealing the determination in their eyes.

"I'm prepared."

Just as Michael Strogoff pulled the leather curtains closed, the tempest struck with full force, rattling the carriage windows like angry fists against glass.

The coachman sprang from his perch to grab the horses' bridles, his boots sliding in the mud as he sensed the grave danger that now threatened them all.

A gust of wind held the tarantass motionless at a bend in the road, the wooden frame creaking under nature's assault. The driver had no choice but to keep the horses facing into the wind. If the carriage were caught sideways, it would flip and plummet down the cliff face into the darkness below. The terrified horses stood on their hind legs, their eyes rolling white with fear as their handler struggled to calm them. His soothing words had given way to angry curses, each one lost in the howling wind. Nothing seemed to work. The poor beasts, dazzled by lightning and startled by the constant thunder, tossed their heads and seemed ready to snap their harnesses and bolt at any moment. The iemschik had lost control of his team, his years of experience rendered useless against nature's fury.

In that instant, Michael Strogoff leaped from the carriage and hurried to help, his coat whipping around him as he fought his way forward. With his extraordinary physical power, he succeeded, though it wasn't easy, in bringing the horses under control, his muscles straining against their panic-driven strength.

The tempest intensified at that point; the wind howling like a thousand angry wolves through the mountain passes. A massive cascade of rocks and fallen trees started tumbling down the mountainside above their position, each boulder threatening destruction as it crashed downward.

"This spot isn't safe," Michael declared, his voice audible above nature's fury.

"Nowhere is safe," replied the coachman, his courage shattered by fear, hands trembling on the reins. "This storm will send us plummeting down the mountain by the quickest route possible."

"Handle that horse, you spineless fool," Michael snapped, muscles tensing as he gripped the bridle, "I'll take care of this one."

Another violent gust that sent leaves and debris cut the conversation short, flying past them like deadly projectiles. Both men had to drop to the earth to keep from being swept away, their faces pressed against the muddy ground. Despite their best attempts, and even with the horses straining against their traces, their vehicle slid backwards with an ominous groan until an enormous tree trunk halted its path toward the steep drop-off, the impact jarring everyone inside.

"Keep your courage, Nadia!" Michael Strogoff called out, fighting to maintain his footing in the treacherous conditions.

"I am calm," the young woman from Livonia answered, her tone steady and composed despite the chaos surrounding them, her hands folded in her lap.

The deafening thunder subsided as the fierce wind rushed down into the ravine below, carrying with it loose branches and debris that whirled past them like deadly projectiles.

"Are we turning around?" the iemschik asked, his voice audible over the howling gale.

"No, we must continue forward! After this bend, the hillside will protect us from the worst of it."

"The horses are refusing to move! They sense the danger!"

"Follow my lead and pull them along. We cannot stay here exposed."

"The storm is coming back! Look at those clouds!"

"Will you follow my command?" Michael's tone grew stern.

"Is that an order?" the driver challenged, squinting through the rain that pelted his face.

"It's an order from the Father!" Michael declared, invoking the Emperor's supreme authority for the first time, knowing the weight such words carried even in this remote wilderness.

"Onward, my swift ones!" the iemschik called out, grabbing one horse's reins while Michael took hold of the other, both men leaning into the wind as they urged the frightened animals forward.

The carriage inched forward as the horses strained against the brutal wind, their muscles trembling with exhaustion and fear. The animals could no longer rear up, their spirits broken by nature's onslaught, and the middle horse, less restricted than its companions, maintained position along the road's center, providing what little stability remained. Both men and beasts struggled against the gale, losing one or two steps backward, for every three gained forward, their determination tested with each painful advance. They stumbled on the rain-slicked ground, falling and rising again in their desperate advance, clothes and harnesses soaked through to crushing weight. The carriage teetered on its wooden wheels, the entire frame groaning and threatening to shatter at any moment against the merciless assault. Extra ropes and bindings secured the hood, or canvas top, preventing the wind from tearing it away earlier and leaving them vulnerable. Michael Strogoff and the iemschik spent over two hours traversing this treacherous half-mile stretch, exposed to the storm's fury, their faces raw from the stinging rain and debris. The peril came not only from the wind's relentless assault on the travelers but also from the deadly barrage of stones and broken tree trunks hurtling through the air like nature's artillery, forcing them to duck and weave while maintaining their desperate grip on the reins.

A brilliant bolt of lightning illuminated the scene, revealing an enormous mass tumbling down the mountainside straight toward their carriage. The driver let out a terrified shout, his voice lost in the howling wind.

Despite Michael Strogoff's desperate attempts to urge the horses forward with his whip, the animals stood frozen in fear, refusing to budge. Their eyes rolled white with terror, hooves planted against the rain-slicked ground as if turned to stone themselves.

In mere seconds, the massive boulder would hurtle past their position. With horror, Michael realized the boulder would demolish the carriage and kill his companion. There wasn't enough time to pull her to safety. The distance between them was too great to cross in the precious heartbeats remaining.

In that moment of crisis, Michael felt an extraordinary surge of power course through him, every muscle and sinew charged with desperate energy. He positioned himself behind the carriage and, with impossible strength, shoved the entire vehicle clear of the boulder's deadly path, his boots scraping against the rocky ground as he strained against the weight.

The massive boulder hurtled past, striking his chest and leaving him gasping for air as if struck by artillery fire. It pulverized the stones beneath with a thunderous crack before plummeting into the dark chasm, the sound of its impact lost to the raging storm below. Fragments of shattered rock peppered Michael's face and shoulders as he stumbled backward, his lungs burning from the exertion.

"Oh, brother!" Nadia cried out, having witnessed the scene illuminated by lightning, her hands clasped against her chest in terror.

"Nadia!" Michael called back, his voice straining against the howling wind, "don't be afraid!"

"It's not myself I'm worried about!" Her words carried the tremor of contained panic.

"God watches over us, sister!" Michael's reassurance rang with conviction despite his exhaustion.

"He watches over me, brother, for He has guided you to my side!" the young girl whispered, tears mixing with the rain on her cheeks.

The momentum of the horse-drawn carriage couldn't be slowed, so the exhausted steeds continued their advance, their flanks heaving with each labored step. pulled along by Michael and the coachman, who gripped the reins with white-knuckled determination, they struggled onward toward a slim mountain passage that stretched from north to south, where they would find refuge from the storm's direct assault. At one terminus stood a massive boulder, its peak surrounded by swirling winds that tore at loose debris like hungry spirits. In the boulder's lee, there was relative stillness, a pocket of calm in the chaos; however, once caught within the tornado's reach, neither human nor animal could withstand its devastating force, which threatened to sweep them all into the abyss below.

Something sliced the tallest fir trees jutting above the barrier, as if a massive blade had sliced through their peaks, sending splintered wood and needles spiraling into the maelstrom. The tempest reached its full fury, transforming the sky into a battlefield of elements. Lightning blazed through the narrow valley in blinding sheets of blue-white radiance, while thunder rolled in an unbroken roar that seemed to shake the very foundations of the earth. Each impact made the earth shudder with increasing violence, suggesting the entire Ural mountain range might crumble from its very core, unleashing an avalanche of ancient stone.

Fortunately, they managed to position the tarantass at an angle to the storm's fury, using the natural contours of the terrain to their advantage. Yet the fierce wind currents, channeled downward by the slope like water through a funnel, proved harder to evade. These gusts struck with such force that the carriage seemed ready to shatter apart at any moment, its wooden frame creaking and groaning under the relentless assault.

Forced to abandon her seat in the vulnerable vehicle, Nadia found refuge in a mining hollow that Michael spotted using a lantern's wavering glow through the tempest. The excavation, marked by deep pickaxe strikes in the living rock, offered a secure shelter where the young woman could rest until they resumed their journey, its rough-hewn walls providing welcome protection from the howling winds that threatened to tear their world apart.

At that moment, one o'clock in the morning, the heavens unleashed a fierce downpour. Combined with the howling wind and crackling lightning, the weather turned into a terrifying tempest. The rain fell in stinging sheets, drumming against the rocky ground with such intensity that it created a deafening roar. Pressing forward was now impossible. Having reached this mountain pass, their path ahead involved descending the Ural Mountains' slopes. Attempting such a descent now, with countless mountain streams tearing apart the road and violent gusts of wind and rain swirling around them, would have been pure folly.

"The waiting is a serious matter indeed," Michael stated, his voice audible above the storm's fury. "But we must do it to prevent even longer delays later. The storm's intense fury gives me reason to believe it won't continue much longer. These mountain tempests often exhaust themselves. Dawn will break around three o'clock, and while we can't risk descending in darkness, we should be able to make the attempt after sunrise, if not easily, then at least with less peril."

"We'll wait then, brother," Nadia responded, pulling her coat tighter around her shoulders as another gust of wind howled through their shelter. "But if you're choosing to delay, don't do it just to protect me from exhaustion or danger."

"Nadia," he said, meeting her determined gaze through the shadows, "I understand your courage, but by putting us both in danger, I'm risking something far greater than just our lives. I would fail my sacred mission, a duty that must come before all else, even my own desires to press forward."

"A duty?" Nadia whispered, her voice audible above the howling wind. Her eyes searched his face with sudden intensity.

A brilliant flash of lightning shattered the darkness at that precise moment, turning night into blinding day. A deafening thunderclap followed, so close it seemed to crack the very air around them. The air grew thick with choking sulfurous fumes as a massive pine tree, struck by lightning mere yards from their carriage, erupted into flames like an enormous blazing torch, sending sparks swirling upward into the tempestuous night.

The force of impact knocked the driver down, but sprang back up without injury, brushing snow from his coat as he steadied himself against the carriage wheel.

As the thunder's final rumbles faded into the mountain valleys like distant drums, Nadia squeezed Michael's hand with sudden urgency and whispered in his ear, her breath warm against his cold skin: "Brother, do you hear those shouts?"

© 01/01/2025

Chapter Eleven

TRAVELERS IN DISTRESS

A brief silence descended, then, from afar, cries pierced the stillness, their sounds carrying with remarkable clarity to the tarantass, a Russian carriage. Someone was calling for help, not far down the road.

Michael listened. Though the coachman also heard the shouts, he shook his head.

"Someone needs our help!" Nadia exclaimed.

"They are beyond help," the coachman stated.

"Why not?" Michael demanded. "Wouldn't we want others to help us if we were in their place?"

"You can't risk the carriage and horses!"

"Then I'll go on foot," Michael declared, cutting off the coachman protests.

"I'm coming with you, brother," Nadia said, rising.

"No, stay here, Nadia. Keep the coachman company. I don't want to leave him by himself."

"I shall remain here," Nadia declared with quiet determination.

"Under no circumstances must you move from this position."

"This is where you'll find me upon your return."

Michael squeezed her hand, then vanished into the inky darkness as he rounded the slope's edge.

"Your brother's judgment is faulty," the coachman commented.

"No, his judgment is sound," Nadia responded with simple conviction.

Strogoff, meanwhile, pressed forward with urgent strides. A dual purpose drove his haste, both the desire to assist the troubled travelers and a burning curiosity about their identity. He felt certain the desperate cries originated from the telga that had maintained its lead ahead of him, somehow defying the tempest that had halted others in their tracks.

Though the rainfall had ceased, the tempest continued with even greater intensity. As: The wind carried clearer cries. The tempest obscured the mountain pass where Nadia waited. The path twisted through the landscape, and the violent gusts of wind, deflected by the sharp turns, created treacherous whirlwinds that Michael could only navigate by summoning all his strength to stay upright.

Before long, he realized the travelers whose voices he'd detected were close by. Despite their proximity, the darkness prevented Michael from spotting them, though their words reached him with perfect clarity.

"Are you planning to return, you fool?" he heard someone shout, much to his astonishment.

"Wait until the next stop. You'll get a good whipping!"

"Listen here, you devil's messenger! Hey! Down there!"

"So this is what passes for transportation in these parts!"

"Indeed, they call this rickety thing a telga!"

"That wretched driver! He keeps going as if he hasn't noticed we're not with him anymore!"

"To think he would dare deceive me, a respectable English gentleman! I shall file a formal complaint with the chancellor's office and see that scoundrel hung!"

He spoke these words with intense fury, but was cut off by his companion's sudden outburst of laughter. "Now that's amusing!" the companion declared.

"How dare you laugh!" the Englishman snapped.

"Of course I dare, my dear colleague," came the reply, "and, too. I must say, I've experienced nothing so ridiculous."

At that moment, a deafening thunderclap echoed through the ravine before fading into the far-off mountain peaks. As the last rumble subsided, the cheerful voice continued: "Indeed, it's hilarious. This contraption most definitely isn't of French origin."

"Not from England either," the other person responded.

Along the road, illuminated by lightning flashes, Michael spotted two travelers about twenty yards away. They sat side by side in an unusual vehicle, its wheels sunk deep into the muddy ruts of the road.

As he drew closer, he recognized them as the two reporters he'd traveled with aboard the Caucasus. One was grinning, while the other looked at their predicament.

"Good morning!" the Frenchman called out. "What a pleasure to see you here. Allow me to introduce my dear adversary, Mr. Blount."

The British news correspondent gave a small bow, and was preparing to introduce his fellow journalist, Alcide Jolivet, as etiquette required, but Michael cut him short.

"There's no need for introductions," he said. "We've already met during our journey on the Volga."

"Oh, of course! Now I remember! Mr?"

"Nicholas Korpanoff, from Irkutsk. But tell me, what's occurred that seems to amuse you so, even though it appears to be at your companion's expense?"

"Indeed, Mr. Korpanoff," Alcide answered. "Would you believe it? Our driver has vanished with the front section of this wretched carriage, leaving us stranded in the rear portion! Here we sit in half a telga, without horses or driver. Don't you find it amusing?"

"Not in the least," the Englishman stated.

"Oh, but it is! You need to see the humor in these situations, my friend."

"And how exactly do you propose we continue our journey?" Blount demanded.

"Nothing could be simpler," said Alcide with a grin. "Just strap yourself to what's left of our wagon. I'll handle the reins and call you my sweet dove, just like a proper Russian coachman, and you can gallop away like a genuine postal steed."

"Mr. Jolivet," the Englishman said, "I find your humor most inappropriate. You're going too far with this..."

"Oh, do hush now, my good man. When you're worn out, I'll take over. And you have my permission to call me a wheezing slug and spineless turtle if I don't get you moving at breakneck speed."

Alcide conveyed all of this with such genuine cheerfulness that Michael couldn't suppress a smile. "My friends," he said, "I have a superior suggestion. We've reached the summit of the Ural mountains, so from here it's all downhill. My carriage is parked nearby, just two hundred yards back. I'll provide one of my horses to attach to what's left of the telga, and by tomorrow, assuming all goes well, we'll reach Ekaterenburg together."

"That's a magnanimous offer, Mr. Korpanoff," Alcide responded.

"You know, I'd be happy to give you spots in my carriage," Michael said, "but it's only built for two, and my sister and I take up both seats."

"That's quite alright," Alcide replied. "Between your horse and our demi-telga, we could travel anywhere."

"We'd be most grateful to accept your offer," Harry Blount chimed in. "Though that coachman..."

"Trust me, you're not the first travelers to run into this kind of trouble," Michael assured them.

"But why wouldn't our driver return?" one of them demanded. "He must realize he's abandoned us here, the scoundrel!"

"Ha! He had no clue whatsoever!"

"You mean to tell me he didn't realize he left half his cart behind?"

"Not at all! He's driving what's left of it toward Ekaterenburg, unaware."

"Didn't I say it would be amusing, colleague?" Alcide said with a laugh.

"Well then, gentlemen, shall we?" Michael suggested. "My carriage awaits..."

"But what about the broken cart?" the Englishman interjected.

"Oh, don't worry about that, my dear Blount!" Alcide exclaimed. "It's stuck in the ground, I dare say if we left it till spring, it would sprout leaves!"

"Let's go, gentlemen," Michael Strogoff called out. "We'll retrieve the carriage together."

The Frenchman and Englishman climbed down from their seats, no longer the rear ones, as the front section had already departed, and followed Michael's lead.

As they walked, Alcide Jolivet kept up his characteristic chatter with his usual cheerful disposition. "My word, Mr. Korpanoff," he remarked, "you've helped us escape quite a predicament."

"I did what anyone would have done in the same situation," Michael responded.

"Well then, sir, you've done us a great service, and if your journey continues further, perhaps our paths will cross again, and..."

When Alcide Jolivet refrained from asking Michael about his destination, Michael volunteered the information to avoid arousing suspicion. "I'm heading to Omsk, gentlemen," he stated.

"As for Mr. Blount and myself," Alcide responded, "we seek wherever danger, and therefore news, can be found."

"You mean the provinces under attack?" Michael inquired, showing particular interest.

"Mr. Korpanoff. Perhaps our paths will cross there."

"I rather doubt that," Michael replied. "I have no desire to face bullets or spears. I'm far too peace-loving to venture into combat zones."

"Please accept my sincerest apologies, sir. It's regrettable that our paths must diverge ! Though perhaps fortune will smile upon us, and we might share the road together after departing Ekaterenburg, even if just for a brief while?"

Michael paused before asking, "Are you continuing to Omsk?"

"Our plans remain uncertain," Alcide responded. "Though we'll proceed to Ishim, and from there, we'll have to let circumstances guide our journey."

"In that case, gentlemen," Michael replied, "we shall be companions until we reach Ishim."

Although Michael harbored a strong preference for solitary travel, he recognized the potential for misinterpretation if he were to avoid the two journalists who happened to be charting a similar course. Since Alcide and his fellow traveler planned to stop at Ishim for a while, Michael concluded it might be beneficial to share this portion of the trip with them.

"Have you received any definite information about locating the Tartar invasion?" he inquired.

"Yes, indeed," Alcide confirmed. "All we have to go on is what was reported in Perm. The Tartar forces under Feofar-Khan have swept through Semipolatinsk province, and they've been moving down the Irtish River these past few days. If you want to reach Omsk before they do, you'll need to make haste."

"You're right about that," Michael agreed.

"Word is also going around that Colonel Ogareff managed to slip across the border in disguise. They say he'll soon link up with the Tartar commander in the rebel territory."

"But where did this information come from?" Michael pressed, troubled by this news which, true or not, affected him.

"Well, you know how news travels," Alcide responded. "Word gets around."

"So you believe Colonel Ogareff has made his way to Siberia?"

"I've heard talk that he planned to travel the Kasan-Ekaterenburg route."

"Is that so, Mr. Jolivet?" Harry Blount perked up, breaking his silence.

"Indeed it is," Alcide confirmed.

"And are you aware he traveled in disguise as a gypsy?" Blount pressed.

"Like one of the Roma people!" Michael burst out without thinking, and the memory of the elderly Bohemian traveler at Nijni-Novgorod flashed in his mind, along with their shared journey on the Caucasus and their arrival at Kasan.

"Only enough to jot down some observations about it in correspondence to my cousin," Alcide responded with a grin.

"You were quite quick during your Kasan stop," the Englishman remarked.

"Indeed, I was, my friend! While they were refueling the Caucasus, I made the most of my time gathering intelligence."

Ignoring the witty exchange between Harry Blount and Alcide, Michael's thoughts wandered to the traveling gypsies. He dwelled on the elderly Tsigane leader, whose features had remained hidden from view, and the mysterious woman at his side who had fixed Michael with such an enigmatic look. His reverie was suddenly broken by the crack of a pistol nearby.

"Quick, gentlemen!" he called out.

"Well, well," Alcide mused to himself, "our cautious merchant friend, who steers clear of gunfire, seems mighty eager to rush toward danger now!"

Racing after Michael came Harry Blount, never one to shy away from peril. Within moments, all three had reached the jutting rock formation that shielded the carriage where the road curved.

The lightning-struck pine cluster continued to blaze. Though they saw no one, Michael's instincts proved correct. A terrifying growl pierced the air, followed by another loud report.

"It's a bear!" Michael shouted, recognizing the unmistakable sound. "Nadia! Nadia!" Yanking his cutlass from his belt, he darted around the stone buttress where the young woman had said she would wait.

Fire consumed the massive pine trees, casting an eerie, flickering light across the landscape. Just as Michael approached the horse-drawn carriage, an enormous creature lumbered in his direction.

Before him stood a colossal bear. Driven from its forest home by the raging storm, the beast had sought shelter in this cavern, its regular den, which was now inhabited by Nadia.

Faced with the massive beast, the terrified horses snapped their restraints and bolted. Focusing on the coachman's actions: Abandoning Nadia to face the bear alone, the coachman pursued his fleeing horses, his concern for his animals.

Despite the danger, the young woman remained courageous and composed. unaware of her presence, the bear had turned its attention to the remaining horse. Without hesitation, Nadia emerged from her hiding place, retrieved one of Michael's revolvers from the carriage, and approached the bear before firing at point-blank range.

She darted behind the carriage as the bear, nursing a minor shoulder wound, spun to face her. But when she noticed the horse straining against its traces, ready to snap them, she knew they'd be stranded if it broke free and they couldn't recover the others. With remarkable composure, she stepped back toward the bear and, just as it lifted its paws to strike, fired her second barrel straight at it.

Michael arrived the moment he heard the news. In one leap, he reached the scene, and with another, he positioned himself between the bear and the girl. A single upward thrust of his arm, wielding his fearsome blade, brought down the massive creature. The bear collapsed, lifeless, after

Michael performed the renowned technique of Siberian hunters, a precise strike designed to preserve the animal's valuable pelt, which commanded high prices at the market.

"Tell me you're unharmed, sister," Michael said, rushing to the young girl's side.

"I'm fine, brother," Nadia answered.

The pair of reporters caught up with them. Alcide grabbed hold of the horse's reins, and with his powerful grip, brought the animal under control. He and his fellow journalist had witnessed Michael's swift action with the knife. "Well done!" Alcide exclaimed. "For someone who's just a merchant, Mr. Korpanoff, you wield that hunting blade like an expert."

"Like a true professional," Blount chimed in.

"Where I come from in Siberia," Michael replied, "we must learn to be skilled at many things."

Alcide studied him. Standing in the harsh light, his knife coated in crimson, his imposing frame towering above with one foot planted on the massive beast's body, he cut quite a striking figure.

"What a fearsome warrior," Alcide muttered to himself. Then, approaching with deep respect, he greeted the young woman.

Nadia inclined her head.

Alcide turned to face his companion. "Now there's a sister who matches her brother's courage!" he remarked. "If I were one of those bears, I'd think twice before tangling with such a brave and graceful pair."

Harry Blount maintained a rigid posture, standing apart from the others with his hat held in his hands. His companion's relaxed demeanor seemed to make Blount even more formal and uncomfortable.

Just then, the coachman returned, having caught his two runaway horses. He looked at the splendid beast sprawled lifeless on the ground, reluctant to abandon it to scavenging birds, before turning his attention to getting his team back in harness.

Michael explained to him about the stranded travelers and his plan to let them use one horse.

"Whatever you prefer," answered the coachman. "Though, mind you, that means two carriages rather than one."

"Fair enough, my good man," said Alcide, catching the driver's hint, "you'll get paid twice the usual rate."

"Then off we go, my swift beauties!" the coachman called out to his horses.

The group resumed their journey, with Nadia settling back into the carriage while Michael and his fellow travelers proceeded on foot. At three o'clock, fierce winds continued to howl through the mountain pass. By first light, they had reached the telga, which remained stuck, its wheels half-buried. The vehicle's condition made it clear why a sudden tug could split it between its front and back sections. They managed to salvage the situation by using ropes to harness one horse to what remained of the telga. The reporters climbed aboard this makeshift transport, and both carriages began moving again. All that remained was the straightforward descent down the Ural slopes.

The two carriages made their way to Ekaterenburg, with the carriage leading to the telga. The six-hour journey down the winding mountain roads was uneventful, save for the occasional glimpse of a majestic eagle soaring overhead or a curious marmot scurrying across the rocky terrain.

As they pulled up to the post-house, they spotted their former driver standing by the entrance, arms folded across his broad chest. The good-natured Russian greeted them with a warm smile, extended his calloused hand, and asked for his customary tip in a thick, gravelly voice.

The outrageous demand sent Blount into a fury, his face reddening like a ripe tomato as he clenched his fists. If the coachman hadn't backed away, he would have received a direct punch, delivered with proper British boxing technique, as payment for his audacious request for "na vodkou."

Alcide Jolivet found this display of temper hilarious, laughing harder than he ever had.

"But the poor fellow has a point!" he exclaimed. "He's right, my friend. We can hardly blame him if we couldn't keep up with his pace!"

He dug into his pocket and pulled out a few copecks. "Here, my friend," he said, offering them to the coachman. "I give these to you."

This only made Mr. Blount more furious, and he started threatening legal action against the telga's owner.

"You're talking about a lawsuit in Russia?" Alcide exclaimed. "Why, those cases drag on forever! Have you heard about that nurse who sued for twelve months' worth of infant care payments?"

"No, I haven't," Harry Blount replied.

"Well, you should've seen how old that 'baby' was by the time the court ruled in the nurse's favor!"

"And what position did he hold?" she inquired.

"He served as a Colonel in the Imperial Guard!"

The response triggered a collective burst of laughter from everyone present.

Alcide, pleased with his clever remark, retrieved his well-worn notebook and jotted down an entry he intended to include in an upcoming French-Russian dictionary he was compiling: "Telga, A Russian vehicle that begins its journey on four wheels but, owing to the appalling state of the nation's roads, arrives at its destination on two." He chuckled to himself, imagining the looks on the faces of readers who would encounter that definition. The indignant expression on Mr. Blount's face only heightened his amusement at poking fun at Russian inefficiency as he watched Alcide scribble away.

Chapter Twelve

PROVOCATION

Ekaterinburg, despite being physically located in Asia beyond the Ural Mountains on their easternmost slopes, is part of Europe. The city falls under the jurisdiction of the Perm government, making it an administrative part of European Russia. This creates an unusual situation where a piece of what is Siberia is technically within Russia's European territory. The local population embraces this duality, often referring to their home as a bridge between continents. Street signs and official documents display both European and Asian influences, while the architecture blends classical European designs with elements inspired by the city's position as a gateway to Siberia. This geographic anomaly has helped shape Ekaterinburg's unique cultural identity, making it a distinctive melting pot where East meets West.

Ekaterenburg, established in 1723, had grown into a significant urban center where Michael and his fellow travelers would find transportation to continue their journey. The city housed the empire's primary mint and served as the administrative hub for mining operations. Its prominence stemmed from its role as the focal point of a thriving industrial region, known for its gold and platinum processing and refinement facilities.

At this time, Ekaterenburg was experiencing a significant surge in its population, with many Russians and Siberians gathering there to escape the looming Tartar threat. While finding transportation into Ekaterenburg had been challenging earlier, departing was now easy, since most people were reluctant to travel on Siberian routes during these uncertain times.

They found it easy to exchange their well-worn demi-carriage, which had carried them as far as Ekaterenburg, for a sturdy telga, a low, four-wheeled Russian wagon designed for rough terrain. Michael, however, kept his tarantass, a light, two-wheeled Russian carriage, as it had weathered the Ural crossing well and proved ideal for traversing the vast expanses ahead. All it needed was a fresh team of three hardy horses to continue their swift journey eastward toward the distant city of Irkutsk, deep in the heart of Siberia.

The road leading to Tioumen, extending as far as Novo-Zaimskoe, features mild elevations and rolling terrain, early indicators of the approaching Ural Mountains. However, beyond Novo-Zaimskoe lies the vast expanse of the steppe, a endless sea of grasslands stretching towards the horizon. The travelers could already envision the challenges that lay ahead as they ventured into this desolate yet beautiful landscape.

The journalists had planned to make Ichim their stopping point, four hundred and twenty miles distant from Ekaterenburg. From there, they would let circumstances dictate whether to continue their journey through the invaded territory together or, depending on how their journalistic instincts guided them in pursuit of news. The prospect of parting ways weighed heavily on their minds, as the bond forged through their shared experiences had become a source of strength and camaraderie in these uncertain times.

The road connecting Ekaterenburg to Ichim, passing through Irkutsk, remained Michael's sole option. However, having no interest in gathering news and wishing to steer clear of areas ravaged by the invading forces, he resolved not to make any stops along the way. The urgency of his mission weighed upon him, fueling his determination to press forward without delay.

"I'm pleased to travel alongside you," he told his fellow travelers, his voice tinged with a hint of regret, "but I must be frank. Reaching Omsk is my utmost priority. My sister and I need to reunite with our mother there before it's too late." He paused, the gravity of the situation etched on his face. "Who knows if we'll arrive before the Tartars overrun the town? Therefore, I can only pause at post-houses to switch horses. We must keep moving, both day and night, lest we risk being caught in the path of the invading forces."

"That's our plan," Blount responded, his expression resolute. "We cannot afford any delays on this perilous journey."

"Excellent," said Michael, his voice tinged with urgency. "But there's no time to waste. Find a carriage that..."

"That has back wheels," Alcide cut in with a wry smirk, "guaranteed to keep pace with the front ones."

Within thirty minutes, the determined Frenchman had secured a sturdy tarantass, and he and his companion took their seats, eager to depart. Michael and Nadia returned to their own carriage, exchanging a solemn glance as they prepared for the arduous trek ahead. As the clock struck noon, its resonant chime echoing through the streets of Ekaterenburg, both vehicles set off together, the wheels crunching against the well-trodden road, their occupants steeling themselves for the challenges that lay before them.

In the depths of Siberia, Nadia found herself traversing the expansive route to Irkutsk, her heart heavy with trepidation. Her mind was consumed with thoughts as three robust, fleet-footed horses pulled her across the exile lands where her father was forced to dwell, for an uncertain duration, far removed from their homeland. The endless steppes rolling beneath the tarantass registered in her consciousness, for her gaze remained fixed on the distant horizon, somewhere beyond which her banished father awaited, a longing ache gripping her soul. Racing at fifteen miles per hour, she remained oblivious to her surroundings and the distinct character of Western Siberia, so unlike its eastern counterpart. This region boasted few farmlands; the topsoil was barren, yet beneath the surface lay abundant treasures, iron, copper, platinum, and gold, a wealth that had drawn fortune-seekers from far and wide. The land's peculiar economy posed a simple question: why till the earth when greater riches waited below? Throughout the region, pickaxes rang out in constant labor, their rhythmic clanging echoing across the desolate landscape, while plows lay idle and forgotten, gathering dust in the arid wind.

Nadia's mind wandered from the Baikal region as she contemplated her current circumstances. The memory of her father grew dim, giving way to visions of her kind-hearted traveling companion as she'd first encountered him on the Wladimir train. She remembered his thoughtful gestures throughout their journey, his unexpected appearance at the police station to secure her release, the warm sincerity with which he'd addressed her as sister despite their forged acquaintance, his protective nature shielding her from harm during their harrowing Volga river descent. But most vivid was his heroic conduct during that frightful night amidst the raging Ural storm, when he'd braved the howling winds and lashing rain without hesitation to preserve her life at the cost of his own safety.

Nadia reflected on Michael with deep gratitude, her heart swelling with affection for this man who had become far more than a traveling companion. She felt blessed beyond measure to have found such a noble guardian, someone who combined unflinching courage with profound wisdom and selfless friendship. In his reassuring presence, she experienced a sense of complete security, knowing his protection was steadfast and unwavering no matter the peril they faced. His dedication to ensuring her safety went far beyond what even a devoted brother might offer. With the major hurdles of their harrowing adventure now overcome, completing her journey to the remote valley seemed an assured conclusion, a question of patience and perseverance until they at last reached her ancestral home.

Michael sat lost in contemplation, feeling grateful that fate had orchestrated his encounter with Nadia. This meeting served two purposes, allowing him to offer help when needed while also providing perfect cover for his true identity. He found himself admiring the young woman's steady courage. Their connection felt almost familial, as if she were his sister. What he experienced toward his capable and valiant traveling companion was more akin to deep respect than romantic attraction. He recognized in her one of those exceptional souls, pure and uncommon, that commanded universal admiration.

The perils now intensified for Michael upon entering Siberian territory. Assuming the reports were accurate and Ivan Ogareff had indeed crossed the border, every move would require utmost vigilance. The situation had shifted as Tartar scouts now patrolled the Siberian regions, their eyes ever-watchful for any suspicious activity. These merciless warriors would end both his mission and his life if his disguise fails or his role as the Czar's messenger was revealed. Michael felt the burden of his duty weighing more heavily than ever before, the stakes higher than he could have imagined when first accepting this perilous assignment. Yet he resolved to persevere, his courage and determination unwavering in the face of increasing danger.

In the second carriage, matters proceeded, the familiar dynamic between Alcide and Blount playing out as it so often did. Alcide was long-winded, constructing complete sentences with his usual flair for embellishment, while Blount's responses were terse and minimal, the man of few words offering only what was necessary. Despite their contrasting communication styles, both men remained vigilant, observing their surroundings from their unique perspectives and documenting the few uneventful happenings during their passage through Western Siberia's harsh, unforgiving territories.

At every relay station, the journalists stepped down from their coach and joined Michael. Nadia remained in the tarantass throughout the journey, only leaving when it was time for meals at the post-houses. During these breakfast and dinner stops, she would take her place at the table but kept to herself, not taking part in any discussions.

The young lady captivated Alcide, though he maintained proper decorum. Her quiet resilience impressed him in enduring the hardships of their challenging journey.

Michael found the required stops quite frustrating, and at each relay station, he worked to speed things along. He would rush the innkeepers, prod the iemschiks to move faster, and ensure the tarantass was prepared for travel. They would consume their meals much too fast for Blount's preference, as he liked to eat at a measured pace before setting off again at breakneck speed, their generous payment ensuring swift service.

Blount showed no interest in the girl during meals. He was known for his single-minded focus and preferred not to multitask. The topic of her was also one of the rare subjects he avoided discussing with his fellow traveler.

When Alcide once inquired about the girl's age, Blount responded with genuine confusion, "Which girl?"

"Nicholas Korpanoff's sister, of course," Alcide clarified.

"Oh, is that who she is?"

"No, his grandmother!" Alcide snapped back, irritated by Blount's apparent indifference. "How old would you say she is?"

"If I had been there when she was born, I might have understood."

The fields were empty of Siberian farmers, their usual occupants having retreated to safer havens. These rural people were known for their distinctive features: light complexions and solemn expressions, which one famous explorer likened to the people of Castile, though without their proud bearing. Scattered across the landscape, abandoned settlements stood as silent sentinels, signaling the advancing Tartar forces that had driven the villagers to flee northward to the plains, taking their livestock, sheep, camels, and horses, with them in a desperate bid for survival. Those nomadic Kirghiz tribes who maintained their loyalty to the old order had also moved their encampments across the Irtych River, seeking to avoid the raiders' plundering and preserve what little they could from the escalating conflict.

Fortunately, the postal service continued to operate without disruption, and telegraph messages could still be sent between locations connected to the network. Fresh horses were available at each relay station under normal terms, allowing couriers to transport mail and dispatches across the vast expanse of the steppe. The telegraph operators, those unsung heroes tasked with maintaining the vital lines of communication, forwarded each message as it arrived at their station, prioritizing only the official government communications that held sway over matters of state and military import.

The journey went well for Michael up to this point. As the Czar's messenger, he had encountered no obstacles, and he felt confident that if he could reach Krasnoiarsk, which appeared to be the furthest extent of Feofar-Khan's Tartar forces, he would beat them to Irkutsk. After departing Ekaterenburg, the two carriages traveled for twenty-four hours without incident, covering two hundred and twenty miles before reaching the small town of Toulouguisk at seven in the morning. They fed and watered the horses and then ate a quick meal before continuing across the vast steppe. Later that same day, July 22nd, they made it to Tioumen, where they would spend the night before continuing their urgent mission on behalf of the Czar at first light.

In those days, Tioumen's population had swelled to twenty thousand, twice its normal size, as refugees poured in seeking shelter from the escalating conflict. As the first Russian industrial settlement in Siberia, boasting an impressive metal-refining factory and bell foundry, the city was experiencing unprecedented bustle and strain on its resources. News correspondents scattered throughout the city, seeking information and eyewitness accounts from the displaced masses. The reports from Siberian refugees fleeing the conflict painted a grim picture of advancing devastation. They revealed that Feofar-Khan's forces were advancing through the Ichim valley, leaving a trail of burned villages and pillaged settlements in their wake.

They confirmed the disturbing rumors that the traitorous Colonel Ogareff would soon join, or perhaps had already joined the Tartar leader's ranks, lending his strategic expertise to the enemy's cause. These developments suggested military campaigns in Eastern Siberia would intensify in the coming days. In response, the steadfast Cossacks under Tobolsk's government were conducting rapid marches toward Tomsk, determined to intercept and cut off the Tartar forces before they could advance further into the heart of the empire.

The travelers arrived at Novo-Saimsk as the clock struck midnight, leaving behind the undulating landscape with its tree-covered hills, the last vestiges of the Ural Mountains. This marked a pivotal transition, for they were now entering the true Siberian steppe, stretching all the way to the outskirts of Krasnoiarsk in an unbroken expanse.

The terrain transformed into an immense, featureless plain, a sweeping grassland that extended to the horizon in every direction, where earth met the sky in a perfect circle as precise as if drawn by mathematical instruments. In this vast, uninterrupted expanse, only the regimented telegraph poles broke the monotony, their wires singing in the wind like an aeolian harp played by unseen hands. The only sign of the road's presence was the fine dust clouds kicked up by the tarantass' wheels, creating a white ribbon that stretched into the distance, disappearing into the infinite flatness. Without this dusty trail to guide them, the travelers might have believed themselves alone in an endless wilderness, adrift in a sea of grass with no landmarks or reference points to steer by.

The group, led by Michael, continued their swift journey. Their driver, the iemschik, spurred the horses onward, making them race across the terrain as if they had wings. With no barriers or hindrances in their path, the tarantass carriage maintained its direct course toward Ichim, where the two journalists planned to make their stop, assuming circumstances didn't force them to change their intended route.

Novo-Saimsk and Ichim were one hundred and twenty miles apart, a distance they could cover before eight o'clock the following evening, provided they maintained a steady pace. The iemschiks, those hardy drivers of the Siberian steppe, while unsure if their passengers were nobility or high-ranking officials, treated them with the deference deserving of such status, if only for their generous tips of "na vodkou", that ubiquitous offering of vodka that greased the wheels of travel across the vast Russian expanse. As the tarantass rattled over the rutted trail, Michael and his companion settled in for the long haul, the endless grasslands stretching out before them like an ocean of wind-rippled green.

The next day, July 23rd, as they drove their carriages within thirty miles of Ichim, Michael's keen eyes spotted another vehicle ahead, visible through the dusty haze kicked up by the churning wheels. His horses, being fresher than those of the traveler ahead, would soon catch up to them at their current pace. The vehicle wasn't a tarantass or the ubiquitous telga favored by peasants, but a post-berlin, a lighter, swifter carriage built for speed over long distances. It showed unmistakable signs of a lengthy journey, its once-gleaming varnish dulled by the relentless Siberian elements. The postillion was whipping the horses, maintaining their gallop only through harsh treatment and constant shouting of indecipherable urgings. This berlin couldn't have come through Novo-Saimsk; it must have joined the Irkutsk road using one of the lesser-known paths that crisscrossed the steppe, those ancient trails known only to the most seasoned Russian travelers.

When they spotted the berlin in the distance, their immediate instinct was to overtake it and reach the relay station first, ensuring they would secure fresh horses before the other travelers. A quick command to their iemschiks, and their tarantasses caught up to the swifter berlin, the horses' hooves thundering across the dusty steppe.

Michael Strogoff took the lead in the pursuit, his carriage inching ever closer to the berlin. As his vehicle drew alongside, someone leaned out of the berlin's window, the wind whipping at their cloak. Before he could make out any details of the mysterious person, he sped past in a blur, but a commanding voice rang out with one stern word that cut through the cacophony: "Stop!"

The three vehicles thundered onward, with the berlin falling behind the pair of tarantasses. Far from slowing, the chase intensified as the berlin's horses, roused by their competitors' speed and presence, found renewed vigor and kept pace for several minutes. All three carriages vanished into a thick dust cloud kicked up by the pounding hooves, from which came the sharp snap of whips cracking through the air and the angry shouts of the drivers urging their mounts on. The cloud billowed and shifted like a living thing as the pursuit raged within its dusty confines, the horses' breath rasping amid the rumble of spinning wheels over the hard-packed earth.

Michael and his group maintained their lead, which could prove crucial if the relay station had limited horses available. The station might struggle to supply enough horses for two carriages, let alone three. This would force the trailing berlin to wait, allowing Michael's caravan to extend its advantage even further.

Thirty minutes later, the berlin had fallen so far behind that it appeared as a tiny dot where the steppe met the horizon, the dust cloud that once enveloped the chase now dissipating in the distance. Michael's driver cracked his whip with renewed vigor, the horses straining against their harnesses as they thundered across the vast, rolling expanse of the steppe, kicking up clods of dirt in their wake as they raced to put even more ground between themselves and their pursuers.

On that evening, two carriages arrived in Ichim as the clock struck eight, their wheels kicking up plumes of dust in the dying light. Reports about the Tartar invasion grew dire with each passing hour. The advance guard now threatened the town, and just two days prior, forces compelled local officials to withdraw to the relative safety of Tobolsk, abandoning

Ichim. The streets stood silent and deserted, not a single officer or soldier remaining within the town's bounds to offer protection or reassurance to those few civilians who had chosen not to flee.

When Michael Strogoff reached the relay station, his first priority was securing fresh horses. He was relieved to have outpaced the berlin. Unfortunately, only three horses were in suitable condition for harnessing, as the remaining animals had just returned exhausted from a lengthy journey.

Since the two correspondents planned to remain in Ichim, they didn't need to concern themselves with transportation arrangements and had their carriage stored. Within ten minutes, Michael received word that his tarantass was prepared for departure.

"Excellent," he replied.

He turned to face the two reporters. "Gentlemen, we must now part ways."

"But Mr. Korpanoff," Alcide Jolivet interjected, "You can spare an hour in Ichim?"

"I'm afraid not," he answered. "In fact, I intend to depart from the post-house before that berlin we outpaced catches up to us."

"Are you concerned the traveler might compete with you for horses?"

"I'd prefer to avoid any confrontation."

"In that case, Mr. Korpanoff," said Jolivet, "allow us to express our gratitude once more for your help, and for the pleasure of your company during our journey."

"Perhaps we'll cross paths in Omsk in the coming days," Blount mentioned.

"That's likely," Michael replied, "as I'm heading there."

“Well then, have a safe journey, Mr. Korpanoff,” Alcide said, “and may you not encounter any more telgas.”

Both reporters extended their hands to Michael, intending to give him a warm handshake, when they heard the sound of an approaching carriage. The door burst open, and in stepped a man.

Standing there was the Berlin traveler, a commanding figure of military bearing who appeared to be in his forties. Broad shoulders marked his imposing frame and a sturdy build, topped by a resolute head adorned with thick mustaches that merged into his reddish whiskers. His attire consisted of an unadorned uniform, with a cavalry saber at his hip and a short-handled whip gripped in his hand. A stern expression creased his weathered features, and his piercing gaze swept over the room, assessing the occupants with a practiced eye honed from years of military service. An aura of authority radiated from his very presence, commanding respect and obedience from those around him.

"I need horses," he declared with the unmistakable authority of someone used to giving orders.

The postmaster responded with a deferential bow, "I have none available, sir."

"I must have them."

"It simply can't be done," the postmaster asserted, his brow furrowing with concern.

The traveler's eyes narrowed, his jaw tightening. "In that case, how do you explain the horses I noticed being prepared for the carriage outside?"

The postmaster swallowed hard, his gaze darting toward Michael Strogoff. "Those belong to him," he explained with a deferential gesture.

The traveler's expression hardened, his mouth setting in a grim line. "Remove them at once!" he commanded, his authoritative voice brooking no opposition. An edge of impatience crept into his tone as he surveyed the room.

Michael stepped forward, his shoulders squared. "I've already arranged for those horses," he stated, meeting the traveler's gaze without flinching.

"That's irrelevant! I require them," the traveler snapped, his eyes flashing with irritation. "Hurry up; I'm pressed for time."

Drawing a steadying breath, Michael responded, "I'm equally short on time." He struggled to maintain his composure, his jaw clenching as he fought to keep his voice level.

Nadia stood close by, composed, but her heart pounding as internal anxiety gripped her over the confrontation that would have been better avoided.

"That's enough!" the traveler declared, his voice cutting through the tension like a knife. Moving toward the postmaster with purposeful strides, he demanded with a menacing motion of his hand, "Have those horses hitched to my berlin."

The harried postmaster found himself in a quandary, unsure whether to follow Michael's legitimate claim or the other traveler's improper request. His questioning gaze fell on Michael, who possessed the lawful authority to challenge such unreasonable demands. Yet the postmaster could do nothing. He could not ignore the forceful demands of an armed traveler.

For a brief moment, Michael weighed his options, his brow furrowing as he considered the potential consequences of each course of action. He was reluctant to present his podorojna papers, as doing so would draw unwanted notice and reveal his identity as an imperial courier. Surrendering his horses would set back his journey, a delay he could ill afford with the pressing importance of his mission. Yet he also recognized that becoming embroiled in a confrontation, especially one involving violence, could jeopardize his vital mission and put innocent lives at risk. Michael's jaw clenched as he wrestled with the tough decision, aware that the tense situation could escalate at any moment.

The two journalists watched him, prepared to back him up if he sought their help. Michael's heart pounded in his chest, but he fought to maintain an outward sense of calm and composure.

"I will keep my horses in my carriage," Michael stated, maintaining the modest tone befitting a store owner from Irkutsk. He hoped this reasonable stance would defuse the tense situation.

The stranger stepped toward Michael and gripped his shoulder, his fingers digging into Michael's flesh. "Is that so?" he growled, his breath hot and sour. "You refuse to surrender your horses to me?"

"That's correct," Michael replied, holding the stranger's gaze despite the menacing proximity.

"Very well then. The horses will go to whoever proves stronger. Prepare yourself, I'll show no mercy!" With a sudden motion, the stranger unsheathed his blade, the steel glinting in the dim light.

Nadia rushed forward without hesitation, positioning herself between Michael and the armed stranger, her own hand resting on the hilt of her sword. The two journalists, Blount and Alcide Jolivet, moved forward as well, ready to intervene and defend their comrade.

"I won't engage in combat," Michael stated, crossing his arms over his chest in a gesture of resolute non-violence. He had no intention of being drawn into an unnecessary confrontation that could derail his vital mission.

The stranger's eyes narrowed, his expression a mixture of confusion and outrage. "You refuse to fight?" he spat, tightening his grip on his weapon.

"Yes," Michael replied, his voice level and unwavering.

"Even after that, you still refuse?" the traveler shouted in disbelief. Then, catching everyone off guard, he swung the whip handle and struck Michael's shoulder with a sharp crack. The blow made Michael's face drain of color and he staggered back a step, grimacing in pain. His fists clenched, every fiber of his being yearning to strike back at his attacker and defend his honor. But through sheer force of will, he held himself in check, his jaw clenched tight. A fight now would mean more than just lost time, it could derail his entire vital mission and put everything at risk. Better to sacrifice a few hours and endure the indignity than risk the collapse of all he had worked towards. And yet, to stand there and endure such humiliation in front of his companions, to be branded a coward... it took every ounce of Michael's restraint.

"Come on then, you lily-livered milksop, fight back if you're not a complete craven!" the traveler taunted again, his words growing even more crude and hostile as he sensed Michael's internal struggle. The cruel lash of his tongue was almost as painful as the blow from the whip handle.

"No," Michael stated, his gaze unwavering as he met the other man's eyes, refusing to be cowed despite the stinging ache from the blow. He would not retaliate, no matter how greatly the insults stung his pride. To do so would only vindicate the bully's taunts about his lack of courage.

"Bring the horses now, you useless layabout!" the man snarled, his face reddening with rage at Michael's stoic defiance. He stormed out of the stables, boots kicking up dust in his wake.

The postmaster, who had witnessed the entire confrontation, trailed after him, shaking his graying head at Michael with an exasperated shrug as if to say "I cannot fathom why you didn't defend yourself."

Michael's passive response to the unprovoked attack unsettled the small cluster of reporters watching this exchange. They struggled to understand how such a capable-looking young man in his prime could accept being struck without demanding swift retribution. Uncomfortable with the tense situation they had stumbled into, they offered Michael brief, awkward nods of... what? Sympathy? Admiration for his restraint? It was impossible to discern their intentions. Then they withdrew, with the eldest among them, Jolivet, turning to make a low comment to Harry Blount as they departed, no doubt dissecting what they had just witnessed.

"How could someone so masterful at hunting Ural bears show such weakness? Can a person be brave one moment and craven the next? It defies understanding," Jolivet muttered, his brow furrowed in consternation as he grappled to reconcile the young man's composed demeanor with the tales of his wilderness exploits.

after, the sound of turning wheels and cracking whips showed the berlin carriage, now pulled by the tarantass's sturdy horses, was speeding away from the station and back toward the heart of the city, leaving the unsettling scene behind. The rhythmic clatter of hooves on cobblestone faded into the cacophony of St. Petersburg's bustling streets.

Nadia and Michael were now alone in the room, she maintaining her composure while he trembled, a visceral reaction he could not seem to control no matter how he willed his body to stillness. The Czar's messenger sat, his arms folded across his chest in a defensive posture, as still as carved marble save for the faint quivering of his hands. His face, once pale, had taken on a new hue that spoke not of embarrassment but of something else: fear, perhaps, or a dawning realization of truths he had never contemplated.

Nadia knew only the weightiest of reasons could have compelled him to endure such degradation from that man. Forces he could comprehend laid low on his once unyielding pride, beating the arrogance from him. She approached him now, just as he had come to her at the Nijni-Novgorod police station those many months ago when their paths had first intersected.

"Let me take your hand, brother," she whispered, her voice hushed yet resonant with an undercurrent of quiet strength. Extending her fingers, she offered a lifeline to anchor him against the turbulence that threatened to sweep him away.

Then, with the tender touch of a mother soothing a frightened child, she reached up and brushed away the tear that had formed in his eye, a solitary droplet of sorrow trailing down his ashen cheek. In that simple gesture, she conveyed a world of empathy and compassion, a balm against the anguish that contorted his features.

© 01/01/2025

Chapter Thirteen

DUTY BEFORE EVERYTHING

Nadia understood, with a woman's intuition, that Michael Strogoff was driven by hidden purposes. She sensed he served something greater than himself, and that in this moment, he had set aside his own feelings, even his justified anger at being wronged in the service of his duty.

Nadia felt a profound respect and admiration for the man before her. Though she did not know the details of his mission, it was clear that Michael was willing to sacrifice his own desires and personal grievances for the sake of a higher calling. His unwavering dedication was both humbling and inspiring. She saw no need to question Michael about any of this. The simple gesture of offering her hand to him had already expressed everything that words could have conveyed between them. An unspoken understanding passed between their souls in that moment, a silent promise to stand together against the trials that lay ahead, no matter the cost.

Michael remained silent all the evening. Because the postmaster couldn't supply fresh horses until the next morning, they had to spend the entire night at the house. Nadia could profit by it to take some rest, and a room was therefore prepared for her.

The young girl would no doubt have preferred not to leave her companion, but she felt he would rather be alone, and she made ready to go to her room.

Just before heading to bed, she felt compelled to approach Michael and bid him goodnight. Nadia moved towards him, her steps soft upon the wooden floor. "Brother," she murmured, the word tinged with a melancholic affection. He responded only with a dismissive wave of his hand, his gaze remaining fixed on some indistinct point in the distance. With a heavy sigh that seemed to carry the weight of their shared burdens, she departed from the room, leaving him to his solitary vigil.

Sleep eluded Michael Strogoff that night. Rest would have been impossible, even for the briefest moment. The spot where the lives of his mother and father had ended loomed large in his mind's eye, an indelible stain upon his memory. The path forward remained shrouded in uncertainty, fraught with perils yet unknown. Still, he steadied his resolve, allowing the embers of determination to burn ever brighter within his breast. For the sake of Mother Russia, he would not falter.

"For the homeland and the Almighty," he whispered, concluding his nightly devotion. The words hung in the still night air, a solemn vow imbued with profound resolve.

A burning curiosity consumed him about his mysterious assailant, their identity, origin, and destination remained unknown. Yet, he remembered their face that he knew he would recognize them, even years later, should they ever meet again? He seared the details of their features and the intensity of their gaze into his memory, an unsettling reminder of the dangers ahead.

Michael Strogoff summoned the stationmaster, his eyes heavy from the sleepless night. An old-school Siberian emerged, regarding the young traveler with concealed disdain as he awaited the inevitable questions. The man's weathered face betrayed a lifetime of hardship and toil in this unforgiving land. His eyes narrowed suspecting this outsider.

"Are you from around here?" Michael inquired, his voice tinged with weariness from the long journey.

"Indeed," came the curt reply, the stationmaster's gruff demeanor betraying little warmth or hospitality.

"Are you familiar with the person who stole my horses?" Michael pressed, undeterred by the man's brusque manner.

"Not at all," the Siberian stated, his eyes revealing nothing.

"Was that your first time seeing him?"

"It was."

"What's your impression of him?" Michael persisted, determined to glean whatever insights he could.

"Someone who commands respect and obedience," the stationmaster said, his gaze hardening as he studied the young traveler. Michael's intense stare bore into the Siberian, but the man remained unflinching, impervious to the scrutiny.

"How dare you pass judgment on me?" Michael burst out, his frustration mounting at the man's enigmatic responses.

"I do dare," the Siberian replied, squaring his shoulders as if bracing for a confrontation. "Some actions demand a response, even from a simple merchant." His words carried the weight of hard-earned wisdom, a lifetime of experience in this unforgiving land.

"A physical response?" Michael challenged, his brow furrowing.

"Yes, young fellow. I'm both old and strong enough to say that to your face." The station master's voice was filled with a strong and quiet confidence born of years spent enduring the harsh Siberian elements. Clearly, nothing would cow or intimidate this man, despite Michael's status and intentions.

Michael went up to the postmaster and laid his two powerful hands on his shoulders.

Then in a calm tone, “Be off, my friend,” said he: “be off! I could kill you.”

The postmaster understood. “I like him better for that,” he muttered and retired without another word.

On the morning of July 24th, at eight o’clock, they harnessed three strong and sturdy horses to the waiting tarantass, ready for the journey ahead. Michael Strogoff and Nadia took their places, and Ichim, with its disagreeable remembrances, was soon left far behind.

At different points during the event, Michael made his way to the postmaster and firmly grasped the man’s shoulders with his powerful hands.

Speaking with eerie calmness, he said: "Leave now, my friend. Leave before I end your life."

The postmaster grasped Michael's meaning. "I respect him more for that," he murmured as he withdrew silently.

When morning came at eight o'clock on July 24th, they hitched three sturdy horses to the tarantass. Michael Strogoff and Nadia settled into their seats, leaving behind Ichim and its unpleasant memories.

During their travels, they made their way between relay posts until reaching Abatskaia at four in the afternoon, another fifty miles along their route. Here, they encountered the Ichim, a major tributary flowing into the Irtych River, which proved more challenging to cross than their earlier passage over the Tobol. The waters of the Ichim rushed swiftly at this crossing point, churning and foaming as they cascaded over rocks and debris. Winter journeys across Siberian rivers were straightforward, as the waterways froze several feet thick, allowing travelers to pass almost without noticing they were crossing a river. The frozen riverbeds lay hidden beneath an unbroken blanket of snow stretching across the steppe, a pristine white expanse broken only by the tracks of sleds and the occasional stunted tree. Summer crossings, however, often presented significant obstacles, with raging currents and slippery embankments posing risks to both man and beast. They needed careful guidance to get the tarantass across the rushing Ichim river without mishap.

Frustrating Michael, the Ichim crossing consumed two full hours, wasting precious time. His anxiety and sense of urgency increased because of the boatmen's troubling reports about the Tartar invasion. Scouts serving Feofar-Khan, the fearsome leader of the nomadic horde, had been spotted along both shores of the lower Ichim in the southern regions of Tobolsk province, placing the city of Omsk in imminent danger. Disquieting word spread of a recent battle between Siberian and Tartar forces near the great Kirghese horde's border, a clash that ended for the outnumbered Russians. Their troops' subsequent withdrawal had triggered a mass exodus of local peasants fleeing the province to escape the invaders' path.

The boatmen described in grim detail the Tartars' savage acts, looting villages, the theft of livestock, burning homes and crops, and the wanton slaughter of any who dared resist. Such brutality and disregard for human life typified the nomads' approach to warfare, as they sought to crush all opposition through sheer force and the ruthless application of terror. With the Tartars drawing ever closer, Michael could only pray they would reach Omsk before the dreaded horde descended upon the city like a ravenous wolf among the flock.

In their panic, the entire population scattered at Feofar-Khan's approach. Michael Strogoff's primary concern wasn't for his own safety, but that the mass exodus from cities would leave him with no way to continue his journey. His urgent need to reach Omsk consumed his thoughts. If he could arrive there enough, he might manage to outpace the Tartar scouts who were advancing through the Irtych valley, and find a clear route to Irkutsk.

As the tarantass traversed the river, it marked the terminus of what military strategists called the "Ichim chain", a series of wooden watchtowers and small fortifications stretching four hundred miles along Siberia's southern border. These outposts, once manned by Cossack units, had served as a defensive line against Kirghese and Tartar incursions. The Muscovite authorities, blinded by hubris and believing that they had subjugated these nomadic peoples, withdrew the garrisons, leaving the fortifications unmanned, a grave miscalculation that left them defenseless when most needed. Invading forces had already reduced several of these strongholds to smoldering ruins, and the boatmen directed Michael's attention to ominous smoke clouds rising on the southern horizon, grim harbingers signaling the inexorable advance of the Tartar horde.

The ferry deposited their tarantass on the Ichim's right bank, and they continued their rapid trek across the vast, undulating steppe. Though Michael Strogoff maintained a stoic demeanor, speaking little, he remained ever-vigilant and devoted to ensuring Nadia's comfort, doing what he could to ease her burden during their relentless journey across the unforgiving terrain. The young woman, for her part, never uttered a word of protest or complaint, wishing only that their sturdy horses could move with even greater swiftness. She sensed that her enigmatic companion's urgency to reach the city of Irkutsk exceeded even her own burning desire to be reunited with her father, and oh, what a daunting, endless distance still stretched before them!

The thought struck her that Michael's mother could be in grave danger if the Tartars took Omsk where she lived. This would explain why her son was so desperate to reach the city, putting his very life at risk with each passing day. Nadia's heart went out to the noble courier, imagining the anguish he must feel at being unable to protect his own flesh and blood.

Finally, unable to contain her curiosity any longer, Nadia mentioned his elderly mother, Marfa, complaining about her vulnerability during these troubled times of violence and upheaval. "Since the invasion began," she inquired, her eyes full of empathy, "have you heard anything from your mother? I can only imagine how worried you must be for her safety."

"No news, Nadia. The last message I received from my mother was positive. Marfa is a resilient woman from Siberia. Despite her years, she maintains her inner strength and fortitude. She understands what it means to endure hardship." A wistful look crossed Michael's weathered features as he spoke of his elderly parent, the worry for her safety etched into the creases around his eyes.

"I will meet her, brother," Nadia responded, placing a comforting hand on his arm. "If you call me sister, then I am Marfa's daughter, too." She offered him a warm smile, hoping to ease his concerns.

When Michael remained silent, his brow furrowed in contemplation, she ventured: "Is it possible your mother escaped from Omsk before the invasion? Perhaps she found refuge elsewhere?"

"I believe so, Nadia," Michael answered, his voice tinged with cautious optimism. "With any luck, she's made it to Tobolsk by now. Marfa despises the Tartars and their brutality, she would never allow herself to be captured without a fierce fight. And she knows these steppes like the back of her weathered hand. Marfa wouldn't think twice about taking her trusty walking stick and following the winding path of the Irtych River to safety. She's traveled every inch of this province over the decades, there isn't a single hidden trail or secluded grove she doesn't know intimately. She and my father explored this entire region countless times in their youth, and I often joined them as a young boy on their adventurous journeys across the vast Siberian wilderness. Yes, Nadia, I'm confident my resilient mother has managed to escape the horrors of Omsk."

Nadia nodded, relieved by his reassurance. "When will you see her again?" she asked.

Michael's expression hardened with determination. "When I return from the battlefield and drive these Tartar invaders from our lands once and for all. Only then can I embrace her again."

"But if she's still trapped in Omsk, you could spare an hour to visit her before we march?" Nadia ventured, her eyes full of concern.

"I won't visit her," Michael stated, his jaw clenched with resolve.

"You're refusing to see her?" Nadia asked, her brow furrowed in disbelief.

"Yes, Nadia," Michael responded, his breathing heavy as he struggled to continue answering her persistent inquiries. An internal battle raged within him, torn between his love for his mother and the duty that now consumed his every waking thought.

"You're saying no? But brother, what likely reason could you have for not seeing your mother if she's still in Omsk?" Nadia pressed, her eyes pleading for an explanation that could justify such a heartless decision.

"What reason?" Michael burst out, his voice so altered by anguish that Nadia flinched. "The same reason that forced me to endure that scoundrel's presence with such cowardice..." His words trailed off, unable to complete the thought as the memories of that fateful night flooded his mind, the night that had changed the course of his life and set him on this perilous path of vengeance.

"Try to be at peace," Nadia whispered to her brother, her gentle words a balm to his tormented soul. "There's only one thing I understand, or perhaps I don't understand it so much as sense it. I believe your actions are now guided by an obligation even holier than the bond between mother and child, if such a thing is possible." Her eyes shone with a profound empathy, an unspoken acknowledgment of the immense weight he carried.

Nadia fell quiet after that, respecting the sacred nature of Michael's burden. From then on, she avoided any discussion that might touch upon his unique circumstances, recognizing the toll it took on him to even contemplate the events that had set him on this perilous path. She understood he carried a private anguish, one that demanded her utmost respect and compassion. And so she honored his silence, offering the solace of her steadfast presence as he navigated the treacherous waters of his quest for justice and retribution.

On the morning of July 25th, as the first pale rays of dawn crept across the horizon, the clock struck three, heralding the tarantass's arrival in Tioukalmsk after a grueling eighty-mile journey from the banks of the Ichim. Although the travelers arranged for fresh horses, their progress stalled when the driver, concerned, hesitated to leave. With a grave tone, he warned of the ever-present threat posed by marauding Tartar bands, who prowled the vast steppe like hungry wolves, eager to seize any unsuspecting travelers, horses, or vehicles that dared to cross their path. The ominous caution cast a pall over the group, yet they steeled their resolve, determined to press on despite the looming perils that awaited them in the wilderness beyond Tioukalmsk's walls.

The only way Michael could overcome the driver's resistance was by offering a substantial payment, as he wanted to avoid showing his travel papers in this situation, like many others. Since the telegraph had sent the latest imperial decree to all Siberian regions, a Russian with special exemption from these orders would have attracted unwanted notice, something the Czar's messenger needed to avoid at all costs. The driver's reluctance either stemmed from trying to exploit Michael's urgency for more money, or from genuine concerns about the journey ahead into the vast, unforgiving steppe, where danger lurked behind every rise and fold of the land. Michael's urgency and the weight of his mission compelled him to agree to the iemschik's demands, though he did so with a furrowed brow and a silent prayer that no further obstacles would impede their progress.

The team made excellent progress in their tarantass, covering fifty miles to reach Koulatsinskoe by 3 PM. The sturdy vehicle, with its pliable suspension and broad wheels, proved well-suited for traversing the undulating terrain of the steppe. Within the next hour, they arrived at the Irtych River, leaving them just fourteen miles from Omsk, their next major waypoint on the long road eastward.

The mighty Irtych River stands as one of Asia's major northern waterways, carving a serpentine path through the continent's heart. Beginning in the majestic Altai Mountains, it traces a southeastern to northwestern route, traveling four thousand miles before joining with the mighty Obi River in a glacial runoff and snowmelt. Along its banks, nomadic tribes have made camp for centuries, following the ebb and flow of the seasons across the vast Siberian expanse.

The rivers in the Siberian basin were at their peak during this season, and the Irtych's waters had risen, swollen with the recent snowmelt from the Altai peaks. The calm flow had transformed into a fierce torrent, the current churning and eddying as it rushed over submerged rocks and sandbars, making any crossing treacherous. Even the strongest swimmer would find it impossible to traverse such roiling rapids, and using a ferryboat carried significant risks of being capsized or swept away.

Despite these dangers, Michael and Nadia remained resolute, refusing to let any obstacle deter them from their eastward journey. Michael suggested a cautious approach: he would first transport the tarantass and horses across the swollen river, concerned that their combined weight might compromise their safety if they attempted the crossing all together. Once he had secured the carriage on the opposite bank, he would return with the small rowboat to bring Nadia across, sparing her from the perils of fording the turbulent waters.

The young woman shook her head, unwilling to accept Michael's cautious proposal. A delay of one hour was too much in her estimation, she wouldn't let concern for her own safety cause such a significant holdup in their eastward journey. With a determined glint in her eyes, Nadia insisted they all cross the raging river together, tarantass and horses included.

Getting everything aboard the small ferryboat proved challenging, as the swollen riverbanks kept the vessel from coming close to shore. Still, with thirty minutes of determined effort from Michael, Nadia, and the crew, they managed to load the bulky tarantass carriage and all three of their sturdy horses onto the precarious craft. Once the intrepid travelers had climbed aboard as well, they pushed away from the muddy bank with poles and set off across the roiling rapids, the ferryboat rocking with each churning swell.

The boat glided through the water for several minutes, the sturdy craft riding the powerful current with ease. They encountered a favorable spot where a lengthy peninsula jutted from the shoreline, creating a gentle eddy that made the crossing straightforward and calm. The pair of boatmen, seasoned veterans of these treacherous rapids, maneuvered their vessel using extended poles, guiding it through the swirling eddies. But as they approached midstream, the water's depth increased, the riverbed sloping away beneath them. Eventually, they could touch bottom with their poles, leaving only about twelve inches of the stout wooden shafts exposed above the surface, which made navigation challenging as they lost their primary means of propulsion and steering. From their position in the boat's rear, Michael and Nadia observed the boatmen's frantic efforts, concerned about potential delays and the prospect of being swept off course by the relentless flow.

"Watch out!" warned one boatman to the other, his voice cutting through the rush of the river.

He had shouted because their vessel was changing course, the current seizing it in a powerful grip. Having drifted into the main flow, the boat was being pulled downstream, the swirling eddies tugging and twisting at the sturdy hull. The boatmen worked their poles, muscles straining as they braced the stout wooden shafts against notches cut beneath the boat's edge. Through sheer force of effort, they managed to resist the relentless force of the river while steering diagonally toward the right shoreline.

Though they expected to make landfall about three to four miles downstream from their intended destination, this mattered little, as long as passengers and animals could disembark onto dry land. The pair of sturdy, weathered oarsmen, further motivated by the promise of twice their usual payment from the wealthy travelers, felt confident they could navigate this challenging stretch of the mighty Irtych River through skill and perseverance.

They didn't expect an unavoidable accident that was beyond their control. Even their dedication and expertise couldn't have differed in this situation. A freak occurrence, an act of nature no mortal could foresee or prevent, was about to unfold before their very eyes.

The current caught their vessel in the middle of the stream, equidistant from both banks, drifting downstream at about two miles per hour, when Michael stood up and stared upstream, squinting against the glare of the sun on the water. He spotted multiple boats approaching their position from upstream, propelled by both oars and the river's relentless current. As the crafts drew nearer, Michael's expression turned to one of grave concern, for the vessels were military, bearing the colors and crests of an elite imperial regiment.

Michael tensed up, letting out an involuntary cry as the blood drained from his face.

"What's wrong?" the girl asked, her voice tight with sudden dread.

But before Michael could answer, one boatman shouted in terror, pointing an accusatory finger upstream,

"Tartars! The Tartars are coming for us!"

Sure enough, a small fleet of sleek boats filled with armed and armored enemy soldiers was closing the distance, propelled by the combined efforts of oarsmen and the river's relentless current. Within minutes, they would catch up to the laden ferry that had no chance of outrunning their lighter craft.

The panic-stricken boatmen cried out, letting their long poles drop into the water with resigned futility. But Michael refused to surrender.

"Stay strong, friends!" he called out in a firm voice that brooked no argument. "I'll give you fifty roubles each if we make it to the far bank before those Tartar dogs catch us!"

The boatmen redoubled their efforts at these words, digging their long poles into the riverbed with renewed vigor, but it became clear they couldn't outrun the approaching Tartars' lighter craft.

There was little chance the Tartars would let them pass unmolested across the river. Indeed, they had every reason to fear what these notorious bandits and raiders might do if they caught the ferry's occupants.

"Stay calm, Nadia," Michael said in a low voice, his eyes narrowing as he assessed the dire situation. "But be prepared for anything."

"I'm ready," Nadia answered, her hand tightening around the hilt of the dagger concealed beneath her cloak.

"Even to jump into the water if I give the word?" Michael pressed.

"Just say when," she replied without hesitation.

"Trust in me, Nadia." Michael reached out and gave her hand a reassuring squeeze.

"I trust you completely!" she affirmed, staring at him with unwavering faith.

The Tartar vessels had closed to within a hundred feet by now. They carried a contingent of Bokharian troops who were scouting the area around the frontier city of Omsk, no doubt on the lookout for any suspicious river traffic.

The vessel was still a short distance from land, the shoreline close yet far. The crew redoubled their efforts, muscles straining as they dug the oars deep into the murky waters, with Michael lending his considerable strength to the cause, grabbing an oar and pushing with extraordinary power. Landing with the carriage and what few horses remained might give them a sliver of a chance to escape the clutches of the approaching Tartars, who were advancing on foot across the riverbank.

But their desperate attempts to outrun their pursuers proved futile, the distance too great to overcome. "Saryn na kitchou!" came the guttural battle cry from the lead boat, the harsh Tartar words slicing through the air like a blade. Rebels and defiant groups use “Saryn na kitchou!” as a cry to catch and subdue all in their path. And here they were, referring to the Tartars coming after them. Michael knew this command well. It demanded immediate and unconditional surrender, with victims expected to prostrate themselves before their captors. The staccato eruption of gunfire shattered the oppressive silence when neither he nor his stalwart crew surrendered; bullets wounded two of the remaining horses.

The ferryboat jolted as the boats crashed into it; the impact reverberating through the wooden hull. Splinters flew in every direction as the vessels ground together, the cacophony of splintering timber and shouts filling the air.

"Quick, Nadia!" Michael called out, preparing to leap into the churning waters in a desperate bid for freedom. His muscles tensed as he steadied himself on the rocking deck.

Just as Nadia moved to follow his lead, a Tartar lance lanced out, burying itself in Michael's side with a sickening crunch. A guttural cry tore from his lips as he pitched forward, sent plunging into the turbulent river. He raised his hand above the churning waters, fingers clawing at the empty air, before vanishing beneath the relentless current that dragged him away into the depths.

Nadia's scream of anguish cut through the chaos, but before she could dive in after him, rough, calloused hands seized her by the arms and dragged her, thrashing wildly, into one of the Tartar boats. The ferrymen lay dead, their vessel abandoned to drift aimlessly downstream, while the ruthless invaders continued their grim journey down the Irtych River, their prize clutched tightly in their grasp.

© 01/01/2025
QuantumDigitalPublishing.io
Book 1 - Chapter XIV

Chapter Fourteen

MOTHER AND SON

Tomsk, another city in the region, surpasses Omsk in size and population, though Omsk serves as the administrative capital of Western Siberia. In Omsk, living in a stately mansion near the center of the administrative district, the Governor-General, who oversees this first section of Asiatic Russia, maintains their residence. Two distinct areas make up the city: one, planned with whitewashed buildings housing government officials and administrators, and Siberian merchants; The merchant quarter, with its wooden houses and traditional architecture, presents a stark contrast to the more European-styled administrative district, though both areas share the same harsh climate that characterizes this remote outpost of Russian civilization.

Numbering between twelve thousand (12,000), and thirteen thousand (13,000), residents, the city's population is modest, befitting its role as a regional administrative center. Although the city possesses defensive walls, they are earthworks only, offering inadequate protection, a common but dangerous compromise in frontier settlements lacking stone and skilled masons. Understanding this vulnerability, the Tartars launched an aggressive assault on the city, managing to capture it after besieging it for just a few days, their mounted forces overwhelming the makeshift fortifications.

The defending forces at Omsk numbered only 2,000 soldiers, who fought with great courage despite being outnumbered. However, the attacking forces pushed them back from the commercial district, as they fought street by street through the wooden buildings, and they had to withdraw to seek shelter in the upper section of the city, where the more substantial government buildings offered better defensive positions.

In this location, the Governor-General had established a defensive position alongside his military personnel. They transformed Omsk's upper district into a makeshift fortress, creating what resembled an improvised "kreml" where they managed to maintain their defense, though with little expectation of receiving the reinforcements they were promised. The narrow streets were barricaded with overturned wagons and furniture from nearby buildings, while sharpshooters took positions in the upper windows of the sturdier structures. The Tartar forces, advancing along the Irtych, grew stronger daily with new troops arriving from the steppes, their campfires dotting the riverbank like countless burning eyes in the gathering darkness. But an even greater threat came from their commander, a man who had betrayed his homeland. This leader was Colonel Ivan Ogareff, whose notorious reputation matched his exceptional boldness in the face of any challenge. His intimate knowledge of Russian military strategy and the city's layout made him an especially dangerous adversary, one whose very name caused whispers of concern among the defending troops.

Ivan Ogareff was a formidable military commander who combined sophisticated military training with the ruthless tactics of Tartar warlords. His maternal Mongolian heritage influenced his preference for cunning warfare, using misdirection and carefully laid traps. He excelled in espionage and infiltration, employing various disguises and deceptions. His moral flexibility allowed him to use whatever means necessary to achieve his goals, including falsehoods when helpful. Known for his merciless nature and experience as an executioner, he served as the perfect lieutenant to Feofar-Khan in their brutal campaign. The soldiers spoke of his ability to appear out of nowhere, striking at the most vulnerable points with devastating precision. His strategic genius lay not just in conventional warfare, but in psychological manipulation, spreading rumors and discord that could tear apart even the most unified resistance. Those who had witnessed his handiwork firsthand told tales of elaborate schemes that would unfold like deadly puzzles, leaving his opponents reeling long before the final blow was struck.

Ivan Ogareff had already seized control of Omsk by the time Michael Strogoff reached the Irtych riverbank. Ogareff was intensifying his assault on the town's upper district, knowing he needed to move on to Tomsk, where the Tartar forces had gathered their main army. His troops swept through the streets, crushing any remaining pockets of resistance with ruthless efficiency.

Several days earlier, Feofar-Khan had captured Tomsk, establishing it as the launching point from which the invaders, now controlling Central Siberia, would advance toward Irkutsk. The city's strategic position and well-stocked armories made it an ideal base of operations, while its network of roads leading eastward would facilitate the rapid movement of troops and supplies. The Tartar banners now flew from every major building, a stark reminder of how quickly the region had fallen to the invading forces.

Ivan Ogareff's true target was Irkutsk, the crown jewel of eastern Siberia. His treacherous scheme involved approaching the Grand Duke using an alias, earning his trust through calculated displays of loyalty, and betraying both the city and the Duke to the Tartars. Such a strategic victory would guarantee the invaders' control over all of Asiatic Siberia, from the Ural Mountains to the Pacific coast, cutting Russia's empire in half. The Czar had discovered this plot through his network of spies and informants and, in response, had dispatched a courier carrying crucial intelligence to thwart it. This explained the courier's strict orders to travel through enemy territory in complete secrecy, concealing his true identity at all costs, for even the slightest hint of his mission would put both his life and the fate of Irkutsk in grave danger.

He had executed his mission until now, but would he be able to see it through to the end? The weight of Russia's fate pressed upon his shoulders with each passing moment.

Though wounded, Michael Strogoff had survived. He swam while keeping himself hidden from view, fighting against the current's relentless pull and ignoring the searing pain from his injuries. Eventually reaching the riverbank on the right side, he dragged himself through the muddy shallows. There, he collapsed among the dense shrubs, his strength depleted, his sodden clothes clinging to his exhausted frame as he struggled to catch his breath in the gathering darkness.

Consciousness returned to reveal he was lying in a peasant's cabin. A kind Russian farmer had found him and nursed him back to health. He had no sense of how many days he'd spent under this generous Siberian's care. As his eyes fluttered open, he saw the man's friendly bearded face hovering above, filled with concern. 'Rest your voice, little father,' the peasant said. 'You don't have the strength yet. Let me explain where you are and what has happened.'

The cabin was modest but warm, with rough-hewn wooden walls and a small iron stove in the corner that filled the single room with the comforting scent of burning pine. Dried herbs hung from the rafters, and through the single window, Michael could make out the silhouettes of birch trees swaying in the wind. A weathered icon of Saint Nicholas hung above the bed where he lay, watching over his recovery with painted eyes that seemed to hold both wisdom and mercy.

The peasant described to Michael Strogoff everything he had seen during the violent encounter, how the Tartar vessels had stormed the ferry, ransacked the coach, and slaughtered the crew. The old man's voice trembled as he recounted the savage efficiency of the attack, the screams that had echoed across the water, and the way the morning mist had turned crimson with blood.

Michael Strogoff had stopped listening, his thoughts turning inward as an icy dread settled in his stomach. Discreetly reaching beneath his clothes, his fingers found the emperor's letter still tucked against his chest, the parchment crackling against his skin. He exhaled with quiet relief, though the weight of his mission seemed heavier than ever considering what he'd just heard.

But there was something else weighing on his mind, something that made his heart clench with worry. "I was traveling with a young woman," he said, his voice hoarse with concern.

"They haven't killed her," said the peasant, seeing the worry etched in his guest's haggard face. "They took her in their boat and continued downstream along the Irtych. She's just one more prisoner being taken to Tomsk with the others, they've been gathering up civilians all along the river these past few days!"

Michael Strogoff couldn't speak, his throat constricting with a mixture of relief and fresh anxiety. He pressed his hand against his chest to steady his racing heart, feeling the precious letter crinkle beneath his palm. Yet despite all these hardships, despite separating from his traveling companion, his sense of duty remained unwavering, like steel tempered in fire. "Where am I?" he asked, forcing himself to focus on his immediate situation.

"On the right bank of the Irtych, about five miles from Omsk," the peasant answered, gesturing toward the north where the city's spires would be visible on a clearer day. "The main road runs parallel to the river, but I wouldn't recommend traveling on it just now."

“How could I have ended up in such a weakened state?”

"You took a lance to the head, but it's healing now," the peasant explained, dabbing at Michael's forehead with a damp cloth. "Rest for a few days, sir, and you'll be fit to travel. You fell into the river, but thankfully the Tartars didn't search you. Your money's still safe in your pocket. The current swept you right to my doorstep."

Michael Strogoff clasped the peasant's rough, weathered hand. Then, with a sudden determination that made him wince from the effort, he asked, "Tell me, friend, how long have I been here in your home?"

"Three days."

"Three days wasted!" Michael's voice cracked with dismay.

"You've been unconscious the whole time. The fever only broke last night."

"Do you have a horse you could sell me?" He struggled to sit up straighter on the straw pallet.

"You want to leave?" The peasant's eyes widened with concern.

"Right now."

"I'm sorry, sir, but I have no horses or carriages. The Tartars took everything when they came through! They didn't leave so much as a mule in the entire village. They stripped us clean, like locusts through a wheat field!"

"I'll walk to Omsk and find a horse there," he declared, already pushing himself to his feet despite his obvious weakness.

"Rest a few more hours first. You'll be stronger for the journey," urged the peasant, reaching out as if to steady him. "The road is treacherous, even for those in good health."

"Not even one hour!" Michael's voice held an edge of steel that brooked no argument.

"Very well then," the mujik conceded, seeing it was pointless to argue with his guest's determination. "I'll guide you myself as far as the main road. Besides," he added, lowering his voice to above a whisper, "the Russians still have a powerful presence in Omsk, you might slip through unnoticed if you're careful."

"My friend," Michael Strogoff replied, gripping the peasant's weathered hand with surprising strength, "may Heaven bless you for your kindness to me!"

"Only fools expect earthly rewards," the mujik responded, already reaching for his worn walking stick and threadbare coat.

Staggering from the hut's doorway, Michael Strogoff nearly collapsed, saved only by the mujik's quick support. His vision swam and darkened at the edges as waves of dizziness washed over him. The crisp outdoor air helped restore his senses, and he touched the head wound, thankful his fur cap had absorbed much of the impact. Blood had matted his dark hair, but the gash wasn't deep. Being the determined man he was, such a minor injury wouldn't stop him. He'd endured far worse in his years of service. His mind focused on one thing alone: reaching far-off Irkutsk. He knew he must pass through Omsk without delay, regardless of the dangers that awaited him there.

"May God watch over my mother and Nadia!" he whispered, his breath forming small clouds in the frosty morning air. "I must put them from my thoughts now! Their safety depends on my success."

Michael Strogoff and his peasant companion made their way into the bustling trading district in the lower section of Omsk. The defensive earthen walls surrounding the area had many gaps and openings created when the raiders accompanying Feofar-Khan's forces had broken through. Inside the city itself, Tartar troops filled the streets and public squares, moving about like colonies of busy insects. However, one could observe they were under strict military control, quite foreign to their usual ways. Rather than wandering, they moved into armed groups to protect against any unexpected attacks. Their boots crunched against broken glass and debris as they patrolled, weapons held at the ready. The morning sun glinted off their polished sabers and the metal tips of their spears, creating an intimidating display of force. Local merchants who would have had their stalls open at this hour instead peered from behind shuttered windows, the usual clamor of commerce replaced by the rhythmic marching of soldiers and occasional barked commands in their harsh foreign tongue.

They converted the sprawling central plaza into a makeshift military encampment, where two thousand (2,000), Tartar soldiers now rested under heavy guard. Their mounts remained saddled while tethered, prepared for immediate departure at a moment's notice. Steam rose from the horses' flanks in the cool morning air as they stamped, their riders sprawled nearby on bedrolls or huddled around small cooking fires. Omsk served as a brief stopover for these Tartar horsemen, who had their sights set on the prosperous eastern Siberian plains, where wealthier cities promised richer spoils from raiding.

The elevated quarter above, which continued to resist Ivan Ogareff's forces despite their fierce attacks, overshadowed the commercial district. The Russian flag still waved atop its fortified walls, a testament to the defenders' successful repulsion of multiple assaults. Scorch marks and impact craters scarred the ancient stonework, while makeshift barricades of overturned carts and furniture blocked the narrow streets leading up to the stronghold. The defenders had proven remarkably resourceful, using everything from boiling oil to improvised explosives to keep the invaders at bay.

With sincere devotion, Michael Strogoff and his companion paid their respects, a gesture filled with justifiable honor, their heads bowed in quiet reverence before the symbols of their homeland's resilience.

Having intimate knowledge of Omsk's layout, Michael Strogoff chose less crowded pathways through the town, weaving through shadowy alleyways and forgotten courtyards that most visitors never discovered. This wasn't because of concerns about recognition. Only his elderly mother, still living there, would have known his true identity beneath his weathered traveler's disguise. Yet he had made a solemn vow to avoid her, and he intended to keep it, no matter how his heart ached at the thought of passing so near without a word. He hoped she had already sought refuge in some remote corner of the steppe, far from the chaos and destruction that threatened to engulf the city.

The mujik knew a postmaster who, if well paid, would not refuse at his request either to let or to sell a carriage or horses. There remained the difficulty of leaving the town, but the breaches in the fortifications would, of course, facilitate his departure.

The peasant was leading his guest to the posting-house when Michael Strogoff halted and ducked behind a protruding wall in a narrow street, his movements swift and silent as a shadow. The weathered stone felt cool against his back as he pressed himself against it.

"What's wrong?" the startled peasant asked, his weathered face creasing with concern.

"Quiet!" Michael whispered, pressing his finger to his lips, his eyes alert and watchful. Just then, a military unit emerged from the main square into the street they had been walking along, their horses' hooves clattering against the cobblestones.

Leading the group of twenty mounted soldiers was an officer in plain uniform, his bearing rigid and purposeful. Though he scanned both sides of the street with keen eyes, sweeping his gaze across doorways and alleyways, he failed to spot Michael Strogoff, who had hidden himself just in time behind the ancient stonework. The soldiers' weapons gleamed in the light as they passed by, unaware of the courier's presence.

The troops galloped down the cramped alleyway, showing no regard for the townspeople. Those unfortunate enough to be caught in their path leaped aside, pressing themselves against weathered walls or diving into doorways. A few terrified screams rang out, silenced by jabbing spears, and the street emptied in moments, leaving only scattered market goods trampled in the dust.

After the riders had vanished around the distant corner, their thundering hoofbeats still echoing off the buildings, Michael Strogoff asked, his face drained of all color and his fingers clenched at his sides, "Who was that, commander?"

"Ivan Ogareff," the Siberian answered in a deep voice filled with loathing, spitting the name as if it were poison on his tongue.

"Ha!" burst out Michael Strogoff, unable to contain his rage. The officer before him was none other than the traveler who had attacked him at Ichim's posting station. Though the encounter had been brief, Strogoff realized this was also the aged Zingari whose suspicious conversation he had overheard in the bustling marketplace of Nijni-Novgorod. Strogoff's mind raced as he connected the dots, realizing this man must be a dangerous adversary who had been tracking him for some time.

Ivan Ogareff was indeed the man Michael Strogoff had suspected. By disguising himself as a Zingari and blending in with Sangarre's traveling group, Ogareff had escaped from Nijni-Novgorod after meeting with his accomplices. He had the complete loyalty of Sangarre and her Zingari companions, who served as his paid informants and carried out his schemes without question. Ogareff was the mysterious voice who had spoken those puzzling words that Michael Strogoff heard at the fairground that night, plotting against the Czar under cover of darkness. He had traveled aboard the Caucasus with the Bohemian group, maintaining his elderly disguise among the dancers and fortune-tellers, and then taken an alternate path from Kasan to Ichim, crossing the treacherous passes of the Urals getting to Omsk, where he now wielded considerable power with the local authorities.

Having spent only three days in Omsk, Ivan Ogareff lagged behind schedule. If not for their unfortunate encounter at Ichim and the three-day delay along the treacherous waters of the Irtych River, where flooding had made crossing impossible, Michael Strogoff would have outpaced him on the journey to Irkutsk.

One could only imagine how much suffering a different fate might have prevented! A different fate could have spared the now ruined towns and villages and the families torn apart by conflict from such devastation. Now, more than ever, Michael Strogoff needed to stay hidden from Ivan Ogareff's calculating sight. Yet when the inevitable confrontation would come, he stood ready to face the traitor, even if by then Ogareff controlled all of Siberia from the Ural Mountains to the Pacific shores.

The peasant and Michael made their way to the posting station, keeping to the shadows of buildings and avoiding the suspicious glances of patrolling soldiers. Once night fell, they could slip through one gap in Omsk's defenses, where the wooden palisades had begun to rot and crumble. Getting another carriage to replace their tarantass was out of the question, none were available for purchase or hire in the war-ravaged city. But Michael Strogoff had no need for a carriage anymore, being alone now, his heart heavy with thoughts of Nadia's fate. A horse would serve his purpose, and, one was available, a sturdy, spirited animal with a dark bay coat and alert eyes that Michael, being an expert rider trained in the imperial courier service, could handle even in the most challenging conditions.

At four in the afternoon, Michael Strogoff found himself waiting at the posting station, studying maps and planning his route while the autumn sun crawled westward. To pass the fortifications, he needed darkness, and wishing to remain unseen from Ogareff's spies who might watch, he stayed inside and took some refreshment, a simple meal of black bread and dried meat that did little to lift his spirits but would fuel his journey ahead.

The crowded public room buzzed with discussions about incoming Muscovite forces. Word had spread that troops would march not to Omsk but to Tomsk, their mission being to wrest the town from Feofar-Khan's Tartar control. The air was thick with tobacco smoke and the sharp scent of kvass, while merchants and travelers huddled in corners, their voices a mix of worry and speculation about the brewing conflict.

Though Michael Strogoff listened, he remained silent amid the chatter, his weathered hands wrapped around a cup of cooling tea as he absorbed every detail of the conversations swirling around him. Then a voice pierced the air, a cry that shook him to his core, two words that thundered in his ears: "My son!"

There stood his mother, old Marfa, trembling yet smiling at him, her lined face illuminated by the dim lamplight that filtered through the station's grimy windows. She tucked her gray hair beneath a worn headscarf, and her work-hardened hands clutched at her shawl. As she reached out her arms, Michael Strogoff rose from his seat, ready to embrace her, his heart pounding with both joy and dread at this unexpected reunion.

The threat of responsibility and the grave risk to both his mother and himself in this chance encounter made him freeze. His self-control was so complete that his face remained completely still. The public room held twenty people, and among them could be informants. After all, wasn't it common knowledge in town that Marfa Strogoff's son served as one of the Czar's messengers?

Michael Strogoff remained motionless.

"Michael!" his mother called out.

"Who might you be, madam?" Michael Strogoff said, his steady voice faltering.

"Who am I? Can it be that you don't recognize your own mother?"

"You must have me confused with someone else," Michael Strogoff responded with icy detachment. "A chance likeness has misled you."

The elderly Marfa approached him with halting steps and stared into his eyes, her weathered face inches from his own. "Are you not the son of Peter and Marfa Strogoff?" she asked, her voice quavering with emotion.

Michael Strogoff would have sacrificed everything to embrace his mother at that moment, to feel her familiar warmth against his chest just once more. But he knew that if he gave in, all would be lost, his mission, his oath, and both their lives. The weight of his duty pressed down upon him like a physical force. With supreme self-control, he shut his eyes, unable to bear the sight of his beloved mother's face contorted with pain, each line of anguish cutting him to his core. He pulled his hands away from her searching, trembling fingers, though every fiber of his being screamed to grasp them tightly. "I'm afraid I don't understand what you're talking about, good woman," he said, taking a step backward, his boots scraping against the wooden floor.

"Michael!" his elderly mother called out once more, her voice cracking with desperation and years of longing.

"I'm not Michael. You are mistaken! I am Nicholas Korpanoff, a store owner from Irkutsk," he declared, each word feeling like broken glass in his throat, the lie tasting bitter on his tongue.

Without warning, he rushed from the public room, shouldering past startled onlookers, as his mother's words echoed one last time: "My son! My son!" The anguished cry followed him down the corridor like a ghost that would forever haunt his memories.

Michael Strogoff summoned all his willpower to depart, his hands trembling and heart pounding against his ribs like a caged bird desperate for freedom. He missed seeing his elderly mother collapse onto a bench in near-unconsciousness; her weathered frame crumpling like autumn leaves. Though the postmaster rushed to help her, his concerned hands steadying her shoulders, she managed to gather her strength and sit up, her breath coming in ragged gasps. A sudden realization struck her with the force of a physical blow. Her own son had denied knowing her! She couldn't accept this possibility, couldn't reconcile the loving boy she'd raised with the stranger who'd stood before her. And there was no chance she had mistaken someone else for him, she was certain it was Michael she had just seen, would know those eyes anywhere, even if they now held a coldness that pierced her soul. If he had pretended not to recognize her, there must have been a compelling reason, something that forced him to act this way, some grave circumstance that demanded such cruel deception. Then, maternal instinct taking over, a single haunting thought consumed her, gnawing at her conscience like a hungry wolf: "Could I have brought about his downfall?"

"I've lost my senses," she declared to those questioning her, wringing her hands in apparent distress. "My vision must be playing tricks! This youth cannot be my son. The voice is all wrong, the mannerisms too foreign. Let's put this behind us, or I'll start seeing him in every face I encounter, haunting me like a ghost."

Barely ten minutes later, an officer of Tartar descent entered the station, his boots clicking against the wooden floor. "Are you Marfa Strogoff?" he inquired, his dark eyes scanning the waiting area with practiced efficiency.

"Yes, that's me," the elderly woman answered, her voice steady and her expression so composed that anyone who had observed her earlier encounter with her son would have thought her a different person. The trembling hands and desperate eyes were gone, replaced by an almost regal bearing.

"Follow me," the officer commanded, turning on his heel without waiting for acknowledgment.

Marfa Strogoff strode behind the Tartar soldier. Within moments, someone brought her to the main square where Ivan Ogareff awaited, already informed of everything.

Sensing there was more to the situation than met the eye, Ogareff fixed his gaze on the elderly Siberian woman and demanded, "What is your name?"

"Marfa Strogoff," she answered, her voice betraying no emotion.

"Do you have a son?" Ogareff's eyes narrowed as he studied her face.

"Yes." The word came out clear and crisp.

"Is he a courier for the Czar?"

"Yes." Her shoulders remained squared, her posture unwavering.

"Where is he?"

"In Moscow."

"Have you heard from him?"

"No."

"How long has it been?"

"Two months."

"Then who was that young man you called your son earlier at the posting-house?" Ogareff's tone grew sharper, more accusatory.

"A young Siberian I mistook for him," replied Marfa Strogoff, her weathered face a mask of weary resignation. "He's the tenth man I've thought was my son since the town filled with strangers. I keep seeing him everywhere." She allowed a tremor to enter her voice, just enough to suggest the desperation of a mother's longing.

"Then this young man wasn't Michael Strogoff?"

"No, it wasn't Michael Strogoff." Her words rang hollow in the tense air between them.

"Listen here, old woman. You know I can torture you until you tell me the truth?" Ogareff leaned forward, his shadow falling across her face like a dark promise.

"I've already told you the truth, and no amount of torture will make me say otherwise." She met his gaze without flinching, her hands clasped in her lap.

"This Siberian wasn't Michael Strogoff?" Ivan Ogareff demanded again, his fingers drumming an impatient rhythm against the wooden table between them.

"No, it wasn't him," Marfa Strogoff repeated, her voice carrying the weight of maternal conviction. "Do you think I would deny my own son, given to me by God himself, for any reason in this world? A mother's heart cannot lie about such things."

With a malevolent glare, Ivan Ogareff studied the elderly woman who dared to defy him, his eyes narrowing as he traced the lines of determination etched into her weathered face. He was certain she had identified her son as the young Siberian traveler, despite her unwavering denials. That this son had first denied his mother, only to have her reject him, suggested something of grave importance, a orchestrated deception that only heightened his suspicions. This convinced Ogareff that the man calling himself Nicholas Korpanoff was none other than Michael Strogoff, the Czar's messenger, traveling under an alias and carrying out a crucial mission, one that Ogareff wanted to uncover. Without hesitation, he pushed back from the table and commanded his men to pursue him, his voice cutting through the tense atmosphere like a blade.

"Take this woman to Tomsk," he ordered, gesturing toward Marfa. "Keep her under close watch."

As his soldiers hauled her away, her head still held high in silent defiance, he muttered under his breath, his words dripping with venom, "When the time comes, I'll make that old witch talk. Every mother has her breaking point."

Chapter Fifteen

THE MARSHES OF THE BARABA

Fortune had smiled upon Michael Strogoff's swift departure from the posting-house. Ivan Ogareff's commands had reached every entry point around the city without delay, with detailed descriptions of Michael distributed to all commanding officers to prevent his escape from Omsk. However, Michael had already slipped through a gap in the fortifications; his mount was now thundering across the open steppe, and the odds of successful flight were tipping in his favor. The hoofbeats of his Siberian horse echoed across the darkening plains as he urged the beast onward, its muscled flanks heaving with each powerful stride. Behind him, the lights of Omsk grew dimmer with each passing minute, and the vast expanse of wilderness ahead promised both refuge and peril. Timing his escape had been crucial. Had he delayed even a quarter hour more, the tightening noose of Ogareff's surveillance would have sealed his fate.

Michael Strogoff departed from Omsk at 8:00 PM on July 29th, the fading summer sun casting long shadows across the city's weathered walls. Located midway between Moscow and Irkutsk, Omsk marked the halfway point of his journey, though the most treacherous stretches still lay ahead. He needed to reach Irkutsk in ten days or fewer to stay ahead of the advancing Tartar forces, a timeline that grew more daunting with each passing hour. Unfortunately, the unexpected encounter with his mother had compromised his secret identity, a moment of filial devotion that might yet prove costly. Now Ivan Ogareff knew well that a Czar's messenger had passed through Omsk in route to Irkutsk, and his spies would already spread word along the road ahead. Given the crucial nature of the dispatches Michael Strogoff carried, he realized they would spare no effort to apprehend him, dispatching their fastest riders and most ruthless agents to intercept him before he could reach his destination.

Little did he realize that Marfa Strogoff had been captured by Ivan Ogareff, and she might pay the ultimate price for her uncontrollable display of emotion upon encountering her son. Perhaps it was a blessing that he remained unaware. Would he have had the strength to endure such devastating news? The weight of such knowledge might have shattered even his iron resolve, forcing him to choose between duty to empire and devotion to family.

Michael Strogoff spurred his horse onward, his own restless urgency flowing into the animal. He asked just one thing of his steed: to carry him to the next station, where he could get a faster mount. The beast's labored breathing and foam-flecked flanks told him it was nearing exhaustion, but there could be no rest until they reached the safety of the imperial post station. Every league gained was another minor victory in this desperate race against time and treachery.

The night had stretched on, and by twelve o'clock, he had covered fifty miles before stopping at Koulikovo station. He confirmed his fears when he found the station without horses and carriages. Tartar patrols had swept through the steppe highway, leaving nothing behind. Everything of value had been taken or commandeered from both the villages and posting-houses. Michael Strogoff could manage to secure minimal provisions for himself and his horse, settling for a handful of dried meat and a small measure of grain that had been overlooked in a dusty corner.

Conserving his horse's strength had become crucial, as finding a replacement seemed unlikely in these circumstances. The animal's coat was dark with sweat, its flanks heaving with each labored breath. Yet, convinced that riders had been sent to chase him, he felt compelled to maintain his lead. Every moment of delay could mean the difference between success and capture. After allowing his horse a brief hour's rest, during which he kept vigilant watch from the shadows of the deserted station, he set off again across the vast steppe, guided only by starlight and his unwavering sense of direction.

Wonderful weather had favored the journey thus far. The climate remained bearable, and moonlight illuminated the brief night's characteristic of this season, making travel across the steppe possible. Michael Strogoff moved with unwavering certainty, his mind sharp despite his troubled thoughts. He advanced toward his destination as if drawn by a visible beacon on the horizon. His only pauses came at occasional bends in the path, where he would stop to let his horse catch its breath. Sometimes he would dismount to give his steed brief relief, or press his ear to the earth, listening for any horses galloping across the steppe. Finding nothing suspicious, he would continue his journey, his muscles tense with vigilance. The cool night air carried the faint scent of wild grasses and distant wood-smoke, while overhead, the stars wheeled in their eternal dance, serving as both compass and timekeeper. Each mile covered brought both satisfaction and anxiety, satisfaction at the progress made, yet anxiety over the vast distance still remaining. His water supply was holding steady, though he rationed it carefully, knowing well the scarcity of reliable sources in these parts.

At nine o'clock on the morning of July 30th, Michael Strogoff moved through Touroumoff station and ventured into the Baraba's marshy terrain, his boots sinking with each determined step into the soft, waterlogged earth.

The next three hundred miles would present formidable natural challenges, treacherous bogs that could swallow a horse whole, swarms of mosquitoes that tormented both man and beast, and deceptive patches of solid ground that could give way without warning. Though well aware of these obstacles, he felt absolute certainty in his ability to overcome them, drawing upon years of experience traversing similar landscapes and an iron resolve that had served him well throughout his career.

The immense Baraba wetlands serve as a natural basin for rainfall that cannot drain into either the Obi or Irtych rivers. With its clay-based ground preventing water absorption, this extensive lowland becomes treacherous to traverse during warmer months. Yet this challenging terrain provides the only route to Irkutsk, where travelers must navigate a path through many ponds, pools, lakes, and swamps. Adding to the journey's perils, these stagnant waters release harmful vapors under the sun's heat, making the passage both exhausting and hazardous. The few local inhabitants who manage to survive here have learned to read the subtle signs of safer passage, certain reeds, slight variations in ground coloration, and the behavior of water birds that avoid the most dangerous areas. But for those unfamiliar with these wetlands, each step forward requires careful consideration and a measure of faith, as what appears solid from above may prove to be nothing more than a thin crust concealing treacherous depths below.

Going through the dense prairie grass, Michael Strogoff urged his horse forward. Unlike the grazed grasslands of the steppe where vast Siberian herds roamed, this terrain featured towering vegetation reaching heights of five to six feet. The damp soil and summer heat had transformed the landscape into a jungle of massive swamp plants. Thick canes and rushes created an intricate maze of vegetation, forming an impassable barrier below. Throughout this wild tangle bloomed countless flowers, their vivid colors painting the landscape in brilliant hues, purple loosestrife stretching toward the sky, delicate white water lilies floating in the scattered pools, and golden marsh marigolds dotting the wettest areas. The air hung heavy with the sweet perfume of these blooms, mingling with the earthy scent of decomposing vegetation. His mount's hooves struck harder ground with a hollow sound, suggesting hidden cavities beneath the surface, while other areas were very soft under their weight, forcing both rider and horse to proceed with heightened caution.

Among the dense thicket of reeds, Michael Strogoff's form had vanished from view of the marshy roadside. The startled water birds that erupted skyward in raucous clouds could only trace his presence, disturbed from their resting places along the path as he thundered past on horseback, concealed by the towering stalks that rose high above him. The rhythmic splashing of his mount's hooves through shallow pools and the swaying motion of the reeds in his wake offered fleeting hints of his passage, like ripples spreading across the surface of a pond. Herons and egrets took flight with indignant squawks, their long legs trailing behind them as they sought refuge deeper in the marsh, while smaller birds darted between the stems in confused, chirping masses.

The path was easy to follow, winding through the marshy landscape. Sometimes it cut straight through thick clusters of wetland vegetation, while at other times it meandered along the edges of enormous pools of water, some so vast they could be called lakes, stretching several miles in each direction. Where the route encountered stagnant waters, travelers would find not bridges but precarious platforms, stabilized with thick clay layers. These makeshift crossings, some extending over three hundred feet, would sway and wobble so much that passengers in horse-drawn tarantasses often felt as queasy as if they were at sea. The wooden planks creaked beneath hooves and wheels, their surfaces slick with algae and morning dew, while beneath them dark water seeped through gaps in the weathered boards. Occasionally, pieces of these ancient crossings would break free and drift away into the marshland, requiring constant maintenance by local villagers who would venture out in flat-bottomed boats to make repairs with whatever timber they could salvage from the surrounding wilderness.

Across stable ground and treacherous terrain alike, Michael Strogoff rode at full speed, his horse jumping over gaps between the decomposing planks. Yet despite their swift pace, neither rider nor mount could evade the relentless biting of the winged pests that swarmed throughout these swamplands. Clouds of mosquitoes and biting flies descended upon them in waves, finding every exposed patch of skin and even penetrating through the weave of his traveling clothes. The horse tossed its head in constant irritation, nostrils flaring against the assault, while sweat-dampened flanks trembled with the effort of maintaining their breakneck pace across such hazardous footing.

In summer, anyone crossing the Baraba must wear special protective gear: horsehair masks with fine wire mesh that extend over their shoulders and wrap around their torsos. Yet even with these safeguards, most travelers emerge with red welts covering their faces, necks, and hands, the skin raised and angry from countless bites. The air seems alive with invisible needles, and one might think that even a suit of armor cannot shield against these flying pests, so determined are they to find any gap or seam through which to attack. Humans and swarms of insects, crane flies, gnats, mosquitoes, horse-flies, and countless microscopic creatures, battle for control of this harsh landscape; the insects' numbers seem to multiply with each passing hour of daylight. Though invisible to the naked eye, these insects make their presence known through merciless stinging, to which even the toughest Siberian hunters have never grown accustomed, forcing even the most hardened veterans indoors during the worst of the swarm seasons.

The stallion beneath Michael Strogoff bolted forward in agony, tormented by the swarm of poisonous insects as if countless spurs had been driven into his flesh. Maddened with pain, the beast thundered across mile after mile at the velocity of a railway engine, whipping his sides with his tail and trying to outrun his tormentors through sheer speed. The horse's muscles rippled and strained beneath its sweat-darkened coat as it charged headlong through the punishing terrain.

Only a rider of Strogoff's exceptional skill could have maintained his seat through the horse's wild plunges, sudden halts, and desperate leaps to escape the relentless attackers. Having pushed beyond physical anguish into a state of singular focus, Strogoff was driven by one guiding purpose: to reach his destination regardless of the cost. Through this frenzied gallop, his mind registered only the landscape rushing past in a blur behind him. His knuckles had gone white from gripping the reins, every muscle in his body tensed to expect the horse's next frantic movement while clouds of the vicious insects continued their pursuit, undeterred by the breakneck pace.

Deep in the Baraba region, where summer brought pestilence and disease, an unexpected sight emerged: human settlements scattered among towering reeds. The inhabitants of these Siberian hamlets, from young children to weathered elders, survived wrapped in animal hides, their faces bearing the marks of harsh living. They tended to their meager flocks of sheep, protecting them from the relentless swarms of insects by creating a barrier of smoke. Day and night, they maintained fires of green wood, the acrid smoke drifting across the endless marshland, a necessary shield for their livestock's survival. These resilient people had adapted to nature's cruelest challenges, their homes built on elevated ground to avoid the worst of the flooding, their daily routines dictated by the endless battle against the biting hordes. The damp air carried not just the smell of smoke but also the pungent aroma of herbs they burned to further repel the insects, creating a haze that hung like a protective veil over their isolated community.

Noticing his exhausted horse was about to collapse, Michael Strogoff stopped at a desolate village, its handful of wooden houses standing silent in the gathering dusk. Setting aside his own weariness, he tended to the beast, massaging its wounds with warm grease as Siberians do, paying special attention to the chafed areas beneath the saddle and around the bit. After feeding the horse well and ensuring its comfort in a makeshift stable fashioned from an abandoned shed, he attended to his own needs, restoring his energy with a quick meal of bread, meat, and a glass of kwass from his dwindling supplies. Within an hour or two, as the first stars began appearing in the darkening sky, he was back on the endless road to Irkutsk, pressing forward with urgency, knowing each moment of rest had cost him precious time he could ill afford to lose.

Traveling through the rugged Siberian terrain, Michael Strogoff reached Elamsk at four in the afternoon on July 30th, his clothes coated in dust from the long journey. His faithful horse needed a full night's rest, as the exhausted creature could not journey any further without risking collapse, its flanks heaving with each labored breath. Like all the villages they had passed through before, Elamsk, with its weathered wooden buildings and suspicious inhabitants, offered no alternative means of transportation, there were neither carriages to hire nor fresh horses available in the stables, which stood empty save for a few scrawny farm animals. The sight of yet another depleted outpost added to Strogoff's growing concern about the delays plaguing his mission.

Michael Strogoff accepted he would need to spend the night in Elamsk, allowing his horse twelve hours to recover its strength. He thought back to his orders from Moscow, to journey across Siberia in secret, reaching Irkutsk without letting speed compromise his mission's success. This meant careful management of his remaining method of transportation was necessary for him. The weight of his responsibility pressed upon him as he secured lodging at the village's only inn, a cramped establishment that smelled of stale beer and wood smoke.

The following day, Michael Strogoff departed Elamsk just as the first Tartar scouts were spotted ten mile behind on the Baraba road. He ventured back into the marshy terrain. Though the path was flat and easy to traverse, it wound, making the journey longer. The surrounding landscape of endless pools and marshes made it impossible to take any shortcuts or alternate routes. Tall reeds swayed in the morning breeze, and occasional water birds took flight at his approach, their wings cutting through the heavy mist that clung to the wetlands. The soft ground beneath his horse's hooves served as a constant reminder that one wrong step could mire them both in the treacherous bog.

Michael Strogoff continued his journey the following day, August 1st, covering another eighty miles before reaching the town of Spaskoe at noon. By two in the afternoon, he made it to Pokrowskoe; the buildings emerging like gray shadows through the hazy summer air. His mount, exhausted from the trek since leaving Elamsk, had reached its limit, its flanks heaving and coat dark with sweat.

At Pokrowskoe, Strogoff had no choice but to stop for the rest of the day and throughout the night to allow for essential rest. The horse's labored breathing and trembling legs clarified that pushing further would risk losing his only means of transportation. Setting off again the next morning across the flooded terrain, where patches of standing water reflected the pale sky above, he pressed on until he arrived in Kamsk at four in the afternoon on August 2nd, having covered fifty miles in that leg of his journey. The town's wooden buildings and modest church spire were a welcome sight after the desolate marshlands.

The village of Kamsk stood as a solitary oasis of life amidst a desolate region. Unlike its surroundings in the Baraba, Kamsk remained viable and wholesome, persisting at the heart of an otherwise uninhabitable expanse. Despite the widespread displacement triggered by Tartar forces, the townspeople had stayed put, believing their central location would afford them adequate warning should danger approach. The village's elevated position on a gentle rise allowed its inhabitants to survey the surrounding marshlands, providing an additional measure of security that had helped maintain their resolve.

Michael Strogoff found himself unable to gather any intelligence during his time there. Had the Governor known the true identity of this supposed Irkutsk merchant, he would have sought him out. Yet Kamsk's remote position had isolated it from the turmoil gripping Siberia, leaving it disconnected from the serious developments unfolding across the region. The villagers went about their daily routines with an almost surreal normalcy, tending to their gardens and livestock as if the political upheaval threatening the empire was nothing more than a distant rumor carried on the wind.

Staying out of sight, Michael Strogoff made every effort to minimize his presence. But mere discretion wasn't sufficient anymore, he yearned for complete invisibility. His experiences had taught him valuable lessons, making him cautious about his current situation and what lay ahead. As a result, he kept to himself, avoiding the village streets and remaining confined within the walls of his chosen inn. The small, dimly lit room became both his sanctuary and his prison, its wooden shutters drawn against prying eyes. He took his meals at odd hours when few others were about, speaking only when necessary and in the muted tones of a man accustomed to blending into shadows. Even his footsteps became measured and deliberate, each movement calculated to draw minimal attention from the inn's other occupants.

The rider had grown quite fond of his horse and had no desire to trade him for another mount. He trusted the animal's capabilities. It had been a fortunate purchase in Omsk, and the kind-hearted peasant who had helped him acquire it from the postmaster had done him an invaluable favor. The bond between Michael Strogoff and his horse had strengthened over time, and the sturdy beast seemed to adapt well to their arduous journey. The animal's steady gait and unflagging endurance had proven invaluable during their long days of travel, and its calm demeanor in the face of unexpected challenges had saved them both more than once. With adequate rest periods of several hours each day, Michael was positive his loyal companion could carry him beyond the territories under siege.

Throughout the evening and night of August 2nd, Michael Strogoff stayed within the confines of his lodging, a quiet inn at the town's edge, far from prying eyes and unwanted attention. He spent the hours reviewing his plans and tending to his horse in the attached stable, ensuring both their needs for the coming day's journey were well met. The distant sounds of the town's nightlife penetrated the thick walls of his refuge, allowing him the solitude he required.

Drained, he retired to his quarters after ensuring his steed was well-tended, yet his rest was restless. His experiences since leaving Moscow had revealed the gravity of his task. The rebellion had reached alarming proportions, made even more dangerous by Ogareff's betrayal. As his gaze fell upon the imperial seal adorning the letter, a document that held the key to easing such widespread suffering and securing peace in this war-torn region, Michael Strogoff felt an overwhelming urge to race across the steppe. He yearned to cover the distance to Irkutsk as swiftly as a bird in flight, to soar like an eagle above all hindrances, to move with the speed of a tempest at a hundred miles per hour, all to stand before the Grand Duke and declare: "Your highness, a message from his Majesty the Czar!"

Sleep eluded him as his mind raced with thoughts of the treacherous path ahead. Each time he closed his eyes, visions of burning villages and rebel encampments flickered behind his eyelids. The weight of responsibility pressed upon his chest, making even the soft bed feel as unyielding as stone. Through the small window of his quarters, the faint glow of distant fires served as a stark reminder of the chaos spreading across the land. His fingers traced the edges of the sealed letter tucked within his coat, its presence both a comfort and a burden that would allow him no true rest this night.

The following morning at six, Michael Strogoff resumed his journey, his muscles still aching from the previous day's rigors. This leg of the trip passed with no problems, owing to his careful vigilance and constant awareness of his surroundings. The terrain, though difficult, offered few surprises, and he encountered only the occasional merchant wagon heading in the opposite direction. Upon reaching Oubinsk, he allowed his horse to rest through the night, tending to the animal's needs and ensuring it had fresh hay and clean water, as he planned to cover the hundred miles between Oubinsk and Ikoulskoe in a single stretch the next day. He set out at first light, the morning mist still clinging to the ground like a ghostly shroud; however, to his dismay, the conditions in the Baraba region had grown even more challenging than before, with muddy paths that threatened to swallow careless hooves and low-hanging branches that required constant vigilance to navigate.

The torrential rains from recent weeks had transformed the lowland between Oubinsk and Kamakore into a vast water basin, turning what should have been solid ground into treacherous wetlands that seemed to mock his urgent mission. The landscape was an endless succession of marshes, ponds and lakes stretching as far as the eye could see, with deceptive patches of firm ground that often gave way to ankle-deep mud. One massive body of water, Lake Tchang, bearing a Chinese name from traders who had long used these routes, required travelers to navigate around its swollen shores for over twenty miles , a painstaking journey at best that involved picking paths through waterlogged grassland and avoiding deeper pools hidden beneath the surface. Michael Strogoff found himself delayed by these challenging conditions, though the setbacks tested his patience, each detour and careful step feeling like precious minutes slipping away from his mission. His earlier decision to forgo taking a carriage in Kamsk had proven wise, as his horse could traverse areas that would have been impassable to wheeled vehicles, its sure-footed instincts helping to detect and avoid the most dangerous spots in the waterlogged terrain.

The night fell as Michael Strogoff reached Ikoulskoe at nine o'clock, where he decided to rest until morning. This secluded Baraba village remained untouched by news of the ongoing conflict. Its unique position between the split Tartar forces, with one branch heading toward Omsk and the other toward Tomsk, had so far shielded it from the invasion's devastation. The villagers went about their simple routines, tending to livestock and small gardens, oblivious to the turmoil that raged beyond their borders.

The challenging terrain would soon be behind him. For barring any setbacks, Michael Strogoff would leave the Baraba behind tomorrow and reach Kolyvan. From there, only eighty miles would separate him from Tomsk. His next moves would depend on the situation, and he would choose to bypass Tomsk, assuming the reports of Feofar-Khan's occupation were accurate. He spent the evening studying his maps by candlelight, plotting alternative routes that might allow him to circumvent the city while still maintaining his heading toward Irkutsk. The thought of being so close to his destination, yet facing such a formidable obstacle, weighed heavily on his mind as he prepared for what promised to be another demanding day of travel.

As Michael Strogoff traveled through the peaceful villages of Ikoulskoe and Karguinsk in the Baraba region, he couldn't help but worry about what awaited him on the Obi River's right bank. The threat from hostile forces there seemed likely to be far greater. If necessary, he was prepared to leave the established route to Irkutsk, even though venturing across the steppe would mean risking a journey without reliable supplies or clear paths to follow. Despite these dangers, he knew he had to press forward without wavering. The contrast between these tranquil settlements, with their simple wooden houses and gentle farmland, and the uncertainty that lay ahead weighed on his mind. He observed the villagers going about their daily routines, tending to their gardens and livestock, untouched by the brewing conflict. Yet the distant sound of birds taking sudden flight or an unexpected movement in the tree line would put him on alert, his senses heightened by the knowledge that each mile brought him closer to hostile territory.

As Michael Strogoff emerged from the final stretches of the Baraba around three-thirty in the afternoon, his horse's hooves began striking the familiar firm, arid ground of Siberia once again, the rhythmic clatter a welcome change from the treacherous marsh terrain he'd endured for days.

His journey had begun in Moscow on July 15th. Now, on August 5th, twenty days had elapsed since he set out, including the three-day delay while stranded along the Irtych River, where rising waters and debris had made crossing impossible despite his desperate attempts to find passage.

He still had a thousand miles ahead of him before reaching Irkutsk, a daunting distance that would take him through some of the empire's most unforgiving territories. The thought of the vast expanse yet to cover made his muscles ache, but there was no time to dwell on physical discomfort.

© 01/01/2025
QuantumDigitalPublishing.io

Chapter Sixteen

A FINAL EFFORT

Michael understood all too well why he dreaded encountering the Tartars in the vast plains beyond the Baraba. The trampled fields, marked by countless hoofprints, provided clear signs of the hordes' passage. One could say of these invaders what was often said of the Turks: "In the wake of their advance, not even grass survives." The earth itself seemed to have been scraped clean, with broken fence posts and scattered debris the only reminder that crops had once grown here.

Taking in the scene, Michael recognized the need for extreme vigilance while crossing this territory. In the distance, wisps of smoke rose against the horizon, marking where villages and homesteads continued to burn. The acrid scent carried on the wind told of destruction both fresh and days old. He wondered whether these fires were set by advance scouts, or if the Emir's primary force had already pushed deeper into the province. The location of Feofar-Khan himself remained a mystery. Had he already reached the Yeniseisk government? Michael couldn't plan a proper strategy without answers to these crucial questions. The landscape appeared abandoned that he questioned whether he could find even a single local Siberian to provide the information he needed. Even the birds had fled, leaving an eerie silence broken only by the whisper of wind through the charred ruins.

Michael traveled for about two miles, encountering no one. He searched for an occupied dwelling, but found every building abandoned and empty, their doors hanging open like hungry mouths, windows staring at the desolate road.

Then he spotted smoke rising from a humble cottage hidden by trees. The thin gray wisps curled against the sky like desperate fingers reaching for help. Drawing closer, he discovered an elderly man some distance from the burned structure, surrounded by crying children. His weathered face was streaked with soot and anguish as he tried to comfort the little ones. A young woman, his daughter and the children's mother, knelt on the ground, staring at the devastation before her. Her clothes were singed and torn, her dark hair matted with ash. She cradled an infant of just a few months at her breast, though soon she would have no milk left to feed the baby. The child's weak cries joined the chorus of despair from its older siblings. Everything around them spoke of complete destruction and despair, scorched walls still radiating heat, the remains of a simple life scattered and smoking in the yard, precious family possessions reduced to cinders and ash.

Michael made his way over to the elderly man, stepping around the smoldering debris that littered the ground between them.

"May I ask you something?" Michael inquired, his voice gentle but urgent.

"Go ahead," the elder responded, his weathered face etched with grief.

"Did Tartar forces come through here?"

"Indeed, you can see my home burning," the old man gestured at the flames still consuming what remained of his dwelling.

"Was it their full army or just a smaller group?"

"The entire army, look around. They've destroyed every field in sight. Not a single stalk of wheat remains standing."

"And was the Emir leading them?"

"Yes, the Emir, that's why the Obi runs red with blood. His presence always brings the worst destruction."

"Has Feofar-Khan made it to Tomsk?"

"He has." The old man's voice was hollow.

"What about Kolyvan? Have his forces reached there?"

"Not yet. Kolyvan still stands unburned. But it won't be long, mark my words."

"I appreciate your help. Is there anything I can do for you?"

"No." The elder turned away, shoulders slumped in defeat.

"Then I'll take my leave."

"Farewell, stranger," the old man murmured, already lost once more in contemplation of his ruined life.

Michael pressed twenty-five roubles into the trembling hands of the destitute woman, who could only stare back in wordless gratitude, tears welling in her weathered eyes, before he urged his mount forward with sharp spurs. The horse snorted and pranced sideways before settling into motion.

His mind was crystal clear on one crucial point: Tomsk must be avoided at all costs. The path to Kolyvan remained viable, as the Tartar forces hadn't yet reached that far. Yes, that would be his course, to rest, regroup, and prepare for the grueling journey ahead. There was no alternative but to cross the Obi, strike out on the Irkutsk road, and give Tomsk a wide berth. The very thought of encountering Feofar-Khan's forces made his jaw clench with determination.

With this fresh route mapped in his mind, Michael knew every moment was precious. Without hesitation, he spurred his horse into a steady, ground-eating gallop, heading toward the Obi's left bank, still forty miles away. Questions plagued him: Would he find a ferry waiting? Or had the marauding Tartars destroyed every vessel, leaving him no choice but to brave the river's waters on horseback? The weight of his mission pressed upon him as the afternoon sun beat down on his shoulders.

This point quite exhausted the horse, its labored breathing and sweat-dampened flanks testament to their hard journey, and Michael planned to use it only for this portion of the journey before getting a fresh mount at Kolyvan. That town would serve as a new beginning, as his journey would take on a distinct character afterward. While traveling through ravaged territories remained treacherous, if he could bypass Tomsk and take the road to Irkutsk through the still-intact province of Yeniseisk, with its dense forests and scattered settlements, he could complete his journey within days.

The arrival of night brought welcome relief from the day's heat, the temperature dropping as stars peppered the vast sky above. By midnight, profound darkness had settled over the steppe, transforming familiar shapes into mysterious shadows. Only the rhythmic sound of hoofbeats broke the silence, accompanied by Michael's gentle words of encouragement to his horse, soft murmurs that seemed to float away into the endless night. The darkness demanded extreme caution to avoid straying from the road, which was flanked by various pools and streams feeding into the Obi, their surfaces catching glimmers of starlight. Michael maintained a careful pace, relying both on his keen eyesight that could pierce the darkness and his horse's proven instincts, developed through countless hours of navigating similar terrain.

Michael had just dismounted to get his bearings when an unusual rumbling sound drifted across the darkened steppe from the west. The noise carried the unmistakable rhythm of multiple horses' hooves drumming against the parched earth somewhere in the distance. Following an old hunter's technique, he dropped to one knee and pressed his ear to the ground, straining to interpret the vibrations.

"Must be a cavalry unit moving along the Omsk road," he thought, his jaw tightening with concern. "They're moving fast. The sound's getting louder with each passing moment. But are they Russian troops or Tartars?"

He listened again, his experienced ear analyzing every nuance of the approaching thunder. "Yes, they're moving at a quick trot, perhaps twenty or thirty horses at least. My horse won't be able to outrun them, not after the distance we've already covered today. If they're Russians, I'll ride to meet them. They could provide valuable intelligence. But if they're Tartars, I'll need to stay clear of their path. The question is, how? There's nowhere to hide in this open steppe, not a tree or rocky outcrop in sight."

Looking around through the darkness, he made out a shadowy mass about a hundred paces ahead on the road's left side. "A copse!" he thought. "Hiding there could be dangerous if they're searching for me, but I have no other option. At least it's better than being caught in the open."

Within moments, Michael had led his horse by the bridle to a small larch of wood that the road cut through. Beyond it lay a treeless expanse of bogs and pools, dotted with stunted bushes, gorse, and heather. The air grew damp and heavy with the scent of rotting vegetation. The terrain on both sides was impossible to traverse, a maze of treacherous mud and half-hidden sinkholes, meaning the patrol would have to pass through this wooded section. They were following the main road toward Irkutsk. He ventured about forty feet in before encountering a stream flowing beneath the undergrowth, its gentle gurgling audible above the rustle of leaves. The darkness was so complete here that Michael had no fear of being spotted unless they conducted a thorough search of the woods. Even the moon's light couldn't penetrate the dense canopy above. After securing his horse to a tree near the stream, taking care to choose a spot where the animal could drink if needed, he crept back to the road's edge to listen and determine what manner of travelers approached. His boots made no sound on the carpet of fallen needles.

Michael had just settled into his hiding spot behind several larch trees when he noticed a dim glow emerging, with brighter, flickering lights moving above it in the darkness. The orange flames cast eerie, dancing shadows against the tree trunks.

"They're carrying torches," he thought, retreating deeper into the dense undergrowth with the stealth of a hunter. His heart pounded as he moved, each step placed to avoid any telltale snap of twigs.

The riders slowed their horses as they neared the wooded area. They seemed to use their lights to examine every bend in the road, the torch flames wavering with each methodical sweep. Their weapons glinted in the firelight, suggesting they were well-armed.

This development worried Michael, who crept closer to the creek's edge, prepared to dive in should the need arise. The water's soft gurgle reminded him it would be cold if he had to use it as an escape route.

The group stopped when they reached the woodland's crest. All fifty or so riders climbed down from their horses, their boots hitting the ground with muted thuds. Around twelve of them held torches aloft, illuminating the path ahead, the combined light creating a bright pool that pushed back the forest's darkness. Their serious expressions and purposeful movements suggested they weren't mere travelers, but men on a mission.

Michael watched with relief as the soldiers made no move toward the copse, choosing instead to set up a temporary camp nearby for rest and sustenance. They removed their horses' saddles, letting the animals feed on the lush grass that blanketed the area. The men sprawled alongside the road, taking out provisions from their knapsacks for a much-needed meal. A few of them stretched their legs and rubbed their sore muscles, while others gathered in small clusters, speaking in hushed tones that didn't quite carry to where Michael hid. The aroma of dried meat and hard bread wafted through the air as they settled in, their weapons kept within arm's reach despite the casual atmosphere. Even at rest, there was an underlying tension in their movements, a readiness that spoke of men expecting trouble at any moment.

Michael identified the approaching horsemen as an Omsk contingent, Usbeck mounted troops with Mongol ancestry. Concealed in the high grass, Michael observed them, trying to discern their words. These formidable soldiers were tall, with hardened, intimidating countenances and weathered faces that spoke of countless days under the harsh steppe sun. Their headgear consisting of traditional "talpak" hats crafted from black sheep's wool, while their feet bore distinctive yellow riding boots featuring elevated heels and pointed tips that echoed medieval styles. The leather of their boots was well-oiled and creased from long hours in the stirrups. woven belts of red leather, each adorned with intricate patterns that marked their rank and tribal affiliations, secured their close-fitting military attire. Each warrior's battle gear included a protective shield burnished to a dull sheen, and the curved blade kept razor-sharp, plus a flintlock rifle attached to their mount with well-maintained leather straps. Colorful capes flowed from their wide shoulders, the fabric rippling in the breeze like battle standards, lending vivid touches to their warrior-like bearing. Their horses, sturdy steppe breeds with powerful haunches and thick necks, moved with the fluid grace that came from years of partnership between mount and rider.

The Usbeck steeds grazed near the forest's edge, sharing their masters' hardy bloodline. Though smaller in stature than their Turcomanian cousins, these mounts possessed extraordinary vigor and moved only at a gallop, knowing no other pace. The demanding terrain suited their compact frames and powerful legs, and their thick winter coats protected them from the bitter steppe winds.

The unit operated under a pendja-baschi, an officer commanding fifty warriors, who was assisted by a deh-baschi, a leader of ten. Both officers were distinguished by their helmets, partial suits of mail, and the small trumpets secured to their saddle-bows, marking their positions of authority. Their armor gleamed with careful maintenance, decorated with brass studs and elaborate engravings that spoke of their elevated status. The trumpets, crafted from polished brass and wrapped with dyed leather cords, could pierce through the din of battle with their sharp, commanding notes.

The commander had no choice but to grant his weary troops respite after their grueling march across the steppes. As he and his lieutenant made their way through the sparse woods, they passed a clay pipe between them filled with "beng," the potent cannabis plant used throughout the region to make hashish. The pungent smoke curled in the still air as they walked. Hidden behind a fallen log just yards away, Michael Strogoff could distinguish every word of their conversation in Tartar, a language he had learned during his years as a courier.

His ears perked up at their first words. They were discussing him, their voices carrying in the quiet forest.

"That courier can't be far ahead," the commander said, exhaling a cloud of sweet-smelling smoke. "And there's no way he could have taken any path except through the Baraba. The marshlands would force him along the primary route."

"Is he even gone from Omsk?" the deh-baschi questioned, scratching his beard. "He could still hide somewhere in the city, waiting for us to pass by."

"Let's hope so. That way, Colonel Ogareff's dispatches would never make it to where they're meant to go." He spat into the dirt with obvious disdain.

"I've heard he's local, from Siberia," the deh-baschi continued, lowering his voice as if sharing a secret. "If that's true, he'd know these lands well. He might have left the Irkutsk road, planning to get back on it later. These Siberians are crafty with their backwoods routes."

"But we'd still be ahead of him," the pendja-baschi countered, adjusting his weapons belt. "We rode out of Omsk an hour after he did, taking the quickest route and riding hard. Our horses are the finest in the regiment. Either he's still in Omsk, or we'll beat him to Tomsk and stop him there. Either way, he won't make it to Irkutsk. The Colonel's orders were quite clear about that."

"That tough-looking Siberian woman must be his mother," remarked the deh-baschi, scratching at his beard. "She had the same stubborn look in her eyes."

Michael's heart pounded at these words, his fingers tightening on his reins until his knuckles went white.

"Indeed," the pendja-baschi replied, a cruel smile playing across his weathered face. "She kept insisting the supposed merchant wasn't her son, but it was futile. Colonel Ogareff wasn't fooled; as he said, he'll know just how to make the old crone talk when the moment's right. He has ways of loosening even the most determined tongues."

Each word struck Michael like a physical blow, leaving him dizzy with dread. His identity as the Czar's courier had been discovered! Mounted soldiers would intercept him now, their nets closing in from every direction. And most devastating of all, his mother was now captive to the Tartars, with the ruthless Ogareff vowing to force information from her whenever he pleased! The thought of what torments that monster might inflict on her made his blood run cold.

Michael was aware of the loyal Siberian woman's willingness to die protecting him. Though he had thought his hatred for Ivan Ogareff couldn't grow stronger, a fresh surge of loathing filled his heart as the traitor who had betrayed their homeland now threatened to inflict pain on his mother. The very thought of Marfa suffering at Ogareff's hands made his jaw clench until his teeth ached.

As Michael listened to the two officers talking, he learned that a battle was about to take place near Kolyvan between Russian forces advancing from the north and the Tartar army. Reports showed that a small Russian contingent of two thousand soldiers had reached the lower Obi River and was moving toward Tomsk. If true, these troops would soon clash with Feofar-Khan's dominant forces and face certain defeat, leaving the invaders in complete control of the road to Irkutsk. The officers spoke with such confidence about their superior numbers that Michael's heart sank. The

Russian soldiers were marching straight into a massacre, unaware of the overwhelming force that awaited them.

Someone had placed a bounty on Michael's head, according to information he gleaned from the pendja-baschi's words. The orders expressly stated that Michael was to be captured, dead or alive, and anyone delivering him would receive a reward.

Time was of the essence. He needed to outpace the Usbeck cavalry on the road to Irkutsk and place the Obi River between them. This meant he had to make his escape before the camp disbanded, while the soldiers were still settling in for their brief rest.

Once Michael reached this conclusion, he set his mind to carrying it out with the same iron determination that had sustained him through his journey thus far.

Little time was available. The pendja-baschi planned only a brief hour's rest for his men, despite their horses being as exhausted as Michael's own mount, having had no fresh replacements since leaving Omsk. The animals' labored breathing and drooping heads testified to their fatigue.

With dawn approaching within the hour, Michael had precious little time. He would need to use the cover of darkness to slip from the small forest and speed along the road. Though the night would provide some concealment, attempting such an escape seemed impossible given the vigilant guards and the open terrain that lay ahead. Still, he had no choice but to try.

Michael refused to act rashly, taking time to carefully consider his options. Analyzing his surroundings, he concluded that escape through the rear of the wood was impossible. A wide and deep stream of treacherous muddy waters blocked that path. Below the water's surface lay an unstable, mucky bottom that would not support weight. Only one route remained available: the high-road. He would need to quietly skirt the wood's perimeter to reach it, then push his valiant horse to its absolute limits in a desperate gallop. The faithful creature would collapse upon reaching the Obi's banks, where Michael would then have to cross the mighty river either by boat or swimming. This was the daunting challenge before him.

The sight of such peril only strengthened his resolve and bravery. His jaw set as he mentally mapped the treacherous path ahead, calculating distances and timing with the precision of a military strategist. The cool night air seemed to sharpen his senses, and the weight of his responsibilities pressed upon him like a physical force.

With his life, his mission, his homeland, and his mother's wellbeing hanging in the balance, there was no room for doubt. Every fiber of his being focused on the task ahead, his muscles tensing in anticipation of the moment when he would need to act. The fate of his beloved Russia might well depend upon his success or failure in the next few crucial hours.

Time was of the essence. A faint stirring had begun among the soldiers, with several riders patrolling the road before the forest's edge. Though most troops still rested beneath the trees, their mounts were working their way deeper into the woods, their hooves crunching on fallen leaves and broken twigs.

The thought of commandeering one of their horses crossed Michael's mind, but he dismissed it, those steeds would be just as exhausted as his own, if not more so after their long march. Better to rely on his faithful companion, which had already proven invaluable throughout this perilous journey. His horse remained well-concealed behind dense brush, still undetected by the Usbecks, who hadn't ventured this far into the forest. The animal stood, its breath creating small clouds in the cool air, as if understanding the need for absolute silence in these tense moments.

Michael crept through the grass to reach his horse, which was lying down among fallen pine needles. He stroked its damp neck and whispered soothing words into its twitching ears, getting it standing and making no sound. The animal's muscles trembled beneath his touch, but it remained steady. By now, the torches had burned out, leaving them in total darkness beneath the towering larch trees. After securing the bit with practiced fingers, Michael checked the saddle straps and stirrups before leading his horse away from their hiding spot. The well-trained animal followed, placing each hoof with deliberate care, not making even the slightest sound against the soft forest floor.

Several Usbeck horses lifted their heads and began moving toward the forest's edge, their nostrils flaring as they caught unfamiliar scents on the night breeze. Michael gripped his revolver, its familiar weight offering some comfort as he prepared to shoot any Tartar who came near. His finger rested on the trigger, heart pounding in his chest. Fortunately, no alarm was raised, and he reached the corner where the woods met the road, the shadows of the forest canopy providing welcome cover from any watchful eyes.

Intending to remain unseen, Michael planned to wait until he was around two hundred feet past the corner before mounting. His heart was still racing from the close call with the sentries, and he knew this next part would require perfect timing. His plans were foiled when, just as he emerged from the wood, one of the Usbeck's horses caught his scent. The horse whinnied and started trotting down the road, its hooves clattering against the packed earth. Its owner chased after it and, spotting a dark figure moving in the low light, called out, "Look out!"

The warning cry sent all the men at the bivouac scrambling to their feet and rushing to get to their horses. Curses and shouts in their native tongue filled the air as they stumbled over their bedrolls in the darkness. Michael mounted his horse and galloped away, the animal's powerful muscles bunching beneath him as they shot forward into the night. Behind him, the detachment's two officers were barking orders in harsh voices, urging their men to give chase.

Michael detected a report and felt something pierce his tunic, the sharp sting of a bullet grazing his shoulder. He remained focused forward, saying nothing as he spurred his horse onward, pressing his body low against the animal's neck. With one powerful leap, they cleared the thick tangle of undergrowth and galloped at full speed toward the Obi, the horse's hooves thundering against the hard-packed earth.

His pursuers' fumbling with their mounts gave him a slight advantage as the Usbek horses remained unsaddled, buying him precious moments. But within two minutes, he could hear multiple sets of hoofbeats closing the gap behind him, the rhythmic drumming echoing through the pre-dawn stillness.

The first light of dawn was now spreading across the landscape in pale fingers of gray, making distant shapes more distinct against the retreating darkness. Michael glanced back and saw a lone rider gaining on him, the man's silhouette growing larger with each passing moment. It was the deh-baschi, who had outpaced his men thanks to his superior mount, a magnificent Arabian stallion whose long strides ate up the ground between them.

Without hesitation, Michael leveled his revolver with deadly precision, his arm steady despite the jarring motion of his galloping mount. His shot found its mark. The Usbeck officer clutched his chest and toppled from his saddle, crumpling to the earth in a lifeless heap, his fine Arabian rearing as its master fell.

The remaining horsemen thundered forward, their weapons glinting in the pre-dawn light. Paying no heed to their fallen commander, they urged each other on with fierce battle cries that pierced the morning air, their spurs biting into their mounts' flanks as they closed the gap between themselves and their quarry. The thunder of hooves seemed to shake the very ground.

For thirty desperate minutes, Michael managed to stay just beyond the Tartars' reach, weaving across the terrain to break their pursuit. But he could feel his horse's strength failing beneath him, foam flecking its heaving flanks as each labored stride brought them closer to disaster. His heart pounded with the terrible certainty that any moment could bring a fatal stumble on the treacherous ground.

Dawn was breaking, though the sun still lurked below the horizon, painting the clouds above in shades of violet and amber. In the growing light, a pale strip of land stretched out two miles ahead, marked by a scattered line of trees whose branches swayed in the morning breeze, their only hope of sanctuary from the relentless pursuit.

The Obi River stretched across the landscape, running from southwest to northeast, its surface distinguishable from the surrounding steppe as its bed melded with the flat terrain, the water's sluggish current marked only by occasional ripples catching the early light.

Michael faced repeated gunfire but managed to dodge the bullets, twisting in his saddle as the lead whistled past. When soldiers pressed too close, he returned fire with his revolver, dropping several Usbeck attackers who fell with angry shouts from their comrades, their bodies tumbling from their mounts into the trampled grass. But time was against him. His horse was reaching its limits, its breathing now ragged and uneven. Though he made it to the riverbank, the Usbeck force had closed to within fifty paces, their weapons raised and ready.

The Obi's waters lay empty before him, not a single vessel in sight that could carry him across, nothing but the endless expanse of dark water stretching into the distance like a great serpent across the plains.

"One last push, my brave friend!" Michael called to his horse as he spurred it into the river, whose width stretched half a mile across, the icy water soaking through his boots as they plunged into the current.

The rushing waters made forward progress impossible. Michael's mount struggled to find purchase on the riverbed, hooves slipping on smooth stones and treacherous mud. He had no choice but to attempt the treacherous swim across, though the current raged like a tempest, its icy fingers clawing at both horse and rider. Such a daring crossing spoke volumes of Michael's extraordinary bravery, born of desperation and an iron will to survive. Though the soldiers had reached the riverbank, they balked at entering the churning waters, their hesitation visible even from a distance.

Raising his rifle, the pendja-baschi aimed at Michael in the stream, his expert eye accounting for wind and current. The shot rang out, sharp and definitive, striking Michael's horse in its flank. The relentless current swept the wounded, screaming animal away, its dark blood staining the surrounding water.

Michael freed himself from the stirrups and struck out for the far shore, his arms cutting through the frigid water with determined strokes. Bullets rained around him like hail, sending up small geysers where they struck the river's surface, yet he managed to reach the opposite bank and vanish into the protective cover of the reeds, their tall stalks closing behind him like a curtain.

Chapter Seventeen

THE RIVALS Modern English PBHC

Exhausted but momentarily safe, MICHAEL faced a dire predicament. His loyal horse had perished in the river's depths, leaving him stranded and wondering how to press onward with his journey.

He stood alone, without food or supplies, in a land ravaged by invasion and crawling with the Emir's scouts. Despite being far from his destination, his resolve remained unshaken. "By Heaven, I will get there!" he declared defiantly. "God will protect our sacred Russia."

The Usbeck cavalry had given up their pursuit, unwilling to brave the river's crossing. Now on firm ground, Michael paused to contemplate his next move. Though Tomsk lay under Tartar control and had to be avoided, he needed to locate a town or posting station to acquire a horse. Once mounted, he planned to abandon the main road, only rejoining the Irkutsk route near Krasnoiarsk. From there, if swift enough, he hoped to find clear passage, intending to traverse the Lake Baikal provinces in a southeasterly direction.

Setting off eastward, Michael followed the Obi for two versts until he spotted a picturesque settlement perched on a modest hill. Several churches with distinctive Byzantine domes in green and gold punctuated the gray skyline. This was Kolyvan, a summer refuge for officials and workers from Kamsk and neighboring towns seeking escape from the Baraba's unhealthy climate. According to recent intelligence available to the Czar's courier, Kolyvan remained free of invaders. The Tartar forces had split into two columns, advancing left toward Omsk and right toward Tomsk, leaving the area between untouched.

Michael's strategy was straightforward: reach Kolyvan ahead of the Usbeck horsemen who would follow the opposite bank of the Obi to the ferry. There he would obtain fresh clothing and a horse before continuing toward Irkutsk across the southern steppe.

At three in the morning, Kolyvan lay silent and seemingly deserted. The local inhabitants had apparently fled northward to Yeniseisk province, knowing they could not resist the approaching invasion.

The sound of distant gunfire caught Michael's attention as he strode quickly toward Kolyvan. He halted, clearly identifying the deep boom of artillery mixed with the sharp crackling of muskets.

"Artillery and musket fire!" he exclaimed. "The Russian forces must be engaging the Tartar army. I must reach Kolyvan before they do!"

The battle sounds grew louder, and a haze began forming to Kolyvan's left—not smoke, but the distinctive white clouds created by artillery fire.

On the Obi's left bank, Usbeck cavalry had positioned themselves to watch the battle's outcome. Michael felt safe from them as he rushed toward the town.

The gunfire intensified and drew closer, transforming from a general roar into distinct shots. As the smoke thinned periodically, it became clear the fighting was moving southward. Kolyvan appeared to face an attack from the north, but Michael couldn't determine whether Russians or Tartars held the town.

When he was just half a verst from Kolyvan, flames erupted from the town's buildings, and a church steeple collapsed amid smoke and fire. The battle had reached Kolyvan's streets. Michael questioned whether to seek shelter there. Could he avoid capture? Would he manage another escape like in Omsk? After a moment's hesitation, he considered finding a smaller town and acquiring a horse at any cost. This seemed his best option, so he left the Obi and headed right of Kolyvan.

The battle intensified, with flames now consuming an entire quarter of the town's left side.

As Michael ran across the steppe seeking tree cover, he spotted Tartar cavalry approaching from the right. Unable to continue in that direction and with the horsemen advancing quickly, he faced limited options.

Then he noticed a solitary house among dense trees, which he might reach undetected. Exhausted and hungry, Michael had no choice but to seek shelter there and find sustenance, whether offered or taken.

He rushed toward the building, which stood about half a verst away. As he drew closer, he recognized it as a telegraph office, with two wires extending east and west, and a third leading toward Kolyvan.

Given the circumstances, he expected the station to be deserted. Even if it was, Michael could shelter there and wait for nightfall before venturing across the steppe dotted with Tartar scouts.

He burst through the door.

Inside the dispatch room sat a single clerk—a remarkably composed man who seemed utterly unaffected by the chaos outside. He waited patiently at his wicket, ready to serve any customers who might appear.

"What news?" Michael gasped, his voice ragged from exhaustion.

"None," replied the clerk with a smile.

"Are the Russians fighting the Tartars?"

"So they say."

"Who's winning?"

"I couldn't say."

Such extraordinary composure amid such turmoil seemed almost unbelievable.

"Is the telegraph line still intact?" Michael asked.

"It's cut between Kolyvan and Krasnoiarsk, but still functioning between Kolyvan and the Russian border."

"For government use?"

"For the government when they need it. For anyone else who can pay. Ten copecks per word, whenever you're ready, sir!"

Michael was about to explain that he needed no telegraph—only bread and water—when the door flew open again.

Fearing Tartar soldiers, Michael prepared to escape through the window, but only two men entered. Neither looked like Tartar warriors. One clutched a penciled dispatch, and hurrying past his companion, approached the unflappable clerk's window.

Michael was astounded to recognize these unexpected visitors: Harry Blount and Alcide Jolivet, the two reporters. Once traveling companions, they were now rivals competing for battlefield stories.

They had departed Ichim shortly after Michael but had reached Kolyvan first, following the same route—Michael's three-day delay at the Irtych had cost him precious time. After witnessing the clash between Russians and Tartars outside town, they had fled just as fighting erupted in the streets, racing to the telegraph office to dispatch their competing reports to Europe, each hoping to scoop the other.

Hidden in the shadows, Michael observed the scene unfold, able to witness everything without detection. This was his chance to gather crucial information about whether he could enter Kolyvan.

Blount had managed to reach the telegraph window first, leaving his competitor behind. Alcide Jolivet, unusually agitated, stood nearby tapping his foot impatiently.

"Ten copecks per word," announced the clerk.

Without hesitation, Blount placed a substantial stack of roubles on the counter, while Jolivet watched in disbelief.

"Very well," the clerk said, then began transmitting the message with remarkable composure: "Daily Telegraph, London.

"From Kolyvan, Government of Omsk, Siberia, 6th August.

"Engagement between Russian and Tartar troops."

The clerk's clear voice allowed Michael to hear every word of the English correspondent's report.

"Russians repulsed with great loss. Tartars entered Kolyvan today." The message concluded there.

"My turn now," Jolivet called out eagerly, ready to send his dispatch to his cousin.

But Blount had other plans. He intended to maintain his position at the window, ensuring he could report events as they unfolded. He refused to yield to his colleague.

"You've finished!" Jolivet protested.

"I have not," Blount replied calmly.

He proceeded to write additional lines, which the clerk read aloud in his steady voice: "John Gilpin was a citizen of credit and renown; a train-band captain eke was he of famous London town."

Blount was cleverly reciting childhood verses to maintain his position and prevent his rival from taking over. Though this tactic might cost his newspaper a fortune in roubles, it would secure them the breaking news. France would simply have to wait.

Jolivet was furious, though under normal circumstances he might have admired such tactical thinking. He tried unsuccessfully to convince the clerk to prioritize his dispatch.

"This gentleman has the right," the clerk stated pleasantly, indicating Blount with a smile. He continued transmitting Cowper's famous verses to the Daily Telegraph.

While the transmission continued, Blount stepped to the window, using his field glass to survey the situation around Kolyvan. He soon returned to add to his message: "Two churches are ablaze. The fire spreads rightward. 'John Gilpin's spouse said to her dear, Though wedded we have been these twice ten tedious years, yet we no holiday have seen.'"

Alcide Jolivet was seething with frustration at his rival, the Daily Telegraph's correspondent, whom he wished he could throttle.

He interrupted the clerk again, who remained unperturbed and simply stated, "He has every right to do so, sir - at ten kopeks per word."

Blount had just delivered this news to be telegraphed: "Russian refugees fleeing the town. 'Away went Gilpin—who but he? His fame soon spread around: He carries weight! he rides a race! 'Tis for a thousand pound!'" He then turned to give his competitor a teasing look.

This only increased Jolivet's irritation.

Meanwhile, Blount had returned to watch through the window, this time genuinely absorbed by the unfolding scene. Seizing this opportunity after Blount's message was sent, Jolivet quietly took his place at the counter. Following his rival's example, he placed a substantial pile of rubles down and submitted his dispatch, which the clerk read aloud: "To Madeleine Jolivet, 10, Faubourg Montmartre, Paris.

"From Kolyvan, Government of Omsk, Siberia, 6th August.

"Refugees fleeing town. Russians defeated. Tartar cavalry in fierce pursuit."

As Blount returned, he heard Jolivet finishing his telegram by singing mockingly:

"Il est un petit homme, Tout habille de gris, Dans Paris!"

Like his rival had done, Jolivet had incorporated a playful Beranger verse.

"Well, well!" remarked Blount.

"Indeed," Jolivet responded.

The situation in Kolyvan had become dire. The battle was drawing closer, with gunfire continuing without pause.

Suddenly, the telegraph office shook violently as a shell burst through the wall, filling the room with dust.

Alcide was just completing his message when this happened. In one fluid motion, he stopped writing, rushed to grab the shell with both hands, hurled it out the window, and returned to the counter.

The shell exploded outside five seconds later. With remarkable composure, Alcide wrote: "A six-inch shell has just breached the telegraph office wall. Expecting more of similar caliber."

Michael Strogoff was now certain the Russians had been forced out of Kolyvan. His only option left was to escape across the southern steppe.

At that moment, another burst of gunfire erupted near the telegraph office, with bullets shattering all the window glass. Harry Blount collapsed, struck in the shoulder.

"Even at this critical moment, Jolivet was preparing to add a final note to his dispatch: 'Harry Blount of the Daily Telegraph has fallen beside me, struck by—' when the unflappable clerk announced with perfect composure: 'Sir, there's been a break in the wire.' Then, stepping away from his station, he calmly picked up his hat, brushed it with his sleeve, and with his perpetual smile, vanished through a small door that Michael hadn't noticed before.

Tartar troops had encircled the building, leaving Michael and the journalists with no escape route.

Alcide Jolivet, still clutching his now-futile dispatch, rushed to Blount's motionless form on the ground. He courageously hoisted his colleague onto his shoulders, intending to make a break for it. But he had waited too long!

They were captured, and in that same moment, Michael, caught off guard as he attempted to escape through the window, was seized by the Tartars!

Epilogue

Michael Strogoff Books I & II

The Horizon of Duty

Irkutsk, Siberia, Twenty Years Later

The frost-laden winds of Siberia still whispered Michael Strogoff's name. To the villagers, he remained the "Courier of Iron," the man who had defied betrayal, blindness, and Tartar savagery to deliver the Czar's warning and save a nation. Yet in the quiet of his stone-hewn home overlooking the Angara River, Michael was simply a husband, a father, and a keeper of stories. Beside him, Nadia Fedor, now Nadia Strogoff, traced the lines of a map unfurled on their oak table, a gift from the Czar himself, its edges gilt with imperial insignia. Their children, dark-haired and sharp-eyed, played by the hearth, their laughter a testament to a peace hard-won.

The Czar's gratitude had been lavish: lands, titles, and a medal struck in Michael's honor. But the courier had asked only for a quiet post in Irkutsk, where he might serve as steward of the frontier he had bled to protect. Siberia, once a jagged tapestry of peril, now hummed with telegraph lines and nascent railways, threads of progress stitched by a regime eager to solidify its grasp. The Emir's rebellion had been crushed, his ambitions buried in the ashes of his own fortresses, but the memory of those flames lingered in Michael's dreams.

Historians would later write of this era as a fulcrum: the moment Russia's eastward march turned inexorable. Scholars marveled at how a single man's resolve had safeguarded Irkutsk, the linchpin of the empire's defenses. Yet in their monographs, they often overlooked the woman who had guided him through darkness. Nadia's diaries, discovered decades later, told a quieter truth, of fear dispelled not by valor alone, but by the unyielding grip of two hands clasped in trust.

On the outskirts of Moscow, a marble monument now stood, engraved with names of those who had perished in the Tartar revolt. Among them, Ivan Ogareff's was etched in smaller script, a cipher of infamy. The Czar, it was said, visited it once, his face unreadable as snow. His reign had grown heavier, tempered by the knowledge that loyalty was as fragile as it was vital.

As twilight draped Irkutsk in gold, Michael walked the riverbank, his steps sure, his gaze, restored by surgeons years prior, fixed on the horizon. Nadia joined him, her arm threaded through his. "Do you ever wonder," she asked, "what might have become of us if we'd faltered?" He smiled, the scar on his brow softening. "We did not falter. And so, the world turned."

In St. Petersburg, engineers drafted plans for a railroad that would one day span the continent, binding east to west. They called it the Trans-Siberian, a steel artery through the wilderness Michael had once crossed on horseback. Progress, he mused, was its own kind of courier.

**** From the journals of Pyotr Vassiliev, Imperial Historian, 1891**

Also by...
Juan José Piedra

The Dreamscape 2032 Steampunk Stillness Project

Coming Soon: An Eight Book Steampunk Science Fiction Novella Series

Pre-Orders Coming Soon ***Where You Can Witness the Birth of Legends!***

In the Age of Steam, the first dreamers dared to defy the earthbound chains of fate.

From coal and gear, spring and fire, they carved a path into the unknown, igniting an unstoppable journey that would stretch beyond the stars. Now, in a sweeping eight-book saga, **Juan José Piedra** unveils the epic chronicle of a civilization's ascent from humble beginnings to celestial destiny.

Across these novellas, heroes are forged in the fires of invention, secret protector races awaken from the ashes of forgotten wars, and the vast, hidden architecture of the cosmos reveals itself to those brave enough to seek it.

In this legendary series, you will find:

- **Worlds Reborn**: Steam-powered cities, lost technologies, and celestial frontiers.
- **Champions of Destiny**: Inventors, rebels, explorers, and guardians who defy the odds.
- **A Tapestry of Wonders**: From the tick of the first clockwork heart to the hum of quantum sails.
- **The Eternal Struggle**: Between freedom and control, vision and destruction, hope and despair.
- **A Journey Across Time and Stars**: Eight volumes, one living legend.

The spark of invention becomes the flame of destiny. The flame becomes a beacon across the void.

Be part of the Legendary Epic Saga! Pre-Orders Coming Soon!

Coming soon to all major bookstores & digital platforms including Book.io on the Cardano Blockchain!

Juan José Piedra

Forging Legends in the Age of Steam and Stars

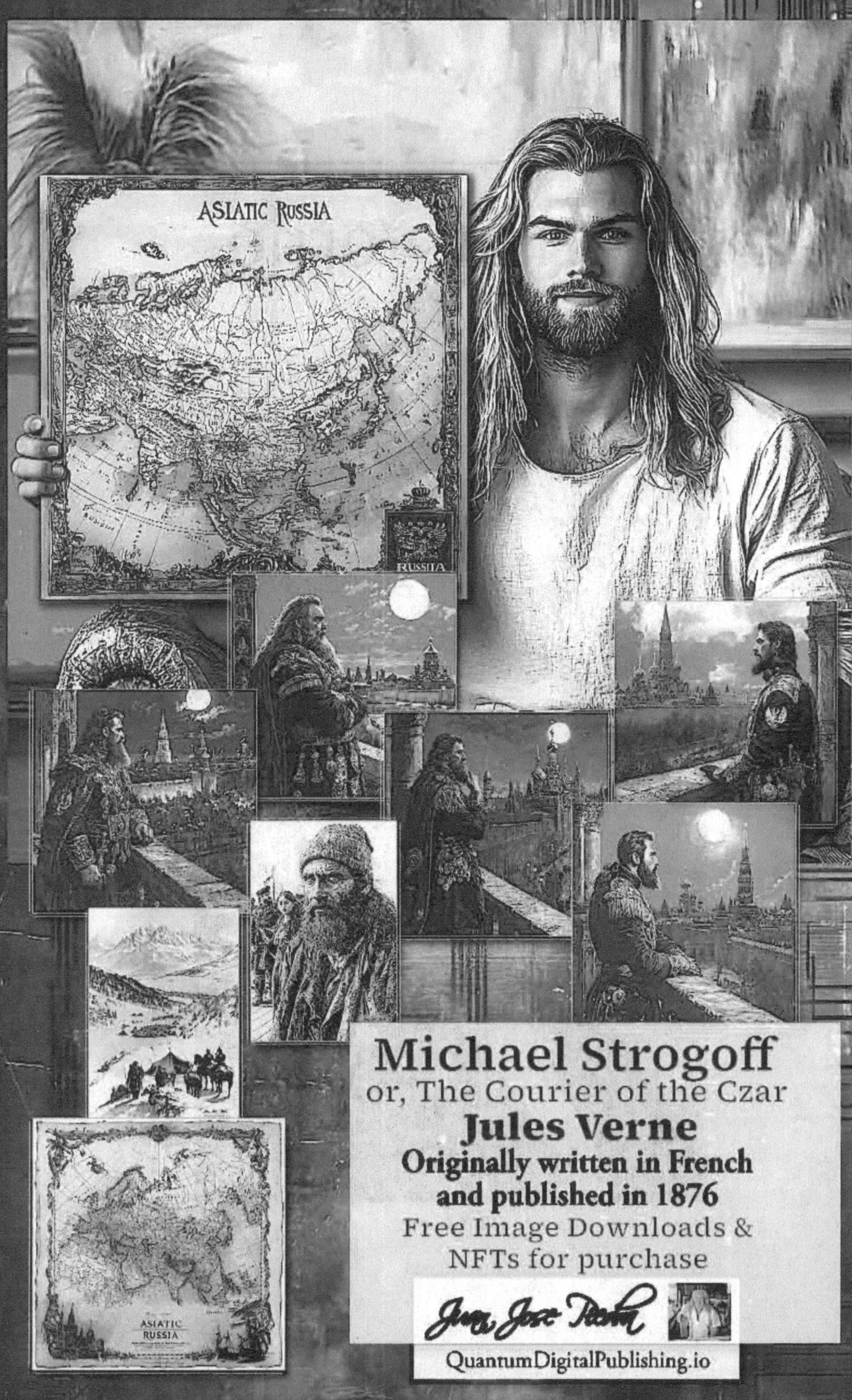
ASIATIC RUSSIA
RUSSIA
ASIATIC
RUSSIA
Michael Strogoff
or, The Courier of the Czar
Jules Verne
Originally written in French
and published in 1876
Free Image Downloads &
NFTs for purchase
QuantumDigitalPublishing.io

About Jules Verne

Jules Verne

Jules Verne, one of the "fathers of science fiction," is renowned for his imaginative and scientifically plausible stories that have captivated readers for generations. Michael Strogoff, or the Courier of the Czar is a prime example of his mastery in blending historical accuracy with thrilling adventure.

Set in the late 19th century during the reign of Tsar Alexander II, the novel takes place in a Russia on the brink of turmoil. The political landscape is fraught with tension, particularly in the Siberian provinces, where a rebellion led by the traitor Ivan Ogareff threatens the stability of the empire.

The story follows Michael Strogoff, a dedicated courier summoned by the Czar to deliver a crucial message to his brother, the Grand Duke, in Irkutsk. Strogoff's journey is fraught with danger, as he must navigate through a war-torn landscape filled with physical and emotional challenges. The narrative explores themes of loyalty, sacrifice, and the resilience of the human spirit, making it a compelling read for fans of historical fiction and adventure.

Verne's writing style is characterized by vivid descriptions and a sense of urgency that keeps readers engaged. Michael Strogoff is a testament to his ability to create a rich and immersive world that resonates with contemporary readers. The book's enduring appeal lies in its timeless themes and the universal human experiences it portrays.

As you embark on this journey with Michael Strogoff, prepare to be transported to a world of intrigue, danger, and heroism. May this classic tale of courage and loyalty inspire and entertain you as it has countless readers before you.

Enjoy your adventure through the pages of Michael Strogoff, or the Courier of the Czar.

Michael Strogoff (Originally written in French in 1876) is an adventure novel set in the vast expanse of the Russian Empire during a fictionalized Tartar rebellion. Though often published as a single volume, some editions split the story into two parts. Below is a consolidated summary of the two-book structure brilliantly written by **Jules Verne**:

Book ONE: The Mission

The story begins in Moscow, where **Michael Strogoff**, a fearless Siberian-born courier for Tsar Alexander II, is entrusted with a critical mission: to warn the governor of Irkutsk, the Tsar's brother, of an impending invasion by Tartar forces led by the ruthless **Feofar Khan** and his traitorous ally, **Ivan Ogareff** (a disgraced Russian officer). The rebellion threatens to sever Siberia from Moscow and overthrow imperial rule.

Michael departs immediately, traveling across Siberia via the Ural Mountains and the vast steppes. Along the way, he meets **Nadia Fedor**, a young Lithuanian woman journeying to join her exiled father in Irkutsk. The two form a bond, and Nadia becomes his steadfast companion.

Their journey grows perilous as Tartar forces, aided by Ogareff's spies, close in. Michael faces natural disasters, betrayals, and ambushes. A pivotal moment occurs when he is captured and tortured by the Tartars. To protect his mission, Michael endures a searing-hot blade that blinds him (or so it seems). Despite this, he escapes with Nadia's help, continuing toward Irkutsk under the guise of a helpless beggar.

Book TWO: The Siege and Resolution

In the second half, the Tartar army besieges Irkutsk. Unbeknownst to the defenders, Ivan Ogareff infiltrates the city disguised as a fisherman, plotting to open the gates to Feofar Khan. Meanwhile, Michael and Nadia, now reliant on her guidance due to his supposed blindness, arrive at the city's outskirts.

Michael reveals his true identity to Russian soldiers and delivers the Tsar's warning, foiling Ogareff's plans. In a climactic confrontation, Michael's "blindness" is exposed as a ruse (his eyes were saved by tears evoked during the torture). He duels Ogareff, kills him, and ensures Irkutsk's defense holds.

The rebellion collapses, and Michael is hailed as a hero. Nadia reunites with her father, and Michael returns to Moscow, honored by the Tsar. The story closes with themes of loyalty, sacrifice, and the triumph of duty over personal suffering.

Key Themes

- **Loyalty and Duty**: Michael's unwavering commitment to the Tsar and Russia.
- **Resilience**: Endurance against physical and psychological trials.
- **Deception and Betrayal**: Ogareff's treachery contrasts with Michael's integrity.
- **Imperialism**: Reflects 19th-century Russian geopolitics and colonial tensions.

Legacy

While less fantastical than Verne's other works (*20,000 Leagues, Around the World*), *Michael Strogoff* is celebrated for its intense pacing, historical flavor, and vivid portrayal of Siberia. It remains a classic of adventure literature, blending political intrigue with a personal odyssey of courage.

Acknowledgements

I wish to acknowledge my wife and lifelong creative partner, Jessie Keener, N.D. A remarkable woman whose wisdom, heart, and intellect have shaped every step of this journey. A Naturopathic Doctor with over 40 years of experience, Jessie brings the world into every conversation. Raised by the sea and seasoned by her early years in Brazil, she is as well-traveled as she is well-read, with thousands of books under her belt and a passion for knowledge that's truly inspiring.

A gifted communicator, Jessie hosted her own public access television show for many years, always championing truth, health, and the human spirit. She's currently working on her own powerful book: Who Will Save Our Doctors? A timely exploration of how today's medical professionals are being compromised by outdated protocols and the overwhelming influence of Big Pharma.

Her brilliance, integrity, and creative fire continue to light the way for thousands.

Glossary Of Terms / Michael Strogoff I & II

- **Hasseurs:** Likely refers to a type of mounted irregular cavalry or horsemen, possibly of Central Asian or Tartar origin, known for their skill in scouting, raiding, and engaging in guerrilla-style warfare. These riders would have been lightly armed and highly mobile, adept at navigating the vast steppes and rugged terrain of Siberia. Their role in the novel aligns with the depiction of Tartar forces, who rely on fast-moving, opportunistic cavalry units to disrupt Russian defenses and terrorize local populations.

Verne's use of such terms reflects the historical reality of Central Asian warfare, where nomadic horsemen played a crucial role in military campaigns, relying on their superior horsemanship and knowledge of the land to conduct swift attacks and strategic retreats. In the novel, such forces would have contributed to the challenges faced by Michael Strogoff on his perilous journey across Siberia.

- **Chef d'oeuvre:** Is a French expression meaning "masterpiece" or "masterwork." It is used to describe something that represents the pinnacle of skill, craftsmanship, or artistry.

In the novel, Verne may use this term either literally, referring to an exceptional work of art or craftsmanship, or figuratively, to highlight a particularly remarkable event, strategy, or achievement, perhaps in the context of military tactics, deception, or a daring feat by Michael Strogoff or his adversaries. The phrase conveys a sense of excellence and perfection in whatever it is applied to.

- **Sang Froid:** Is a French term that translates to "cold blood" in English, but it is used figuratively to mean composure, self-control, or unshakable calmness in the face of danger or crisis.

In the novel, characters like Michael Strogoff exhibit sang-froid by maintaining a steady, fearless demeanor even in life-threatening situations, such as when he faces the Tartars, endures torture, or executes his mission under extreme pressure. His ability to think clearly and act decisively, without letting emotions overwhelm him, is a defining trait of his heroism.

- **Imperturbable:** describes a person who remains calm, composed, and unshaken, even in the most difficult or dangerous situations. It refers to an unyielding steadiness of mind and an inability to be disturbed or flustered by external pressures.

Michael Strogoff himself embodies imperturbability, as he endures extreme hardships, braving the vast Siberian landscape, outmaneuvering enemies, and even facing torture, without losing his resolve. His imperturbable nature allows him to complete his mission with unwavering focus, making him a true model of resilience and self-discipline.

- **Provençals:** Refers to people from Provence, a region in southeastern France known for its distinct culture, language, and traditions. The term typically evokes imagery of lively, warm-hearted individuals, often associated with Mediterranean influences, music, and storytelling.

In the novel, Provençals might be referenced to describe a particular character's background, temperament, or expressive nature. Given Jules Verne's attention to regional characteristics, a Provençal character would likely exhibit traits such as vivid storytelling, warmth, enthusiasm, or a strong sense of identity linked to their homeland.

- **Corps Diplomatique:** Refers to the collective body of diplomats representing various nations within a foreign country or at a government's court. This term encompasses ambassadors, envoys, ministers, and other diplomatic officials responsible for managing international relations and negotiations.

Jules Verne often uses such terms to highlight the presence of high-ranking foreign representatives or to emphasize the political and strategic elements within the novel's setting. In Michael Strogoff, the "Corps Diplomatique" would likely refer to the gathering of officials, correspondents, and representatives who observe and report on events unfolding in Russia, particularly regarding the Tartar invasion and the Czar's response. Their role in the narrative underscores the political weight and international implications of the conflict.

- **Physiognomists:** Refers to individuals who study and interpret facial features and expressions to determine a person's character, emotions, or intentions.

Physiognomy was a widely accepted pseudo-science in the 19th century, based on the belief that a person's physical appearance, particularly their facial structure and expressions, could reveal their inner nature or even predict their fate. In Michael Strogoff, Verne may use this term to describe characters who observe and assess others based on their facial traits, especially in tense or strategic moments when someone's true identity, trustworthiness, or intentions are in question. This aligns with the novel's themes of deception, disguise, and the ability to read people accurately in high-stakes situations.

- **Chasseurs:** Wore the simple uniform of an officer of chasseurs of the guard - "Chasseurs" refers to a type of light cavalry or infantry soldier in the Russian or French military, known for their speed, agility, and reconnaissance abilities.

The term "chasseur" (French for "hunter") was used in European armies to denote elite troops specialized in skirmishing, scouting, and rapid movements. In the Russian context, Chasseurs were often associated with Cossacks or other mobile forces that played crucial roles in frontier defense and rapid deployment during military campaigns.

- **Facade:** Refers to the front or outward appearance of a building, often designed to be impressive or decorative.

The term can also metaphorically signify a deceptive outward appearance, where something or someone presents a false or misleading exterior to conceal true intentions or feelings. However, in the novel, it is most commonly used in its architectural sense, describing the exterior of structures in Russian cities such as Irkutsk or Moscow, which are depicted with detailed attention to their grand and imposing designs.

- **Polonaise:** Refers to a traditional Polish dance of a stately and processional nature, characterized by a moderate triple meter and elegant, flowing movements.

It can also refer to a type of music composed in the style of this dance, often used to evoke a sense of grandeur and national pride. Given Verne's detailed descriptions of cultural elements throughout the novel, the term might appear in reference to a formal event, a piece of music played in a Russian or Polish setting, or even as an allusion to the refined customs of the aristocracy.

- **Imperial Fête:** Refers to a grand celebration or festivity organized by or in honor of the Russian Emperor (Czar) and the imperial court.

Such events were often elaborate and lavish, featuring ceremonial banquets, music, dancing, and military displays, reflecting the wealth, power, and grandeur of the Russian Empire. These fêtes could be held on various occasions, such as official visits, victories, coronations, or national holidays, showcasing the splendor and dominance of the ruling monarchy.

- **Steppes:** Refers to vast, treeless plains that stretch across Siberia and Central Asia. These landscapes are characterized by their flat or gently rolling terrain, covered mainly with grasses and sparse vegetation, and are subject to extreme weather conditions, including harsh winters and scorching summers.

In the novel, the steppes of Siberia serve as a significant setting for Michael Strogoff's journey. These vast, open expanses emphasize the great distances he must travel, the dangers he faces from both natural elements and enemy forces, and the isolation of the Russian frontier. The steppes are both a physical and symbolic obstacle, representing the endurance and resilience required to complete his mission.

- **Iemschik:** (or Yamshik), refers to a Russian postilion or coachman who drives a horse-drawn vehicle, such as a tarantass, along the czarist empire's postal roads.

The Iemschiks were an essential part of the imperial postal and transport system, responsible for ferrying travelers, couriers, and government officials across vast distances, particularly in remote regions like Siberia. They often worked at relay stations, known as "yam" stations, where fresh horses could be quickly harnessed to allow for continuous travel. These drivers were known for their hardiness, familiarity with the rugged terrain, and ability to handle their horses skillfully.

- **Versts:** Killometers or versts, Refers to a Russian unit of distance measurement, approximately equal to 1.066 kilometers (0.662 versts).

The verst was commonly used in the Russian Empire to measure long distances, particularly in the vast and rugged expanses of Siberia, where Michael Strogoff's journey takes place. Given the immense scale of Russia, travel distances were often measured in versts rather than versts or kilometers.

- **Tarantass:** Is a traditional Russian carriage or traveling vehicle, designed for long-distance journeys across the vast and rugged terrain of Siberia.

Description:

The tarantass is a large, four-wheeled carriage, typically constructed with a suspension system made of leather straps or wooden springs, allowing it to absorb shocks on rough roads.

- **Cravat:** A neckcloth; a piece of muslin, silk, or other material worn about the neck, generally outside a linen collar, by men, and less frequently by women.

"cravat" refers to a piece of cloth worn around the neck, typically tied in a knot or bow, serving as a decorative and functional accessory.

- **Kibick or Telga:** The term "kibick" is likely borrowed from Russian киби́тка (kibítka) and is an obsolete synonym for kibitka, a type of vehicle. "Telga" refers to a type of four-wheel horse-drawn vehicle used primarily for carrying loads in Russia and other countries. The telga is nothing but an open four-wheeled cart, made entirely of wood, the pieces fastened together by means of strong rope.

"kibick" (also spelled kibitka) and "telga" refer to types of Russian horse-drawn vehicles commonly used for travel across Siberia and the vast Russian Empire.

- **Overawe:** Means to intimidate, subdue, or control someone through fear, authority, or an imposing presence.

Explanation in Context:
The term "overawe" is often used to describe how powerful figures, military forces, or intense situations instill fear or submission in others.

- **Khanat:** Khanates were typically nomadic Turkic peoples, Tatar and Mongol societies located on the Eurasian Steppe.

"Khanat" refers to a territory or political entity ruled by a Khan, a sovereign leader of a Mongol, Tartar, or Central Asian tribal state.

- **Damascus Blade:** Refers to a sword or dagger made from Damascus steel, a highly prized metal known for its exceptional strength, sharpness, and distinctive wavy pattern.

Explanation in Context:
Damascus steel was historically renowned for its superior quality, capable of cutting through lesser weapons and maintaining a sharp edge.

- **Sesame par excellence:** Is a figurative phrase derived from the famous magical command "Open, Sesame!" from Ali Baba and the Forty Thieves in One Thousand and One Nights.

Definition in Context:
"Sesame" symbolizes a powerful key, something that grants access or opens doors effortlessly.

- **Podorojna Papers:** Refers to an official travel permit or passport issued by the Russian government, granting the bearer the right to travel freely and requisition transportation along their journey.

Definition in Context:
"Podorojna" (or Podorozhnaya Gramota in Russian) was an official document in Imperial Russia, primarily used for government couriers, military personnel, or officials traveling on state business.

- **Kwass:** A jug of kwass, the ordinary Russian beer.

"Kwass" (also spelled Kvass) refers to a traditional Russian fermented beverage made from black or rye bread, which is mildly alcoholic and widely consumed by people of all social classes in Russia.

- **Zingaris or Tsiganes:** Refers to Gypsies, or the Romani people, a nomadic ethnic group known for their distinct culture, traditions, and lifestyle.

Definition in Context:
The terms "Zingaris" (from Italian) and "Tsiganes" (from French and Russian) both refer to the Romani people, a traditionally itinerant group spread across Europe and Russia.

- **Copecks and Roubles:** Refers to the units of currency used in the Russian Empire during the 19th century.

Definition in Context:
Rouble (₽ or рубль): The primary unit of Russian currency.

- **Eccentric Curvette:** An eccentric curvette refers to an unusual or irregular version of a curvette, which is a light leap performed by a horse where both hind legs leave the ground just before the forelegs are set down. In the context provided, the horses in question galloped continuously but also executed many unconventional curvettes as they moved along.

"Eccentric Curvette" refers to a sudden, exaggerated movement made by a horse, particularly a spirited or well-trained one, while galloping or changing direction.

- **Na Pravo: To the right, Na Levo:** Are Russian directional commands used primarily to guide horses or riders.

Definition in Context:
"Na Pravo" (На Право) – Russian for "To the right" or "Turn right."

- **En Règle:** Is a French phrase that means "in order" or "according to the rules."

Definition in Context:
"En Règle" is used to indicate that something is legitimate, proper, or compliant with official regulations, laws, or procedures.

- **Moujik:** (also spelled "Muzhik") is a Russian term referring to a peasant or laborer in Imperial Russia.

Definition in Context:
A Moujik is a common Russian peasant, typically a serf or free farmer, belonging to the lower class of society.

- **Postilion:** Refers to a horse-mounted guide or driver who rides one of the lead horses to steer and direct a carriage, tarantass, or postal relay coach.

Definition in Context:
A Postilion is a rider who controls a team of horses pulling a carriage or relay post vehicle, often without reins, relying on voice commands, a whip, and their own riding skills.

- **Confrere:** Is a French term meaning "colleague" or "fellow member of the same profession."

Definition in Context:
In the novel, "confrère" is used primarily by the French journalist Alcide Jolivet to refer to his British counterpart, Harry Blount.

- **Na Vodkou:** Is a Russian phrase meaning "with vodka" or "to vodka."

Definition in Context:

It is typically associated with Russian drinking customs, where vodka is a central part of social gatherings, toasts, and celebrations.

- **Tsigane:** Refers to a member of the Romani people, also commonly known as Gypsies.

Definition in Context:
The term "Tsigane" (or "Tzigane") is derived from the Russian and French words for Roma people, who have historically been nomadic communities spread across Europe and Asia.

- **Pour-Boire:** Refers to a small gratuity or tip given as a token of appreciation for a service rendered.

Definition in Context:
"Pour-boire" is a French term that literally translates to "for drink", implying a sum of money given to someone, traditionally to buy a drink but more commonly as a tip.

- **Postmaster:** Refers to the official in charge of a postal station, responsible for managing horses, carriages, and relay services for travelers, particularly couriers and government officials.

Definition in Context:
In Imperial Russia, especially along the vast and rugged roads of Siberia, post stations were crucial for long-distance travel.

- **Discomfiture:** Refers to a state of frustration, defeat, embarrassment, or distress caused by an unexpected failure or setback.

Definition in Context:

The term is often used to describe the feeling of being thwarted in one's plans, whether in battle, strategy, or personal ambitions.

- **Incendiarism:** Refers to the deliberate act of setting fire to property, buildings, or other structures, often as a method of warfare or destruction.

Definition in Context:
In the novel, incendiarism is used as a strategic tool by the Tartars and their allies to cause chaos and destruction, particularly during their invasion of Siberia.

- **Saryn na kitchou!:** Is a Tartar battle cry that can be roughly translated to "Down on your knees!" or "On your faces!" in English.

Definition in Context:
This phrase is shouted by the Tartar invaders as a command to those they are attacking, demanding immediate submission.

- **Kreml:** The term "kreml," Often spelled as "Kremlin," refers to a major fortified central complex found in historic Russian cities.

"Kreml" refers to the Kremlin, which is a fortified central complex found in many Russian cities, most famously in Moscow.

- **Bivouacked:** A site where people on holiday can pitch a tent temporary living quarters specially built by the army for soldiers.

"bivouacked" refers to the act of setting up a temporary encampment in an open area, usually without tents or permanent shelter, often for the purpose of resting or preparing for further travel or battle.

- **Dipterals:** Refers to large swarms of insects, specifically two-winged flies or mosquitoes, which are commonly found in the Siberian wilderness.

Definition in Context:
The word "Dipterals" derives from the biological classification Diptera, which is the scientific order for insects with two wings, such as flies, gnats, and mosquitoes.

- **Deh-Baschi:** Is a Tartar military title referring to an officer or commander, likely in charge of a group of ten soldiers.

Definition in Context:
The term "Deh-Baschi" is derived from Turkic and Persian origins, where:

- **Pendja-Baschi:** Is a Tartar military title, referring to an officer in charge of a group of fifty soldiers.

Definition in Context:
The term "Pendja-Baschi" is derived from Turkic and Persian origins, where:

- **Beng:** Is a Tartar term meaning "prince" or "chieftain."

Definition in Context:
"Beng" is a title used to denote a high-ranking leader or noble among the Tartars.

- **Il est un petit homme, Tout habille de gris, Dans Paris!:** Is a French nursery rhyme that appears in the novel.

Definition in Context:

This lighthearted French song is sung by the French journalist Alcide Jolivet, one of the two European correspondents in the novel.

To Those Who Ride Into the Storm

A Poem for Michael Strogoff

Through winds that howl and rivers wide,
Where frozen specters stalk and hide,
Beyond the reach of hearth and home,
The lone courier dares to roam.

His steed is swift, his course unknown,
A shadow cast where few have flown.
The road is cruel, the night is deep,
Yet duty wakes where others sleep.

The sky is torn with icy breath,
The path ahead is laced with death,
Yet forward still, his fate is sworn,
For he who rides must face the storm.

No banners raised, no songs resound,
No gilded halls, no laurel crowned,
Yet kingdoms rise and wars are stayed
By those who ride and are not swayed.

So let the tempest rail and roar,
Let lightning lash the barren shore,
For empires stand, as they have sworn,
On those who ride into the storm.

www.ingramcontent.com/pod-product-compliance
Lightning Source LLC
LaVergne TN
LVHW031924090826
845145LV00018B/2830